OUT OF THE FRYING PAN . . .
INTO THE BELLY OF THE BEAST

"The odds are twenty-to-one against you surviving the Grokorian cave lizard," announced the wizard.

"Is that what it is? I thought it was a subterranean elephant or something."

"I wasn't able to find one of those."

A questing paw of the lizard swished the air above my head, missing my scalp by inches. I couldn't stay here long.

I didn't. A slimy, spongy tentacle reached up from below, snared my legs, and pulled me off the ledge without so much as a how-do-you-do. I didn't so much fall as ride down the tentacled monster's lair.

"Congratulations," said the wizard. "You seem to have escaped the grok. Quite cleverly too."

"Hardy har har," I said as the tentacle dragged my lower body through a hole in the cliff face. I clung to the edges of the opening, resisting with all my might the inexorable pull of whatever it was at the other end.

ROYAL CHAOS

Dan McGirt

A ROC BOOK

Dedicated to the original Jason Cosmo fans:

Dan Burer
Tim Drury
Vince Hammond
Paul Hansen
Chris Heine
David Philips
Laura Skelton Roberts
and others

ROC
Published by the Penguin Group
Penguin Books USA Inc., 375 Hudson Street,
New York, New York 10014, U.S.A.
Penguin Books Ltd, 27 Wrights Lane,
London W8 5TZ, England
Penguin Books Australia Ltd, Ringwood,
Victoria, Australia
Penguin Books Canada Ltd, 2801 John Street,
Markham, Ontario, Canada L3R 1B4
Penguin Books (N.Z.) Ltd, 182–190 Wairau Road,
Auckland 10, New Zealand

Penguin Books Ltd, Registered Offices:
Harmondsworth, Middlesex, England

First published by Roc, an imprint of Penguin Books USA Inc.

First Printing, June, 1990
10 9 8 7 6 5 4 3 2 1

1

It was perfect weather for an outdoor wedding. The late summer sky was clear and blue, and the gold dome of Rae City's Dawn Chapel gleamed brightly in the morning sun. The air was warm and mild. A gentle breeze made the jeweled banners in the surrounding park snap and flutter. It was a souvenir postcard kind of day, and the committee of meteorological magi responsible for all this were as justifiably proud of their handiwork as the wedding guests were appreciative.

Over one hundred notables of the Eleven Kingdoms had gathered to witness the marriage of Raella Shurbenholt, Queen of Raelna, to the wizard Mercury Boltblaster. Among the guests were kings, queens, dukes, earls, and lesser nobles by the dozen. The High Council of the League of Benevolent Magic was on hand, as were a good many diplomats and a few private citizens like me, Jason Cosmo. Thankfully, there was no horde of obnoxious tabloid photographers underfoot, as neither tabloids nor photographs had yet been thought of in the magical world of Arden.

Though most of the guests were already seated on cushioned benches beneath a pair of billowing red-and-gold silk canopies erected in the chapel garden, my companion and I had not yet taken our places. We stood outside the Crystalfire Gate, which pierced the high goldenberry hedge surrounding the chapel grounds, and awaited the start of the wedding procession. Thousands of cheering Raelnans lined the route from the fabulous Solar Palace to the courtyard in front of the Crystalfire Gate. Many more waved from the balconies and windows of Rae City's multicolored, terraced towers. I hadn't figured out exactly who they were waving to, but their excitement mounted with each passing moment. The land of Raelna had not witnessed a royal wedding in almost forty years, and the people were enjoying the spectacle. You would never know this same city had been attacked by legions of Day-Glo orange demons just a few months ago. Joy ruled the day, not fear. At least not yet.

"We're running late," I remarked for the fifth time in as many minutes.

"Weddings always do, Jason," said Sapphrina, my lady love. She was a gorgeous young woman with honey-blond hair, glittering blue eyes, a perfect figure, and a golden tan.

"It's expected," added her sister Rubis as she stepped through the gate to join us. Rubis was also a gorgeous young woman with honey-blond hair, glittering blue eyes, a perfect figure, and a golden tan. No observer could have told them apart if they hadn't been color-coded. Sapphrina wore an azure gown and Rubis one of fiery scarlet, both low-cut and frosted with hundreds of tiny diamonds.

"I thought you were talking with Uncle Dwide," said Sapphrina. She referred to Dwide Ikanglower, President of Zastria. He was a longtime friend of the twins' father, Corun Corundum, a wealthy merchant and a member of the Zastrian Senate. The girls had known President Ikanglower since childhood.

"I was," said Rubis. "He wants to see both of us during the reception."

"About Father?"

"Yes. Uncle Dwide is trying to play peacemaker again."

"Lost cause," snorted Sapphrina. Corun Corundum had disowned his daughters two years ago when they refused to go through with arranged marriages. Needless to say, they were not on the best of terms with him.

"I wonder what the holdup is?" I asked, discreetly refraining from comment on the domestic situation. "I don't like this standing around and waiting."

"Standing around and waiting is also traditional," said Sapphrina patiently. "You're supposed to make small talk with the other guests."

"We tried that, remember? The Duchess of Claxony fainted as soon as I told her my name."

"That must have upset the Duke," said Rubis.

"He fainted too," said Sapphrina.

It wasn't my fault that I was the most feared man in the Eleven Kingdoms. A cabal of evil wizards was responsible for that. By a campaign of deliberate misinformation they had painted in the minds of millions a false image of Jason Cosmo as a terrible marauder who ate babies for breakfast and drank blood for wine. In most places, my name was spoken only in fearful whispers, if at all. I was actually a warm, generous, kind-hearted, likable fellow, but my vile reputation was a real burden in social settings.

"It shouldn't be much longer, darling," said Sapphrina, pointing down the Avenue of Morning.

Protocol demanded that the royal procession not proceed until all the guests reached the chapel. Even now a lone coach drawn by black horses hurtled down the avenue with unceremonial haste to deliver a late arrival.

"Who could that be?" I wondered aloud. "I thought everyone was here already."

A small child chasing an errant ball darted into the path of the carriage. The driver did not slow his reckless pace and would have run the little boy down had not an alert soldier snatched him to safety at the last instant. The otherwise jubilant crowd booed and hissed as the coach passed.

"Must be the Dark Duke," I said softly. The black mace emblem on the carriage door confirmed my guess.

Thule, Duke of Nethershawn, emerged from his coach and stalked through the Crystalfire Gate without greeting anyone. It was just as well, because no one greeted him. He was a tall, grim man with silver hair and a scowling graveyard face. He was the leader of those reactionary nobles who opposed Queen Raella's efforts to create a kinder, gentler kingdom through such reforms as outlawing slavery and banning torture. Her union with Mercury was a serious blow to Thule's plans. He was not a happy camper.

"What is he doing here?" I asked when he had passed. "He was invited only as a necessary formality. No one expected him to actually show up." The twins didn't have an answer and neither did I.

After a moment of disturbing silence, a thunderous shout shook the air. It was followed by a majestic trumpet fanfare at the far end of the avenue. The wedding procession had finally begun.

General Vixen Hotfur, Supreme Commander of the Armies of Raelna, led the procession astride a great roan charger. Nearly forty, Hotfur was lean and hard-muscled, with fox-red hair and sly amber eyes. The She-Fox, as she was known due to her tactical cunning, would have preferred leading something more stimulating, like a reckless cavalry charge against the center lines of a vast horde of bloodthirsty foes. But long-standing tradition demanded that the Supreme Commander head up all state processions. This had been the rule since 534 A.H., when King Raeford the Moose was murdered by rebellious nobles during the parade kicking off the annual Partially Hydrogenated Sunflower Oil Festival.

The 85th Ceremonial Showcase Brigade of the Royal Mounted Lancers followed Hotfur. The unit hadn't seen battle in over a century, but when it came to parades they were unsurpassed, riding in perfect formation with studied stiffness and deadpan faces. They had bright red pennons attached to their weapons and bobbing scarlet crests on their shining silver helmets. With flawless precision the colorful troopers peeled off into two columns, lining the last hundred yards of the avenue on either side to await the rest of the procession. Hotfur and the trooper bearing the state banner of Raelna rode alone to the Crystalfire Gate and dismounted. The trooper planted the flag, which bore a smiling golden sunburst on a scarlet field, to the right of the gateway.

I greeted Hotfur as a soldier led her horse away. I had to shout in order to be heard over the deafening roar of the crowd:

"You're looking sharp today, General."

"I damn well should, decked out in all this frippery." She slapped disgustedly at her scarlet dress uniform. She preferred well-worn buckskins. "Can you believe the hoopla? Pomp and ceremony is all very well, but this! My boys can barely keep the bystanders out of the street to let the parade go by. And the din, man! I've seen quieter battles."

"The people love their Queen."

"That they do, The Gods save her! Still, I'll be glad when this is over. There is yet work to do before the city defenses are restored. Those gutter-sucking demons raised merry hell last spring, you know."

"Indeed."

"And the campaigning season is far from over. Ganth has been making noises, Orphalia could come apart any day, and we've had constant skirmishing along the Brythalian frontier since we blunted their spring offensive. This army needs a good shakedown and, by Death and Spittle, it's going to get it once the fun and games are over!"

"You're militarily compulsive, General."

"That's my job, lad."

The lancers were followed by the 15th Processional Festive Pike Regiment, which also split into two columns and lined the perimeter of the court. Behind the foot soldiers was the Royal Strategic Marching Band, which worked in many triumphal flourishes as it marked time for the marchers. The band gave way to the groom's open coach.

"Here's Merc," I said.

"He looks sour for a man about to wed a queen," said Hotfur, noting his scowl.

"What else is new?"

The coach halted and Mercury alighted before us. The future Prince Consort of Raelna was a small-framed man with olive skin and dark green eyes. His bushy eyebrows, long hair, and neatly trimmed beard were black as coal. He wore a scarlet cape over a cloth of gold tunic trimmed with black velvet and sewn with bright emeralds.

Mercury Boltblaster was my best friend. I owed him my life a few dozen times over. Together we had defied death, demons, despair, and doom. We had faced the full might of the dreaded Dark Magic Society and prevailed, something few people could honestly say. We were like brothers and no one was happier for him today than I.

"We're running late," he said as he exited the coach.

"Weddings always do," I said. "Or so I've been told."

"Just so. Well, I'm glad I got another chance to talk to you before the ceremony, Jason. I've got a bad feeling about this."

"I think that's normal."

"I'm not talking about routine prenuptial jitters. I have a premonition of total disaster. I want you to keep an eye out for trouble."

"Merc, everything has been planned to the last detail. What could possibly go wrong?"

He gave me a pained look. "The best-laid plans of gods and men invariably go awry. Consider, for example, Raella's last wedding. A complete debacle, as weddings go."

"Wasn't that your fault?"

He shrugged. "She was marrying the wrong man. That was her father's fault." For political reasons, the late King Raegon had arranged for Raella to marry Prince Halogen, obnoxious heir to the throne of neighboring Orphalia, despite her love for Mercury. "What could I do?"

"Disrupt the ceremony, kidnap the bride, blast your way out of the city, and ride hellbent for leather to Caratha with half the Raelnan army in hot pursuit?"

Merc shrugged again. "See what I mean? You never know what might happen. Raella and I have many enemies. What better time for them to strike at us than today?"

I shook my head in exasperation. "Merc, be optimistic for once! You're about to be married!"

"I certainly hope so." With that, he passed through the gate and entered the chapel to await the start of the ceremony.

"Cynical to a fault," I said.

"He's got naught to worry about, lad," said Hotfur. "There are no less than six hundred of my boys on the scene. We'll have no trouble today."

"Here comes the Queen!" said Sapphrina.

The crowd doubled its cheers as the Queen came into view. A band of trumpeters and the mounted members of the Queen's Very Own Personal Guard preceded her coach, which was drawn by ten white horses. The trooper bearing the Queen's personal standard rode forward and planted it to the left of the Crystalfire Gate. It was similar to the state banner, but with inverted coloring and the addition of a crown and a pattern of roses.

The coach halted, and I lent Her Majesty a hand as she disembarked. Raella Shurbenholt looked like a young goddess. This was natural since she was directly descended from the Goddess Rae, whose son Blaze Shurben had founded Raelna nearly one thousand years ago. She wore a glittering gown of gold brocade embellished with rubies, topaz, and diamonds. It lent a regal aura to her delicate, girlish figure. Her fine, pale, elfin face was offset by reddish-blond hair piled high on her head and apparently held in place by magic. Her most striking feature, however, was her haunting blue eyes. They were like ancient and timeless doorways to a hidden realm of wisdom. When she looked at me I felt she was seeing into my very soul.

"Thank you, Jason." Her voice was sweet and silvery as a well-played harp.

"My pleasure, Your Majesty."

"Is Mercury still fretting?" she asked as a bluebird lit on her outstretched finger and chirped happily. Mice, squirrels, chipmunks, and a couple of rabbits peered at her adoringly from the cover of the hedge. I had noticed before how birds and cute little furry animals were drawn to Raella. She radiated that kind of wholesome goodness. I expected the whole scene to break into a choreographed musical number at any moment.

"Of course," I said.

"It won't be long now." She smiled and went through the gate, escorted by a dozen lovely ladies-in-waiting. Hotfur, the twins, and I followed a moment later, heading for the canopies and our seats on the front row, near Prince Ronaldo of Caratha and his party and just across the aisle from venerable Mage Timeon and the other members of the High Council of the League of Benevolent Magic. The Deputy High Priest of Rae, who would perform the ceremony, was already in place. Raella was the High Priestess of the Church of Rae, but it would be awkward for her to officiate at her own wedding. The task had thus fallen to a lesser member of the religious hierarchy. All was ready.

We waited fifteen minutes before the trumpeters cut loose with another fanfare, silencing the chatter of the seated guests. As the echoes of the blast died out, more artful minstrels took up a stately wedding march. Mercury walked alone down the aisle between the canopies to the outdoor altar. He had refused the traditional escort of noble men-at-arms, not wanting to give one of Thule's admirers a chance to slip a knife between his ribs.

Raella's ladies-in-waiting came next and lined up to the left of the altar. They were followed by the Queen herself, who took her place at Mercury's side. The Deputy High Priest then offered up a prayer of thanksgiving to the all-wise, all-knowing, all-seeing Goddess Rae. I had met her and knew better. She was actually somewhat shallow and scatterbrained. On the other hand, she was also my patron deity. I tried to think less blasphemous thoughts.

The prayer was followed by a long hymn of praise from the Holy Sunlight Chorus. The priest then delivered a lengthy sermon on love, devotion, marriage, and the healthful benefits of fresh air and sunshine. This was followed by another hymn. I stifled a yawn. Respect for The Gods was one thing, but this was ridiculous. We were already thirty minutes into the ceremony. Hotfur was visibly restless. Merc was annoyed. The twins were pictures of composure.

The priest gave another prayer, urging the Sun Goddess to shower favor upon the royal couple and their kingdom, including its principal cities and towns and the various duchies, earldoms, and counties, which he listed for Divine Rae's convenience. The chorus sang its third hymn.

Finally the priest spoke the words we were all waiting for.

"And so let us now, before The Gods and humanity, perform the task for which we have gathered here on this twentieth day of the Sixmonth of the year 990 in the Age of Hope. Let us seal this favored couple together in holy matrimony. Let us rejoice as they begin a new life together. Let us—"

"Let us get on with it," growled Merc.

"Ahem. Do you, Raella Shurbenholt, Queen of Raelna, Princess of the Silver Sands, Daughter of the Sun, et cetera, take this man Mercury Boltblaster to be your lawfully wed husband for life, to share your fortunes and dominion, and promise to cleave to him to the exclusion of all others as commanded by the Holy Scripture of Rae, Revised Edition?"

"With all my heart, I do," said Raella, gazing fondly at the wizard.

"Do you, Mercury Boltblaster, Arcane Master and Honorary Lord of this kingdom, take this woman, Raella Shurbenholt, to be your lawfully wed wife for life, to share in her fortune and dominions to the extent provided by law and custom, and promise to cleave to her to the exclusion of all others as commanded by the Holy Scripture of Rae, Revised Edition, in supersession of any contrary credal provisions derived from the teachings of whichever other of The Gods you may honor?"

"I do," said Mercury with a trace of a smile. Despite his fears, it looked as though we were going to get through the wedding without incident.

"Then by virtue of the power bestowed upon me by the Church of Rae, and before The Gods and humanity as witnesses, I do hereby solemnly proclaim you, from this moment forward, to be—*urracht!*"

A crossbow's steel quarrel suddenly appeared in the Deputy High Priest's chest. He stiffened, staggered backward while clutching the shaft, and fell dead across the altar. Merc and Raella turned to face the horror-stricken crowd. Hotfur and I sprang to our feet, as did many of the guests.

The assassin, a man of dark olive complexion, stood at the opposite end of the aisle, behind the canopies, his crossbow poised. A long white scar ran across his left cheek. He wore a red turban, bright orange pantaloons, a wide green sash, and a loose purple shirt open at the chest. A dozen similarly garbed men and women stood behind him.

"By order of Zaran Zimzabar, Supreme Commander of the People's Army of the New Glorious Order, you are all sentenced to death!" he proclaimed. "Death to all monarchists! Death to all capitalists! Death to all neo-conservative trilateral monetarist running dogs! Down with all outmoded forms of government! Long live the new world order of the liberated masses! Long live PANGO!"

His second quarrel sped toward Raella. Merc snatched it from the air just before it reached her breast.

"I knew it! I knew something like this would happen!" Merc said, hurling the arrow to the ground. "It was too much to expect a simple little wedding without some psychotic megalomaniac disrupting things!"

Merc stretched forth his arms and sent jets of scarlet flame from his hands toward the terrorist. Unexpectedly, an invisible force deflected the streams of fire, which ignited the canopies instead of Zaran.

The terrorist sneered. "You ignorant tool of imperialistic repression! You cannot halt the ordained flow of history with your paltry spells! PANGO is destined to remake the world!" Zaran gave a signal and laughed madly as his followers opened fire on the crowd.

Total panic. Terrorists appeared out of thin air, completely surrounding us. They were armed with sophisticated self-winding crossbows, the latest technology, with which they cut down guests in a withering cross fire. Those with the presence of mind to dive to the ground escaped harm, but many panicked and ran. They died swiftly, including Raella's ladies-in-waiting and the Holy Sunlight Chorus.

Raella surrounded Mercury, me, Hotfur, the twins, and herself in a protective nimbus of energy, granting us temporary respite from our attackers' missiles.

"How did they get in here?" demanded Raella.

"I don't know, Majesty!" said Hotfur. "This area is supposed to be sealed!"

"Where in the Assorted Hells are your soldiers?" asked Merc. "They must hear the screams."

"I don't know!" Hotfur was visibly dismayed.

The Raelnan troopers just outside the park made no

move to help us. I could see them through the trees and the hedge, standing at attention as if nothing unusual was happening. I looked askance at General Hotfur. Was she in league with Zaran? It seemed improbable, but I knew from experience that improbable didn't mean impossible.

Several PANGO raiders hacked down the canopy poles. The flaming fabric enveloped the cowering guests. Crossbowmen pumped quarrels into anyone who moved beneath the covering.

"We're on our own," said Merc.

"It looks that way," I agreed.

"You might need this." He reached into the folds of his cloak, which contained what he called a pocket universe, and withdrew my sword, Overwhelm. The blade was a yard of gleaming miraculum, a metal harder than steel and lighter than air. Well, perhaps not lighter than air, but much lighter than the average sword. I had given it to him earlier for safekeeping.

"Take these too," said Merc, handing me my helm and hauberk. These were also forged of miraculum. The hooded tunic of mail hung to my knees and covered my arms to the wrist, where the gauntlets took over. The helmet had nose and cheek guards. As a whole, the suit would turn aside any normal weapon and absorb the impact of the mightiest blows. The twins helped me struggle into it.

"Shield," I said.

"Shield," said Merc, handing it over. My shield, also miraculum, was kite-shaped today. Sometimes it was round. Sometimes oval. It seemed to shift form whenever I wasn't looking. I knew there had to be a way to control the transformations and select the best shape for a given situation, but I hadn't figured it out yet and it wasn't convenient to do so now. A kite shield would do.

"I'm ready," I said. My entire outfit had once belonged to the Mighty Champion, the legendary hero credited with bringing an end to the Age of Despair a thousand years ago. With it, I was as close to invincible as a mortal warrior could be.

"What of Timeon?" asked Raella, peering through the cloud of quarrels for some sign of the old wizard.

"Your League friends seem to have been roasted along with the rest," noted Merc sourly. He had a long-standing dislike for the League and had a hard time concealing it. Not that he tried. "Are you ready to take the offensive, love?"

"Aye," said the Queen.

"Let's do it," I said.

"Yes!" said Hotfur. "I'll gut that little netherfrogging butterslimer and roast him on a spit!"

"Sapphrina, Rubis, you must lie down," said Raella. "I am going to lower the protective screen." The girls gracefully hit the dirt.

Zaran laughed at the carnage. "Thus will perish all who oppose PANGO! From the purifying flames shall emerge a new age of nationalization, collectivization, and universal brotherhood! Cower in your magic bubble while you may! You too shall die! Yes, you wizard! You and your wench of a Queen! I shall flay you alive!"

"That tears it," said Merc. "Drop the shield now."

The bubble vanished and Merc attacked with a blue bolt of death, five streams of azure energy emanating from the fingers of his right hand to converge on the terrorist's chest. The bolt fizzled before reaching Zaran.

"I do not fear your magic, fool! I am Zaran! I am invincible!"

"He may have a point," I said. Raella brought her defensive screen back up just in time to stop the next volley of arrows.

"I'll just have to use a stronger spell," said Merc. "Maybe Oppenheimer's Nuclear Nullification will do the trick."

"Absolutely not!" said Raella. "I want my capital to remain standing, if you please. You always overreact."

"I don't know. He's got a powerful force field. Perhaps the Crimson Claws of Chaos?"

"You may try that," said Raella. "But be careful."

We were the only ones still standing against the attackers. About forty terrorists stood in a loose ring around us. At a signal from Zaran, they ceased firing and glared at us.

The terror commander spoke. "If you surrender, grovel

before me like the diseased dogs you are, and beg for mercy I will grant you swift deaths. If not, you will die slowly and painfully. Choose swiftly."

"Gods," said Merc, rolling his eyes. "How many times have I heard that line?"

"Four hundred and seventy-five," I said. "We figured it out last week, remember?"

"*You* must surrender!" bellowed Hotfur angrily. "My forces have the park surrounded! You cannot leave this place alive!"

"Your witless soldiery did not prevent my entrance! They will not hinder my departure when my work is done!"

"You will not depart," said Raella wrathfully. "I have waited over ten years for this, my wedding day. Woe to you who have dared to defile it!"

She dropped her shield again, and her body glowed with golden fire. In the same instant Merc used telekinesis to wrench the crossbows from the hands of the terrorists and send the weapons flying out of the park. Hotfur and I rushed at the startled PANGO raiders.

They reached for their clubs, swords, daggers, and axes and closed in. But, before we could engage, the flaming canopies rose up and whirled through the air like great fiery sheets to reveal Timeon and his fellow Leaguers, Ormazander, Valence, and Episymachus standing together amid the dead and dying.

Hotfur and I stopped in our tracks. The League wizards engulfed half a dozen terrorists in the burning fabric before the flames gave out. The others panicked and fled through the Crystalfire Gate or over the hedge, abandoning their leader. Zaran didn't seem troubled.

Hotfur and I had yet to use our swords. "I feel about as useful as a butcher at a vegetarian's convention," I said.

"Where in the Assorted Hells are my mother-loving, spittle-kicking, misbegotten, horse-son troops!" Hotfur demanded.

"With Merc and Raella, who needs troops?"

Raella, feet firmly planted and arms outstretched, poured wave after wave of golden light at Zaran. The arcane energies she summoned scorched the very air. Zaran's dome of force was in danger of collapsing. Its wavery outline was visible as Raella's spell washed over it like water poured on an inverted bowl.

At the same time, Mercury attacked with the Crimson Claws of Chaos, which resembled the disembodied talons of a gigantic red eagle from the aeries of Upper Hell. By a quirk of metaphysics, that is exactly what they were. The hovering claws mimicked Merc's hand motions, raking Zaran's force field as Merc raked the air. The protective dome could not last long under the dual assault.

The next events seemed to happen in slow motion. Zaran still had his crossbow, which Merc's telekinesis had not touched. He now loaded it with a silver quarrel inscribed with glowing runes, and aimed it at the Queen. Hotfur and I could do nothing. Mercury and Raella, intent on their attacks, did not sense the danger.

Zaran fired. Raella's spell did not hinder the enchanted quarrel as it flew toward her. It struck between her breasts. An instant later, her torso exploded in a spray of gore and white light. Her body flew several feet into the air and dissolved into greenish vapor. Only the tatters of her gown fell to the ground.

I turned to confront Zaran. He was gone.

Someone, I don't know who, spoke the words we all dreaded to hear:

"The Queen is dead!"

2

For a long, horrible moment there was utter silence. The Crimson Claws of Chaos dissolved into red vapor as Mercury fell to his knees. Tears gushed from his eyes and spilled across his pain-frozen face to gather in his beard as he clutched the shredded remains of Raella's gown. I put my hand on his shoulder in a sympathetic gesture, but Merc shrugged it away.

"Merc—"

"Leave me alone, Jason." His voice vibrated with raw pain and awesome menace. I backed off.

The lawn was ablaze. Through the black smoke and crackling flames, I glimpsed the distraught twins huddled together nearby, badly shaken but unhurt. Bodies littered the park. A handful of survivors milled about in shock and confusion, weeping and screaming. Others were silent. Hotfur ordered the soldiers now pouring through the Crystalfire Gate to tend the wounded, search for possible hiding terrorists, and put out the flames. Timeon and his fellows aided in those efforts.

The Raelnans watching the wedding from atop nearby towers saw the carnage. The news would spread through the city like a virus, a plague of rumors and distortions that would grow, exaggeration upon exaggeration, until the citizens worked themselves into a frenzy of fear and anger. There would be riots, looting, panic in the streets. The murder of a ruler as beloved as Queen Raella always had dire consequences.

Hotfur loudly and colorfully berated her bewildered officers for failing to come to our aid during the attack. The soldiers claimed to have heard and seen nothing. They were surrounded by slaughter and could not understand how or why.

The death toll was high. Prince Ronaldo of Caratha escaped without harm, but his fellow heads of state were not so lucky. King Stron Astatine of Orphalia, only months into his reign, was dead. President Ikanglower died with a bolt through his neck. The ambassadors of Brythalia, Ganth, Xornos, Cyrilla, and the Malravian tribes all perished. The great nobles of Raelna, who made up most of the guests, were all but eradicated. Many fiefs and titles would pass to eldest sons and daughters in the days to come. Moreover, most of the chief officials of the realm had perished. With one bloody stroke PANGO had effectively destroyed the upper levels of the Raelnan government. In all, Zaran's raiders took over a hundred lives. We had killed only eight terrorists in return.

I knew the trouble wasn't over when a black-suited, jack-booted regiment of Thule Nethershawn's personal army, the Maceketeers, jogged into the park to surround Hotfur and her junior officers. The lank and greasy leader of the ducal storm troopers, Bobhe Skuldrudge, ordered the regular army officers to throw down their weapons. None obeyed.

"What is the meaning of this?" demanded Hotfur.

"General Hotfur, you are under arrest for crimes of high treason and regicide on orders of His Majesty, Thule I, King of Raelna," sneered Skuldrudge.

"What?"

Thule Nethershawn, unscathed in the attack, strode toward the beleaguered general. Like most villains of his ilk, he had a booming bass voice. "It is obvious that the terrorist scum could not have reached this park and perpetrated this appalling massacre without your cooperation, General. Your troops stood by while they did their bloody work, but your PANGO allies failed to kill us all. Now you will pay the price for your treachery. Your attempted coup has failed."

"Madness!" said Hotfur, brandishing her sword. "Do you expect anyone to take that load of goat dung seriously? I'm no traitor and you're no king!"

The Raelnan regulars in the park, noting the confrontation, moved to attack the Maceketeers and rescue their general, only to halt in their tracks as more of Thule's men arrived to give the Maceketeers a three-to-one advantage. The rest of the regulars in Rae City had their hands full trying to control the frightened masses outside. No reinforcements would come to Hotfur's aid.

"You are wrong, General. The laws of succession specifically state that in the event of a female monarch's death by enchanted crossbow quarrel during the course of a royal wedding taking place in the Sixmonth, the Prism Throne falls to her father's eldest third cousin by marriage twice removed. In this case, myself."

"There is no such provision!"

"But there is. It was passed by the Council of Nobles and approved by Raella herself. You can find it in Paragraph Six of Section C of Part Twelve of Article Nine of Chapter Eleven of the Annual Routine Update of the Official Authorized Wagon Axle Specifications and Stan-

dards which Her Just Departed Majesty signed over a
month ago. We may be thankful that Her Now Late
Majesty had the wisdom and foresight to provide for this
tragic eventuality. It is so important to maintain continu-
ity of leadership during a crisis."

"It will take more than a regulation to make a king of
you, you grease-licking ghoul! You're not even of the
Blood Royal!"

"I have a drop or two. Most nobles do."

"The choice of a ruler belongs to the Council of Nobles!"

"The Council has just confirmed my selection by a
unanimous vote."

"Impossible! Most of the Council lies dead at our
feet!"

"They abstained. But I live. Duke Monfort of Corona
was not with us today. My vassals Count Nightgaunt and
Lord Blackspear arrived late."

"They weren't invited."

"In any event, they are here, as am I, and we just met
in emergency session. Three-fourths of the surviving Council is a quorum, so our action is official. I am King and I
command you to put down your weapon. If you do not,
you will be killed on the spot, traitor."

"She's no traitor and you're no king!" I cried, interposing myself between Hotfur and the Maceketeers.

"Didn't I just go over that point?" said Thule.

In the first moments of the attack I suspected Hotfur
of treachery, but all I had seen and heard since convinced me of her innocence. Thule was making a blatant
grab for power. If he succecded, all that Raella stood for
would be destroyed. This had to stop now. "Call off your
dogs, Thule, and slink back to your filthy lair! Your
claim is worthless!"

Thule turned his cold gaze upon me. "Jason Cosmo. A
name almost as feared as my own. You are said to be a
mighty warrior, boy, but you are no match for me."

"Try me."

"Ahem. I didn't mean me personally, but me and my
heroic Maceketeers." Thule was playing it cool, but the
Maceketeers didn't look so sure of themselves. At the
mention of my name, all went pale and several fainted.

"Bring them on," I sneered. "Who'll be the first to die?"

"Your Zastrian harlots. Tell me, Cosmo, are their lives of any value to you?"

"What?" I glanced to one side and saw a pair of burly Maceketeers roughly yank the tearful twins to their feet and point daggers to their throats.

"Unhand them at once, you vermin!" I started toward the twins.

"If he takes one more step, kill them both," ordered Thule.

I skidded to a halt and whirled to face him. "You will regret this, Nethershawn."

"I doubt it. I enjoy this sort of thing. As I suspected, you are not so merciless as the tales would have it. You are soft. You are weak. So quit your posturing and put down your sword."

I dropped Overwhelm. Thule smiled thinly as the Maceketeers regarded him with new respect. He had forced Jason Cosmo to back down. His followers were more convinced than ever of his power and rightness. His opponents were overawed. Thule milked the moment for all it was worth.

"Heads of state have died here. The rabble are in a panic. A dangerous terrorist is loose. Treason is in our midst. I have no time for your effrontery, Cosmo. Do not utter another word in my presence."

"As you wish."

"As you wish, *Your Majesty*," prompted Thule.

"Look, don't push it."

Thule turned to the She-Fox. "General Hotfur, you have three seconds to follow Cosmo's example."

"If you want my sword, you fornicating lump-monger, come here and I'll give it to you."

"I was hoping you would say that. Take her."

Maceketeers with crossbows cut down the junior officers standing with Hotfur. A dozen storm troopers with iron maces then closed in on her. She pivoted to and fro in an effort to fend them all off and gutted three before they clubbed her senseless. I watched in rage and frustration, but was not willing to sacrifice Sapphrina and Rubis to save Hotfur. I couldn't think of a way to help them all.

The Raelnan regulars were divided. Some moved to rescue their leader and quickly fell. Others stood idle, either from cowardice or confusion about which side was in the right. They knew Thule to be a schemer, but his claim to the throne had at least a veneer of legality to it. If he was indeed the King of Raelna now, the army was pledged to his service.

"Take her to the dungeon beneath the palace," commanded Thule. "Unseal the old torture chamber and prepare it for use. I will supervise the interrogation later. We'll have a full confession out of her before long. General Skuldrudge, I appoint you Supreme Commander of my armies. Your first task is to clear the streets. Use whatever degree of force is necessary, but restore order. Announce a curfew. Anyone out after dark is to be put to death on the spot. With relish."

"With relish, Your Majesty?"

"With extra relish."

"As you command, Your Majesty."

"I am thankful that my loyal Maceketeers chose to attend today's festivities."

"Quite convenient," I muttered.

"We are proud to serve," said Skuldrudge. He saluted and hastened to carry out his orders.

"This kingdom has grown soft and permissive," said Thule to no one in particular. "I intend to restore it to its former strength and glory. The lesser classes must be put in their proper place so that those who were meant to rule them may enjoy the privileges which are theirs by ancient right."

"You mean you want to rob, rape, torture, and murder the common folk like you did in the bad old days," I said.

"Precisely. Peasants exist for the amusement of their betters."

"That's news to me."

"Didn't I command you to silence?"

"I think so, yes."

"Then be silent."

Mage Timeon approached Thule, followed by the other League wizards. "Duke of Nethershawn, I must protest this—"

"Enough, old man! I am King now and your niggling League is no longer welcome here! Raella was taken in by your simpering ways, but I will give no ear to your blandishments. Begone, the lot of you! Get out of my kingdom with all due haste and do not return if you value your lives!"

"Sorry to bother you," said Timeon curtly, bowing and backing away. He and his fellows turned heel and departed. Confrontation was not the League's strong suit.

"Maceketeers!" said Thule. "Seize the scheming wizard who sought to usurp power in Raelna by wedding my gullible, soft-headed predecessor!"

"Do you mean Boltblaster, Your Majesty?" asked a hesitant Maceketeer.

"Of course I mean Boltblaster, you dolt!"

"Ah . . . don't you think he might use magic on us if we try to seize him?"

"He might. Do you know what I will do to you if you don't?"

"Right. Let's get him, boys." Four storm troopers hurried to seize Merc.

"That's probably not a good idea just now," I said. Through all of this Merc remained kneeling where Raella had fallen, lost in tears and sorrow.

"Really?" said Thule. "Why not?"

The first Maceketeer to lay a hand on Mercury suffered a broken arm, a dislocated shoulder, and a broken neck in rapid succession. Before his nearest companion could react, Merc grabbed his tunic and yanked him off balance. As the startled soldier fell, Merc took to the air. He vaulted over the two remaining men and disabled them from behind. The four troopers hit the ground together. Only one was still conscious, albeit barely.

"Just a hunch," I said. Thule blanched, but only slightly.

Merc glared at the Dark Duke. "Thule! Zaran may have pulled the trigger, but you pulled the strings! You killed Raella!"

"Who? Me?" said Thule innocently.

"Now you're in for it," I said, ducking.

The heavy maces of Merc's fallen foes flew toward Thule as if hurled by invisible hands. He never flinched. Four loyal Maceketeers threw themselves into the paths of the missiles, shielding their master with their own bodies. Two would never rise again.

Merc wasn't finished. Bolts of azure lightning flew from his fingertips to crackle around Thule's form and send the usurper to his knees. The bolts danced and twisted in the air, avoiding those of Thule's men who attempted to break the circuit by interposing themselves between wizard and prey. The Dark Duke screamed as the spiritual lightning scorched his very soul. He clawed at the air like a madman and his hair stood on end. Bright blood flew from his nose and ears. Having suffered such an attack myself once, I knew what he was going through. But I wasn't sympathetic.

At my mental command, Overwhelm flew to my hand. In an instant I was at the side of the twins. The Maceketeers quickly realized that killing the girls would not prevent their own deaths and roughly shoved their captives aside to meet my attack. Their knives were no match for Overwhelm. I killed both men in seconds.

"Are you two okay?"

"Alive and whole, but that's all I'll claim," said Sapphrina.

"That's good enough. Now stay down."

The rest of the Maceketeers rushed at Mercury, but he held them off with a display of power worthy of an arcane master. Without allowing his attack of Thule to waver, he pelted the soldiers with flying weapons, shields, corpses, and heavy clumps of earth. Merc surrounded himself with a whirling wall of levitated objects as he slowly advanced on his helpless victim.

"For the sake of your own vile ambitions, Nethershawn, you destroyed the one thing in this world that I loved." His eyes glittered with cold fury. His face was a stony mask of hate. "You have ripped my heart and soul out, Thule. I will do the same to you. And then you can rot in the Blackest Pit of Hell forever!"

Rather than reply, Thule reached out imploringly to

me. "Cosmo! Whatever Raella . . . and the wizard paid you . . . I will double. Just slay him now!"

"You have got to be kidding."

It looked as though King Thule's reign was going to be the shortest on record. Unfortunately, a smart storm trooper got past Merc's defenses by crawling low to the ground. He suddenly rose up and hit Merc in the back of the head with his mace. The wizard's reflexes saved him from a messy death, but he was momentarily stunned. His spells faltered and a dozen soldiers pounced on him before he could recover. Others lifted their stricken master and carried him from the park with manic haste.

"Kill them all!" bellowed Thule as he was borne through the Crystalfire Gate. A hundred fresh Maceketeers rushed into the park to do just that.

"This doesn't look good," said Sapphrina.

"Don't worry," I said. "We'll get out of here somehow."

"Yes," said Rubis. "Dead."

"Thanks for the vote of confidence."

Even my magic sword and shield would not be enough to protect me and two unarmed women from the number of foes we faced. By the blessing of Rae, I had the strength of at least ten men by the light of day. Even so, I would eventually tire or someone would get lucky and then the show would be over. Rubis was only being realistic.

"I'm only being realistic," said Rubis.

"Well, I guess this isn't exactly a bake-off."

The onrushing soldiers disappeared beneath an avalanche of frosted layer cakes, steaming pies, hot puddings, and sticky pastries which fell from the sky as if the bakeries of Paradise had exploded.

"Of course, I could be wrong."

We looked up. Timeon and his fellow wizards swept over us aboard a large flying carpet. They skimmed down to ground level.

"Quickly! Get on!" said Timeon. His fellows helped Sapphrina and Rubis mount the hovering rug. I hesitated. I hated flying.

"What kind of spell was that?"

"We call it Sarilee's Just Desserts. It is only non-lethal catering magic and won't hold them for long. Get on!"

"I'm not partial to flying carpets. I think I'll just fight my way out."

"Don't be an idiot!" Merc snarled, emerging from the wall of sweets. He was covered with whipped cream, blood, chocolate frosting, and shredded coconut. "Thule has eluded me for now. We've got to get out of here!"

He dragged me aboard the carpet, which shot high into the air with vertigo-inducing swiftness. From this altitude we could see that all of Rae City was in chaos. Fires raged in several sections of the city. Panicked crowds choked the streets, alternately fleeing and fighting the brutal Maceketeers. Regular army troops and city guards attempted to control the mobs. Some cooperated with Thule's men. Others attacked them. It looked like every man for himself down there.

We streaked away to the southwest, bound for Caratha.

"I'm sorry you were caught in our attack," Timeon told Mercury. "We didn't see you amid all your foes."

"That's because I was at the bottom of the pile." Merc whiped his face clean with a towel from his cloak. "You know I don't think much of your League, Timeon, but thanks for the rescue. I guess you guys aren't such cream puffs after all."

We reached Caratha in a little over three hours. My villa was located in the wealthy northeast section of town, just west of Pantheon Park. The Leaguers touched down on the tennis court, allowing the rest of us to disembark before speeding across town to League headquarters. Before their departure, Timeon hinted that he had something important to tell me. I promised to visit the League office later that day and meet with the High Council.

In the meantime, Merc and I had other matters to discuss. The girls left the two of us alone in the garden.

"She's dead, Jason. Gone forever." Merc's features collapsed.

"I'm sorry, Merc. I know how you must feel."

"I doubt that. Do you know what it means to have half

your soul wrenched away? To have your still-beating heart torn from your breast without anesthesia and put through a rusty meat grinder right in front of you? To have the Doorway to Happiness slammed in your face and be thrust instead into the Pit of Absolute Despair?"

"Okay. Maybe I don't know exactly how you feel. But I feel bad for you."

"It's Raella you should feel bad for. She is dead, and her precious blood cries out for vengeance. Listen!" He cocked his head and cupped a hand around his ear.

I did likewise. "Yes, I hear it. Look, I'll help you avenge her, Merc. You don't have to do it alone."

"I can do this alone, Jason. There is no need for you to get involved."

"Of course there is! You're my friend and so was Raella. I couldn't possibly stay on the sidelines."

He sighed and squeezed my shoulder. "I knew I could count on you."

"We'll get Thule and Zaran."

"Damn right we will. And the illusionist too."

"And the illusionist too. We'll hunt them down wherever they—Wait a minute. What illusionist?"

"Think about it. Why didn't the soldiers aid us? How did PANGO get in and out so easily? Why did no one outside the park notice what was happening until it was all over?"

"Why?"

"Illusions. A strong field of illusion that made everyone outside the attack zone believe nothing was amiss."

"That would explain how the terrorists seemed to pop out of thin air. Terrorists don't usually do that."

"Assuming they were indeed terrorists and not Maceketeers in disguise. Natalia Slash supposedly killed Zaran before she came after us this past spring. So we assumed. Whether or not Zaran was actually involved, Thule masterminded the attack. And he had an illusionist to help him bring it off."

"Good illusionists are hard to find, are they not?"

"Yes. All spellcasting involves an exercise of imagination, but illusion magic takes ten times as much. The illusionist creates a false reality in his mind and projects it into the world around him. That takes an unusual combination of imagination, willpower, and raw talent. Less than ten known illusionists in all of Arden are capable of creating the effect we experienced."

"That certainly narrows the range of suspects."

"I can narrow it even more. The only ones who would be willing to work with Thule are known members of the Dark Magic Society."

"It figures," I said with a resigned air. "I mean, a rematch with them is almost *de rigueur*, isn't it?"

The Dark Magic Society was the most ruthless and powerful organization in Arden. It was an ancient order dedicated to the goals of world domination and the restoration of the ancient Empire of Fear. If its shadowy lords were involved in Raella's death, it added a dangerous dimension to our quest for vengeance. The sinister schemes of the Society were invariably more complicated than was readily apparent.

"Yes, this smacks of one of their pernicious plots," Merc said. "We know the Society has financed Zaran in the past, so that piece fits. Thule would bargain with the Demon Lords themselves for the Prism Throne. It all fits together into a tidy little package."

"Odd how it always does."

"Yes. Of course, the Society has been divided since we eliminated their former Overmaster, Erimandras. Perhaps only one faction was responsibile for this day's atrocities. But which one?"

"The one with the illusionists?"

"Brilliant, Jason. The Society illusionists hate each other. We won't find them working together."

"Oh. I knew that."

Merc waved the matter away. "We can figure that angle out later. First, I want Thule. I wounded him today. I need to finish him off before he can recover and consolidate his position. We'll return to Rae City in the morning. I hate to delay so long, but we'll need a good night's rest before storming the ramparts."

"Are you suggesting we—just the two of us—ride back to Rae City, fight our way through thousands of Maceketeers to Thule, kill him, and then battle our way out again? Just like that?"

"Of course not. Don't be ridiculous."

"What a relief. That would be a real suicide mission."

"We're going to *fly* back to Rae City, fight our way through thousands of Maceketeers, kill Thule, and get away."

"Even better," I said weakly. "What about Hotfur?"

"What about her?"

"You missed that part in your grief. Thule made her the scapegoat for Zaran's attack and had her thrown in the dungeon. We ought to rescue her while we're in Rae City. After all, she saved our lives last spring."

"Yes, I suppose you're right. We do owe her a favor. Well, my plan is flexible."

"You already have a plan?"

"I just explained it."

"That was a *plan*?"

"You know, we may need a little help on this," Merc mused, stroking his beard.

"I was going to suggest that," I said, breathing a sigh of relief. "As usual, you're one step ahead of me. Maybe Prince Ronaldo will loan you his army."

"No, I know just the man for the job."

"Man? Singular?"

"I need to think this through," said Merc distractedly.

"A very good idea."

"I'm sure that I'm overlooking something important."

"Self-preservation?" I suggested.

"It would be best if you left me alone for a while."

"I'll do that. I have to visit the League anyway."

"Good," said Merc. "Learn all you can from them. And borrow a flying carpet. When you get back I'll have all the details worked out. Then the payback can begin."

3

I took a cab across town to the League tower. News of the Rae City massacre had not yet reached the citizens of Caratha, so it was business as usual here. The streets were crowded and the air full of shouts, songs, and laughter.

Caratha, the City at the Center of the World, was a place of unceasing activity, myriad sights and sounds, innumerable experiences, and a great deal of litter. The Prince of Caratha ruled over a million people packed into an area almost ten miles across and filled with towers, temples, tenements, parks, palaces, piers, and every other kind of structure imaginable. The broad, brown waters of River Crownbolt flowed through the very heart of the city and emptied into the Great Harbor, where hundreds of ships arrived each day. This morning and every morning, from the docks to the shops to the Grand Bazaar, buyers and sellers haggled over products from all across the world of Arden.

Here could be had Ganthian beef, Raelnan linens, Brythalian ores, and prized Malravian wool. From Cyrilla came precious gold, ivory, and strange wooden carvings. Zastrian fruit, wine, and cheese commanded high prices, as did pearls and other sea treasures from the sunken kingdom of Aqualon. Venturesome merchants boasted exotic wares from such half-mythical lands as Rhelt, Kalish, and Manjiphar. Furs, nuts, perfumes, crayons, spices, party favors, garments, ceramic ducks, furnishings, tools, weapons, books—everything that could be bought was bought in Caratha. Including, unfortunately, slaves of every race and nation, sold in the Market of Chains like any other product.

The slave trade disturbed me, but otherwise I enjoyed living there. The city never slept, never rested, never slowed down. It was a far cry from the rustic village of

Lower Hicksnittle where I was born. The complexity, the confusion, and the sheer size of the place daunted me at first, but I soon got into the swing of things. I developed a great affection for Caratha and its ways. I enjoyed relaxing in the public baths on the East Bank of the river. I liked strolling through Pantheon Park or talking with the learned dons at the University. The Royal Carathan Library held more books than I could read in a dozen lifetimes. The Consolidated Temple of The Gods was as awe-inspiring as it was intended to be. The beauty of the fabulous Alcazara Palace defied description. With Sapphrina, and sometimes Rubis, I enjoyed dancing, dining, plays, concerts, and sporting events. I loved every minute of it.

Even so, I was ready to put aside my life of luxury and take up the sword again. As the hackney crossed the river on the ancient North Bridge, a broad span of white granite and polychromatic road tiles, I felt a dormant part of myself awakening and shaking off the stiffness of sleep. A great evil had been done. An avenger was needed. Someone had to strike back in the name of truth, justice, and goodness. And that someone would be me. The Gods had plucked me from obscurity and made me a hero. It was time to do the job I had been selected for.

I passed the stately Bank of Caratha, an imposing block of green-veined marble surrounded by colossal gold columns. The League building was a few blocks farther west. It was a conical blue tower decorated with yellow stars and crescent moons so as to resemble an old-fashioned wizard's hat. I paid the cabbie and was about to pull the bell cord when someone behind me shouted my name.

I turned and faced a scowling blue-skinned warrior wearing a shirt of ringmail over a leather tunic. He was bald except for a topknot bound with a gold ring. He bore a shield and a toothed ,weapon that looked more like a saw than a sword.

"Who are you, Cyrillan?" I snapped, placing my hand on Overwhelm's hilt. Wearing my invincible armor, I didn't feel threatened. His odd weapon couldn't hurt me.

"I be Rothgar Headhacker and I challenge you to a death duel, here and now."

"Why?" As if I had to ask.

"To prove I'm the better man. You've got a big reputation, Cosmo, but I say you're nothing but a slimesucking son of a mud dog."

I suspected he would say something like that. This was the downside of my unearned infamy. Most men had the good sense to be afraid of me, but there were a few hotshots eager to make a name for themselves by slaying the great Jason Cosmo. This had happened every couple of weeks since I came to Caratha. I usually tried to disarm and disable my attackers and turn them over to the city guard; but I had unavoidably killed three Ganthian mercenaries and a Sanskaaran assassin in separate incidents sixteen days ago. No one had challenged me since then, and I didn't have time to play that game again now.

"Listen, Rotgut, I'm not in the mood today. Why don't you just go home and maybe we'll get together some other time."

"Cowardly cur! Spineless sea urchin! Fight me like a man or be shamed forever!"

"Get lost." I turned my back on him and raised my hand to ring the bell. Predictably, he attacked. His weapon met my matchless armor and shattered into tiny fragments. I pulled the cord and heard the muffled sound of the chimes within. I also heard the slap of boot leather on pavement as Rothgar fled. Not bothering to look back, I stepped inside as the great brass doors swung silently inward. The antechamber was round, with a domed ceiling of gold. The black and white floor tiles were arranged in patterns to form magic symbols of warding and protection.

Timeon awaited me within. He was a wizened little gray man with wispy white hair. He wore a pale blue robe embroidered with gold thread and clutched a gnarled wooden staff.

"Welcome, Jason Cosmo," he intoned formally, bowing from the waist. "We are honored by your visit."

"Hello, Timeon."

I was always ill at ease in the League offices and therefore didn't come here often. Timeon and his colleagues treated me like a visiting king or demi-god. They bowed and genuflected and spoke gravely. It made me nervous. I finally decided to ignore their little ceremonies and treat my visits as the informal events they really were in hopes that the League would eventually catch on. It hadn't worked so far.

"Follow me, Master Cosmo. The others await you."

He led the way to a levitation disk. We rode swiftly to the second level. The carpet in the curved hallway was dark red and the walls were covered with ivory silk shot through with gold threads. We entered the conference room. Episymachus, Ormazander, and Valence awaited us within.

"As you might imagine," said Timeon, once we were seated around the conference table, "the death of our dear friend and colleague, along with so many others, disturbs us greatly. I knew Raella all her life, and the loss I feel is monumental. I know you share our grief."

"Yes. But I'm not here to talk about grief."

"Nor are we. We cannot dwell upon it. Our danger is too great. I am certain you suspect, as do we, the insidious hand of the Dark Magic Society in this sorry affair."

"Yes. I was hoping you could tell me more about that."

"For centuries, this League fought to protect Arden from the evil of the Society. We thwarted their plots, exposed their deceptions, countered their offensives, and matched their magical might spell for spell. The struggle continues to this day. Yet, while the League was worn down by the endless strife, the Society grew stronger than ever. Until recently, it seemed that our foes were poised on the brink of total victory. You, of course, won us a respite by destroying the Society's headquarters and eliminating many of its leaders."

"Just trying to be helpful," I said.

"You have thrown the enemy into confusion," said blue-skinned Ormazander. "When you slew the Overmaster, the Society broke into warring factions. Eventually a new Overmaster will emerge. Today's attack is the first sign that one of the contestants may have already won."

"Far sooner than we anticipated," Timeon added.

"What do you mean?"

"When the Society is involved in an internal power struggle, it typically suspends all other activities. Its leaders are too busy fighting one another to commit resources to anything else. But if one of those leaders is secure enough to plan an operation like the one in Rae City, it suggests that the succession struggle was short-lived. There may already be a new Overmaster. The wedding massacre may only be the beginning."

"The beginning of what?"

"The beginning of the final offenseive against the League and the free peoples of Arden," said Episymachus, a dark-haired Xornite magician. He was a new addition to the High Council. "The beginning of the end."

"I don't follow you."

Episymachus explained. "One person in ten thousand has the potential to work magic. Only one in a hundred thousand has the talent required to reach master status. Many of these people never discover or develop their aptitude for magic. This leaves a very small pool of magic-users compared with the total population. There are less than fifteen hundred practicing magi in all the Eleven Kingdoms. Less than two hundred of them are masters. Yet the potential power of this minority is beyond calculation. If they banded together in a common purpose, no force in Arden could withstand them. They could level any fortress and annihilate any army."

Timeon continued. "The League numbers less than one hundred despite our recent international membership drive and offer of free toasters and portable grills to anyone who signs up. The four of us are the only arcane masters now that Raella is dead. The Society has at least fifty masters and over eight hundred known members. We suspect it commands the loyalty of many more."

"The Society is riddled with jealousy and dissent, which has prevented our foes from taking the concerted action that would crush us," said Ormazander. "But that may be at an end."

Timeon spoke again. "Under Erimandras, the Society aggressively recruited new members and killed many who would not serve its cause. Raella was one of our key members, powerful both magically and politically. We fear that her assassination heralds a return to Erimandras's tactics of attrition."

"The Society's goal is to achieve a complete monopoly on the practice of magic," said Episymachus. "If that is accomplished, it will be well on its way to world domination."

"I see what you mean," I said. "But what I don't understand is how this situation came about. For centuries, League and Society were evenly matched. How is it that the League has dwindled while the Society has grown strong?"

The wizards exchanged wary glances. Then Timeon nodded. "That is a perceptive question. In part it is because of the contrasting natures of our organizations. The Society has great wealth got by theft and plunder. We rely on tax-deductible contributions, bake sales, celebrity golf tournaments, and other legitimate modes of funding. The Society deals in treachery and deceit. It subverts and corrupts. Many people are willing to do the bidding of the Overmaster in return for the wealth and pleasures he can offer. We eschew such tactics. Our scruples thus give the Society certain advantages."

"But that was so for centuries and you matched them."

"True," said Timeon. "Yet we always seemed a step behind our foes. Ever on the defensive, lurching from crisis to crisis without a chance to launch our own initiatives."

"That sounds like some foreign policies I've heard of."

"Many leaders of the League grew frustrated by this. In 970 A.H. Dominatus of Auban was elected Councillor, which was what we then called the leader of the League. He advocated fighting fire with fire, turning the Society's own tactics against it. Under him, the League employed murder, torture, and extortion. Many members protested and moved to oust him. Dominatus used the same brutal tactics against his opponents within the League."

"A real motivator, eh?"

"Among those murdered was the great Pencader, to whom your friend Boltblaster was apprenticed. Eventually Dominatus was himself killed by an unknown assassin. The office of Councillor was abolished and greater authority given the High Council to prevent such abuse of power in the future. But the damage was done. The League lost much of its credibility as a force for good. Whether Dominatus was an agent of the Society or merely psychotic, he crippled our order. Our recovery has been slow and difficult."

"Now I see why Merc says there isn't any difference between the two groups. For a time there was none."

Timeon nodded sadly. "Mercury suffered because of that, as did many others. The League lost its appeal to an entire generation of magi. Meanwhile, the Society grew unchecked, with no effective opposition until the return of the Mighty Champion in your person."

I rolled my eyes. "You're not going to start that again, are you?"

During the Age of Despair, which lasted a thousand years, the Eleven Kingdoms were controlled by the demon-serving Empire of Fear. Eventually The Gods sent a Mighty Champion to liberate Arden from the clutches of evil. The sword and armor I bore once belonged to him. According to The Gods, who ought to know, I was his descendant. We even shared the same name. But the League believed I was more. They thought I was the Mighty Champion reborn, sent by The Gods to aid them in their uphill struggle against the Society. That was why they treated me with such elaborate respect. I tried to disabuse Timeon and his fellows of this ridiculous notion. The Gods themselves denied it. But the Leaguers persisted in their belief.

Timeon fixed me with a stern gaze. "You are clearly destined to play a vital role in the struggle between the light and the dark. You have already accomplished much, but more remains to be done. Our work—*your* work— will not be finished until the Dark Magic Society has been utterly stamped out.

"In less than a decade a new millennium will begin. The oracles and the soothsayers have read the signs in the bright heavens and the still waters and the greasy entrails of chickens. They tell us that our endless war with the Society will soon end. One side will emerge victorious and will determine the character of the Next Age. The other will be obliterated, wiped from the face of Arden. You, Jason Cosmo, cannot stand idle as you have done these past months. You are the key to victory or defeat. The infallible Luminous Oracle of Mount Suradel has said so. You must take action."

It was time for a speech. "I'm *not* the Mighty Champion," I said firmly. "But I will accept that I am his heir. I am of his bloodline. I carry his weapons. Perhaps I have inherited his mission as well. Maybe everything for the next thousand years depends on me. I hope it doesn't. I'm not sure I'm equal to such a great responsibility. But you're right about one thing. I have to act. I have to oppose the Society and all it stands for. That's why I'm here today. A terrible crime has been committed. Those responsible must be punished. But to see justice done, I need your help."

"What do you require?" said Timeon.

"I want all the information you have on the various factions of the Society and their leaders. We must figure out which group was responsible."

"There are four main factions," said Episymachus. "We believe Necrophilius the Grave has the upper hand. His rivals are Sinshaper, Vectoroth Plaguecaster, and Rom Acheron."

"We will give you copies of their files," said Timeon.

"I also want information on master illusionists known or suspected to be Society members."

"Those files also will be given to you," said Timeon.

"I will need a flying carpet," I said weakly.

"Pardon? I didn't quite hear that."

I swallowed. "A flying carpet. I need a flying carpet."

Timeon smiled sympathetically. "You shall have our best one. What else?"

"I think that will do it."

"Very well," said Timeon. He paused. "I hinted earlier that we had something important to bring to your attention. Now is an appropriate time to do so. Valence, you have the floor."

The youngest member of the High Council was a handsome, slender, fair-haired man barely into his thirties, quite young for a master wizard. He flashed a brief smile. "Master Cosmo, I recently returned from an expedition to Everwhen Keep, where I conferred with the Mnemonic Monks and conducted extensive research on the life and deeds of the Mighty Champion. I learned much that will be of interest to you, but which will have to wait for a quieter time. One item, however, is of immediate importance. The monks allowed me to study a portion of the ancient Pnarkotic Manuscripts. From them I deciphered a brief and doubtlessly incomplete description of the Ring of Raxx."

I held up my right hand and studied the gold ring set with a clear purple amethyst. It belonged to the Mighty Champion of old and had been in the keeping of the League for centuries. In all that time, the League experts were unable to discover any of the ring's special properties, though it was said to be a talisman of immense power. In a moment of desperation I discovered that it could be used to activate ancient imperial teleportal booths. But that wasn't the sort of power I had an everyday use for. Valence's discovery of other powers after so many had failed marked him as a scholar of the first rank.

"What did you learn?" I asked eagerly.

"The ring apparently enables the wearer to communicate with squirrels."

"Squirrels?"

"And maybe chipmunks. The text was unclear."

"Communicates with squirrels?" This wasn't what I expected.

"Yes. You should be able to understand their chattering as intelligible speech."

"What a breakthrough."

"I'm glad you realize that. Mages have tried for centuries to devise spells that would allow speech with the lower animals. Such magic was well known in the Age of Peace, but was lost. In the modern period, we have met with only partial success, achieving limited talk with cats, dogs, and horses. But never rodents."

"I share your excitement," I said with as much enthusiasm as I could muster. "So how does this work?"

"I don't know. The fragment was incomplete. When

this crisis passes, I will return to Everwhen and study the manuscripts further."

"You mean I have this frivolous—that is to say, fabulous—power and there is no way to activitate it?"

"There is a way. We just don't know what it is. But now that you are aware of the power you may discover how to use it through experimentation."

"Of course. Of course. Thank you, Valence."

"You are welcome. I hope that my discovery will serve you well."

"I'm sure it will."

A lesser mage discreetly entered the room and handed Timeon a sealed envelope. He slid it across the table to me. "Here are the files I promised you."

"Thank you. If that is all, I must be going."

"I will add only this word of advice," said Timeon. "Your friend Boltblaster is understandably upset by today's tragedy. He may throw caution to the Great Whoosh in his hunger for revenge. It will be your part to counsel caution and restraint. Do not let him lead you into destruction. Too much is at stake."

"I understand. Don't worry. Merc and I will do just fine."

"Then may The Gods be with you."

4

It was almost dusk when I returned to the mansion. Merc wasn't there, but I found the twins watching orbavision in the living room. Orbavision, developed by the master technowizard Grammbel, was a variation on the crystal balls commonly used by wizards to view persons and events at great distances. With a few refinements and modifications, Grammbel had turned the arcane scrying device into a novel new mode of entertainment and communication. Thus far, only the wealthy could afford orbavision, but Grammbel spoke of a day when every peasant would have one in his hut. That I would have to see to believe.

"Hi, ladies. Where is Merc?"

"He left soon after you did," said Rubis. "He said he had preparations to make. He didn't say when he would be back."

"I see." I pulled off my surcoat, peeled off my hauberk, and dropped onto the couch between the twins. "How are you two holding up?" I noticed they had both been crying.

"Okay, I suppose," said Sapphrina. "I still can't believe that Uncle Dwide and Queen Raella and all those others are dead."

I wrapped my arm around her. "Neither can I," I said. "It's hard to understand how people like Zaran can snuff out so many lives and actually enjoy it. I don't know why The Gods allow things like that to happen."

"We're going to Zastria," said Sapphrina abruptly. "Uncle Dwide's funeral should be in a couple of weeks, once his body is sent back. We have to be there."

"I understand."

"Uncle Dwide was Father's closest friend," added Rubis.

"We must try to bridge the gap with Father now," said Sapphrina. "He'll need us. It's probably a hopeless task, but we've got to try."

"Of course. How will you get there?"

"The Corundum Trading Company has ships leaving for Port Kylas every day. We'll take passage on one tomorrow. We should return in about a month."

"What if he wants you to stay?"

"My life is in Caratha now," said Sapphrina seriously, squeezing my hand and kissing me on the cheek.

"Mine too," said Rubis with a wink. "We'll be back."

"Hopefully, I will too."

"Don't talk like that," said Sapphrina, frowning. "I'm already afraid I'll never see you again."

"You should be," said Merc as he strode into the room. Garbed entirely in black, he glided across the floor like a renegade shadow cut loose from its owner. A stern-faced shadow with hard green eyes.

"Where have you been?"

"We have no time for talk. We must go."

"Now? I thought we were leaving tomorrow."

"We've had a change of plan. Did you get the flying carpet?"

"It's by the front door."

"We don't need it."

"We don't?"

"No. Why are you still sitting there? Put on your armor. Grab your weapons. We have to leave now."

"Calm down, Merc." Sapphrina helped me pull on the hauberk, while Merc paced the floor feverishly. "You aren't making any sense."

"I don't have time to make sense."

"Of course you don't. Silly me." I strapped on my sword belt as I turned to the twins. "He doesn't have time to make sense."

"Come on," said the wizard.

"At least give me time to say goodbye."

Merc tapped his foot impatiently. "Well, hurry up and kiss her. Kiss both of them. But come on." He stalked out of the room.

I embraced Sapphrina. "I must go."

"Promise you'll be careful." Her eyes were misty.

"I promise," I said, wiping away a tear. "What's this?"

"I'm afraid you're going to die."

"Don't sweat it. Statistically speaking, I've got a good chance of survival. According to a study of heroic literature conducted by the University of Caratha, the success rate for missions of vengeance by certified heroes is almost seventy percent on average. Rescue missions are successful almost eighty percent of the time. This mission is a little of both, so I figure the odds are three-to-one in my favor."

"Really?" she said, brightening a little.

"Really. Look it up for yourself."

"Are you coming or not?" called Merc from outside.

I gave Sapphrina a heartfelt kiss, paused to hug and kiss Rubis, and followed Mercury into the night. He was waiting for me in the garden, crouching warily behind the rose bushes.

"What's the big rush?" I asked.

"Quiet! Get down!" He pulled me down beside him.

"Have you gone crazy, Merc?"

"No. But I nearly forgot something important. This is a quest for revenge. We have to leave at night. Preferably by sneaking out of town."

"What difference does that make?"

"It's traditional. If you're going to do something, do it right. A friend reminded me of the relevant customs."

"Who?"

"You'll meet him. He has the horses."

"Horses? Why aren't we flying? Not that I'm complaining, but I thought—"

"If we fly, we'll get there too soon."

"Too *soon*?"

"We could upset the karmic balance and overaccelerate the plot lines if we arrive in Rae City too early in the scheme of things. I overlooked that important consideration when we talked earlier, but realized it after you left."

"Karmic balance? What are you talking about?"

"Just trust me, Jason. It's not wise to flout the Laws of Narrative. We don't want to get caught in a plot inversion or a thematic breakdown, do we?"

"We don't?"

"Absolutely not."

"Therefore we are taking horses to Rae City," I said, trying to follow his logic. "So that we don't arrive too soon."

"Now you understand."

"Actually, I don't. If we're trying not to hurry, why are *you* in such a hurry?"

"Because we have to leave tonight. I already told you that."

"Oh. Of course. I forgot."

"Now come on, will you?" He crept through the shadows beneath the garden wall.

"May I ask where we're going?" I whispered loudly.

"To the Gate of Moonstones," he said without looking back.

Moonstone Gate pierced the east wall of the city. It was about four miles away.

"Why don't we take a cab?"

"Weren't you listening? We have to sneak out of town. You can't sneak in a cab."

"Who's looking for us?"

"No one that I know of, though you can never be too cautious. It doesn't matter. We're going to sneak."

"I'm not too good at sneaking."

"Just follow my lead."

We crept through the garden and out the back gate used for deliveries. We moved stealthily down the street, stepping carefully from one pool of darkness to the next. For the most part, the moon was hidden by silvery clouds. This aided our efforts to move unnoticed, not that there was anyone around to notice us. When the clouds broke, we froze in place until they consumed Lune's disk once more. I soon understood why Merc was in such a hurry to depart. At our rate of progress it would take several hours to exit the city. If the Moon God was watching, I'm sure he was amused.

We dashed across the boulevard into Pantheon Park, dodging pools of lamplight as we went. The park was quite active in the evening. Lovers strolled hand-in-hand along its graveled paths. Others walked alone, cherishing their solitude. City watchmen whistled as they made their rounds. Crickets chirruped, frogs croaked, and night birds sang. Drunks mumbled to themselves. Brooks gurgled. Fountains splashed. Leaves rustled in the breeze.

"We must cross the park without being seen," said Merc as we crouched at the base of the well-endowed statue of Gemgarde Highpeaks, the Goddess of Hills and Mountains. Studying her figure, I could see where she got the idea for sculpting those particular geological formations.

"There are a lot of people here at night. Why don't we go around the park?"

"That defeats the whole purpose of the exercise."

"Of course. We're sneaking."

"At least I am. Your armor clinks too much."

"Well, we can't all be wizards running around in silly robes, can we?"

"Silly?"

"That came out wrong. I meant to say—"

"Shh—h!"

The gravel crunched as someone approached.

"They're just around the curve," said Merc. "Come."

We sprinted swiftly, if not silently, in the opposite direction. Once out of sight of the statue, we ducked through a hedge to reach the grassy playing field beyond. We would have to cross two hundred yards of open space to reach the edge of the lake in the middle of the park. We could then work our way around the shore using the numerous trees and shrubs at the water's edge for cover.

"Shall we make a run for it?" I asked.

"Of course not," said Merc. "We must cross on our bellies."

"Stupid question. Stupid me."

We dragged ourselves across the ground with our knees and elbows, stopping whenever the moon came out. It had rained the night before and the ground was still soft and moist. Our fronts were soon coated with damp grass and sticky mud. Twenty-five minutes later we reached the path beside the lake.

"Which way?" I asked. My voice startled a group of ducks sleeping in a nearby clump of bushes. They flew across the water, quacking irritably. A dog barked, then another.

"You're a true master of stealth," observed Merc. "We go south."

We got to our feet and headed for the south end of the lake. We hadn't gone a hundred yards before we spotted a jogger coming our way.

"We can hide in these bushes," hissed Merc.

Ecstatic sighs and moans emanated from the bushes in question, which began to shake violently. I could just make out unidentifiable body parts thrashing in the foliage.

"Maybe we should try those bushes instead," I said, indicating another clump.

We let the jogger pass, then continued on our way. Thirty minutes later, we emerged on the east side of the park. It took another forty-five minutes to reach the Moonstone Gate. The gate area was well-lit and well-guarded.

"Can we walk through the gate or do we have to scale the wall blindfolded or something?"

"Follow me," said Merc. He pried open a manhole and led the way down iron rungs into a sewer tunnel. There was a narrow stone walkway beside the stinking river of filth. We went fifty yards north to a cross-tunnel, passed through a hidden door, climbed down another set of rungs, slide down a chute, and did a thirty-foot chimney climb to emerge from a freshly dug grave in the little cemetery outside the city wall. We were both covered with mud and grime from head to toe, but Merc's magically self-cleaning garments grew cleaner by the second. I wasn't so lucky.

"I think I have earthworms in my pants," I said.

"Probably just beetles," said Merc. "I wonder where Rif is?"

"Who's—*gahhh!*"

A leering, wild-eyed, glowing apparition popped up inches from my face. I stumbled backward, tripped over my feet, and sat down hard. The apparition bowed gracefully.

"Rifkin Wildrogue at your service. You may call me Rif."

He was taller than Merc, but shorter than me by a head. His narrow, faintly glowing face had a cadaverous look, but there were worlds of life in his pale blue eyes. His horrible grimace softened into an engaging smile. His hair was like silky threads of midnight drawn back and bound into a tail that hung between his shoulder blades. With his sable cloak wrapped close to his body he was nearly invisible in the darkness. All I could see was his faintly luminous face.

"What are you?" I said weakly. "A vampire or something?"

"A ghost actually."

"You're not serious," I said, feeling my short hairs stiffen.

"I'm quite serious. I'm not a real ghost, of course. I have recently been conducting a liaison with the lovely, passionate, but gullible daughter of one of Caratha's leading citizens. I have the girl quite convinced that she is being romanced by the famous troubadour Trencavel."

"He's been dead for three hundred years."

"Yes, I know. That's why I'm a ghost. Her father is a collector of antiquities. He owns a magical golden harp which once belonged to Trencavel. Eventually I hoped to convince her to place it in my hands, at which time I would fade away like a true phantom and sell the harp to a certain interested party for a pretty penny. However, it appears I shall have to abandon the affair. Something more exciting has come up."

"You're coming with us?"

"Yes," he said gravely. "To avenge the lovely Queen. I owed her much. My life, in fact."

"I'm sure your paramour will miss you."

"She doesn't even know I'm alive," Rifkin laughed. He had just admitted that he was a clever thief and calculating con artist, but I liked his wit and easy manner. And his reverence when he mentioned Raella was genuine.

"You're right on time," he said to Mercury. "I trust your obligatory sneaking went well?"

"Well enough. Now that we've done our bit to ward off bad luck, I'm ready to get moving."

"The horses are over there," said Rif. "Just give me a moment to wipe off this luminous makeup." He dabbed at his face with a wet cloth.

"I haven't introduced myself," I said. "I'm—"

"Jason Cosmo, Son of Chaos, Prince of Darkness, Third Cousin of Death, and Menace to the Civilized World. I know."

"Libel and slander," I protested.

"I know that too."

"Why all this ghost business?" I said, suddenly curious. "Wouldn't it be simpler and safer to just steal the harp?"

"Probably. I would only have to break in once, rather than every night. But the path that leads through the bed of a beautiful woman, even when not the most direct, is always to be preferred. A fortune teller once told me that women shall be the death of me. I try to cooperate with fate."

"I see."

"Of course, it's unpleasant to coat my entire body with this stuff." As the powder came off, Rifkin was revealed to be a handsome man with a face both young and mature. He might have been my age, or even ten years older. It was difficult to tell.

"How can she possibly think you're a ghost? She must know you have substance."

Rif laughed merrily. "She knows it right well. It is, of course, only her fervent love and her promise to keep my nocturnal visits a secret that allow me to take material form for a short while. I come alive in her arms, as it were." He winked. "And she in mine, I assure you. As I said, gullible." He removed the last of the makeup. "Well, gentlemen, shall we ride?"

It was thirty miles from the city wall to the Raelnan border. We kept to the main highway, urging our horses to maintain a steady pace through the night. For several miles the road skirted the north fringe of the broad sea marshes, where the air had a salty tang. Gradually, however, the road curved inland toward the Raelnan plain.

"Merc, you never explained the details of your plan to me," I said.

"That's because I'm still working on it," he said.

"We don't have a plan yet?"

"I've found plans are usually a waste of time," said Rif. "Something always goes wrong and you end up improvising anyway. I like to make things up as I go along."

"We do a lot of that too," I said glumly.

"Tell him about Zaran," said Merc. "We'll talk about the plan later."

"Zaran," said Rifkin, shaking his head sadly. "A contemptible creature. Utterly psychotic. I have access to the files of the CIS—Carathan Intelligence Service. Unauthorized, of course, but that's beside the point."

"Let me guess. You're on intimate terms with one of their female agents."

"Several actually. The extent of their training is remarkable."

"Stick to Zaran please," said Merc.

"My apologies, great wizard. As I was saying, I have access to the CIS files. When Mercury contacted me this afternoon he asked me to check on the beloved leader of PANGO's last known whereabouts. So I dropped by CIS headquarters, which is beneath a certain barber shop on Shield Row. After a little friendly persuasion, I learned that Zaran was captured by Lady Natalia Slash five months ago in Darnk. CIS hired her for this purpose, but failed to specify in the contract that she must personally conduct her prisoner back to Caratha. She opted to subcontract that task in order to give prompt attention to the swamp trolls of the Great Mucky. She was eager to dispense with her outstanding contracts so that she could pursue more lucrative ventures."

"Like me." Like just about every mercenary and bounty hunter in the Eleven Kingdoms, Natalia had wanted to cash in my head for the promised prize of ten million in gold put up by the Dark Magic Society. She eventually caught up with Merc and me in the Incredibly Dark Forest, but ended up fighting at our side against Erimandras. She was swallowed by the Jaws of Death for her efforts.

"Just so. The subcontractors were the Sons of Blood, a crack mercenary unit. They brought Zaran down the Brythalian Corridor and were ambushed south of Fenmar. The unit was killed by magic, crushed beneath several tons of conjured whale blubber. Somewhere in the wide sea swims a very emaciated whale."

"This morning was the first sign of Zaran since his escape?"

"Yes. I also learned that several crates of the newly developed self-winding crossbows disappeared from an armory in Caratha two months ago. CIS traced them as far as Nerak."

Nerak was a small port at the south end of the Brythalian Corridor. It was a haven for pirates, smugglers, and slavers. Brythalia was a landlocked kingdom except for a narrow strip of land, the Corridor, which connected it to the Indigo Sea. King Rubric had deluded dreams of challenging Caratha, Zastria, and Xornos for control of the sea-lanes, but legitimate traders shunned Nerak since they could get better prices for their goods elsewhere.

"Thule Nethershawn's lands are adjacent to the Corridor, are they not?" I asked, remembering my geography.

Rif smiled. "A most salient observation. His seat of Ravenrock is, in fact, a mere twelve leagues from Nerak."

"The pieces are starting to come together," I said. "They make quite an ugly picture."

5

We reached the border just after dawn. It was sunny on the Carathan side, but the sky was thick with black clouds over Raelna, a sign of the Goddess Rae's anger and of dark days to come. Or at the very least a sign of rain.

Farming was important in the outlying areas of the Carathan principality and the adjoining southwestern region of Raelna. Amber fields of grain and green fields of vegetables lined the roadway. Raelna and Caratha had been at peace for over twenty years, so neither nation devoted many soldiers to border duty. A few troops were stationed here to discourage bandits and smugglers, but that was easy duty.

News of the events in Rae City spread across the Eleven Kingdoms like a wildfire on a dry plain, but it spread unevenly. Wizards had the most rapid means of communication. Through the use of certain spells and devices they could transmit messages across vast distances almost instantly. The League broadcast the news to all its members and the Dark Magic Society certainly did the same. Though many wizards worked in solitude, others were attached to the courts of kings and princes with whom they shared what they learned. I knew that every Raelnan embassy had a wizard on duty to send and receive spell-a-grams. Other kingdoms had similar networks. Less than twenty-four hours after the event, every head of state in the Eleven Kingdoms knew of the wedding massacre and Thule's coup, with the probable exception of Fecal IV in distant Darnk.

Lesser mortals learned of these happenings by slower means. Gossip filtered out of the palaces, of course. Raelnans who had been in Rae City for the wedding took the sad news back to their hometowns. It moved through the grapevine in inns, taverns, and marketplaces. The accuracy of knowledge would vary, but by the end of the week, nearly everyone in the Eleven Kingdoms who might care would know what had happened.

Our immediate concern was what the border troops knew and how they were reacting to the news. Thule had ordered our deaths. Did his commands have any meaning here?

A pair of Carathan troopers in purple uniforms stopped us at the border and extracted an exit toll of two brass bits a head, handed us pamphlets inveighing against banditry and smuggling, and waved us through. Nothing unusual here.

Fifteen yards down the road, two red-garbed Raelnan soldiers stopped us again.

"I need to see your papers," said the sergeant. "Proof of identity and citizenship."

"This is a new procedure," said Rif pleasantly.

"The Queen was killed yesterday. We're checking everyone's papers."

"Why?"

"What?"

"Why does the fact the Queen was killed lead you to check everyone's papers?"

"Standing orders. The Queen dies, we have to check papers. That's just how we do things."

"I see," said Rif. "So who is running things in Raelna now?"

"It's hard to say," said the sergeant. "The Dark Duke is claiming the throne. Her Majesty's intended, the wizard Boltblaster, nearly did for him, though. I'm not sure if he's dead or alive. Dead, hopefully." This elicited a brief, bitter smile from Merc.

"And what news of General Hotfur?" I asked.

"Locked in the dungeon, some say. In league with Thule, say others, though I can't credit that. Who really knows? Feri Haleheart is my general and that's who I'll answer to until further notice." General Haleheart commanded the Raelnan Army of the South, responsible for defending this part of the kingdom.

"I see."

"I hope you aren't bound for Rae City. There's rioting there and massacres in the streets."

"Actually, we're headed for Sunfare," Rif said.

"That's mighty close to Brythalia," said the sergeant. "Mark my words, we'll have an invasion soon. I hope the Reaver is on his toes." General Ercan the Reaver commanded the Army of the North, which guarded the Brythalian frontier. "It wouldn't do to get caught up there when it happens."

"We'll be careful," Rif assured him.

"Do that. By the way, you fellows wouldn't be planning on any banditry or smuggling, would you? We try to discourage those sorts of things."

"Certainly not," said Rif, sounding slightly insulted. "We are honest men."

We were three miles down the road before I realized we hadn't shown the soldiers any papers. I remarked on this.

Rif laughed. "If you can get a man like that sergeant talking, he'll forget what he's all about. I have plenty of papers to say I'm anyone I want to be, but you're just as well off to have none at all. I fail to see how a scrap of paper can prove anything."

We stopped at an inn offering an all-you-can-eat breakfast buffet and discussed our plans as we ate.

"We should reach Rae City in two days," said Merc between bites of sausage and eggs.

"Is that soon enough?" I asked. I was working on a steaming stack of blueberry pancakes smothered in maple syrup. A platter of bacon, eggs, and fruit and a couple of apple tarts awaited my attention. "Or still too early?"

"Soon enough. The capital is in chaos. Thule isn't going anywhere until he gets Rae City under control. With all the fighting, we should have no problem slipping into the city."

"What about Hotfur?"

"If Thule wants her dead, she's dead already and there is nothing we can do. If he wants her alive for some reason, she'll still be there when we arrive. Let's look at those files the League gave you."

"Excuse me," said Rif, rising to follow a pretty serving girl beckoning him into the back room. "I'll look at the files later."

I shook my head. "Is he real?"

Merc shrugged. "He suffers from a bit of a sweet tooth, but he's a good man to have around."

"Suffering is not the word that comes to mind. Let's see what Timeon and company have for us."

I opened the packet and withdrew the carefully written reports. We studied the four factional leaders first.

Necrophilius the Grave was the most powerful contender for the office of Overmaster. He was currently one of the Three, the rank in the Society's Ruling Conclave just below the top spot. His speciality was death magic and he was known to work with vampires, ghouls, and other ghastly creatures. He didn't fit the typical mold of a Dark Magic Society leader. He was affiliated with the Forbidden Church of Undeath, which preached that a world of ghosts was preferable to a world of living things. This gave him a base of power outside the Society, albeit a small one. The Forbidden Church had a habit of sacrificing its own members to the greater glory of Death, making recruitment a little tricky. Unlike his fellow Society members, Necrophilius was contemptuous of the Demon Lords. He believed the Society was capable of dominating the world without kowtowing to the Hellmasters. If anything, he felt the demons should serve the Society. Necrophilius was an enemy of Erimandras, but the former Overmaster had been unable to eliminate him. That said a lot about his power and why he was the favorite to emerge as the new Overmaster. It was doubtful that he was involved in Raella's death, however. His style was more subtle.

Sinshaper was also one of the Three, and had been an Erimandras loyalist. He would likely continue the policies of trying to recover the Superwand and free the arch-demon Asmodraxas from his otherdimensional prison. Sinshaper specialized in transformation magic. No one was certain of "his" true form, race, age, or sex. Sinshaper was Necrophilius's strongest rival and had the support of perhaps a third of the Ruling Conclave and the rank-and-file members. The attack in Rae City fit Sinshaper's history of bold moves, but that wasn't conclusive evidence that he was behind it.

Traditionally, the race for Overmaster was between members of the Three. When a victor emerged, the Seven battled to fill the resulting vacancies among the Three, the Twelve battled for a place among the Seven, and so forth. The system had a certain ruthless logic to it and was rigorously adhered to. But in the current power struggle, two low-ranking Conclave members were breaking with tradition and shooting for the main chance.

Rom Acheron was a cipher. He was one of the Twelve, the lowest rank in the Ruling Conclave, having been elevated by Erimandras. Not much was known about him. As an illusionist, he was a prime suspect, but he was also the weakest of the contenders. He couldn't afford to expend his resources on an outside operation unless he were already Overmaster. And that was highly unlikely.

Vectoroth Plaguecaster specialized in disease magic. He was one of the Seven, a former lieutenant of Necrophilius who had betrayed his master in order to seek power for himself. He billed himself as a compromise candidate, a middle ground between the two main players. He had succeeded in attracting some support among those disenchanted with both Necrophilius and Sinshaper, but his campaign was losing momentum. He might have engineered the Rae City massacre as a show of strength, but it seemed unlikely. Like Acheron, he couldn't afford to waste effort on outside operations unless and until he was proclaimed Overmaster.

Studying the other files, we learned that there were

only three Society illusionists who could have directed the Rae City operation. One was Acheron. The mage Phantasm was allied with Sinshaper. Eloisa Mirrorsmoke was thought to favor Necrophilius. The dossiers put us no closer to determining which faction was behind Raella's death, but we would identify the culprit eventually. Then we would make the race for Overmaster a little less crowded.

As we rode, it became evident that the Army of the South was on the move. Several times that morning we were forced to yield the road to passing cavalry squadrons. At midday, with rain pouring down, we overtook several thousand foot soldiers near the town of Zunik. General Haleheart, we soon learned, was marching on Rae City in conjunction with Duke Monfort of Corona, who was raising an army at his seat of Granhill to challenge Nethershawn for the Prism Throne.

"Corona has probably as valid a claim as anyone," said Rif. "He is related to the House of Shurbenholt through both parents. Raella's second cousin, I believe. And he hates Thule."

"Aye," said Merc. "But not so much as I."

Despite the rain, we traveled over thirty miles that day, reaching the peaceful town of Mirpax soon after dusk. At the Inn of the Mystic Mare we dined on goat steaks, steamed mushrooms, and ale while discussing the big news of the day with the crowd. It was not the actions of Feri Haleheart they debated, but those of General Cull Crossmaster, Vixen Hotfur's hand-picked successor as commander of the Army of the Longwash. He had invaded neighboring Orphalia, apparently of his own volition. His fifteen thousand crack troops could have a decisive impact on the civil war which had broken out there upon the death of King Stron in the Rae City massacre. Crossmaster's motives were the subject of heated debate. About half the crowd believed he acted on orders from Thule. Another third thought he planned to seize the Orphalian crown for himself. A small minority felt Crossmaster was doing his duty as he saw it by intervening in Orphalia before Brythalia could.

"A well-timed move," observed Merc thoughtfully, and that was the extent of his commentary.

"Stron Astatine was a straw king," said Rif. "None of the great barons of Orphalia were ready to take power when they deposed Halogen, so they crowned the weakest candidate they could find. Stron's personal holding wasn't any larger than your living room."

"By the 'great barons' I assume you mean Baron von Zinc, Nulf Tungsten, and Baron Bismuth," I said.

"I see you've been doing your homework," said Rif.

Another interesting bit of news was the sudden climb in the death rate among eldest children of recently deceased nobles. Apparently, an army of assassins had decided to kill the heirs of the dukes, counts, earls, and so forth who fell in the wedding massacre, further disrupting the social and political fabric of the realm. No one needed three guesses to figure out who paid the assassins.

"What good does it do Thule to kill another whole generation?" I asked.

"It just adds to the chaos," said Rifkin. "He wants to keep everyone else off balance until he can consolidate his power. The risk, of course, is that the whole kingdom might break apart."

"I understand that. But I thought most of the nobles supported Thule's views. It looks as though he is killing off his own supporters."

"The nobles may have supported Thule's views, but they still respected Raella as their rightful Queen," explained Merc. "Very few shared his extremism or his ambitions. The full Council of Nobles would never have chosen him as King, as he well knows. Only by preventing a new Council from forming can he maintain the fiction of having been duly elected."

"So he is simply eliminating anyone who might get in his way," I concluded. "Typical totalitarian tactics."

"Yes," agreed Merc. "But he's wasting his time."

*   *   *

The rain ended the next day, but the sky remained overcast. By mid-afternoon of our third day in the kingdom, we sighted Rae City. Normally, it rose from Raelna's central plain like an explosion of colors. Its terraced towers were organized in concentric rings around the usually gleaming mountain of white stone, mirrors, and glass that was the Solar Palace. But now the typically bright and joyous city was grim and somber. A haze of thick black smoke stained the air above its walls. The dead bodies of humans and animals lined the roadway. A constant stream of ragged refugees poured out of them. Few persons headed into the city.

We were well ahead of the Army of the South, which probably wouldn't arrive here for another day or two. We passed through the southwest gate without incident. The guards didn't recognize us, which wasn't surprising. Our deeds were well known. Our looks were not. Even Mercury wasn't a familiar face to the average Raelnan, though he was to have wed their Queen.

We immediately noticed that Maceketeers, not Home Guards, patrolled the streets in this part of town. The citizens had long faces and shocked eyes. They did not want to believe that their beautiful, benevolent young Queen was gone. Nearly every door was hung with black ribbons. It was the color of Death and, not coincidentally, of Thule Nethershawn. Mercury clenched his teeth and glowered at no one in particular as we rode through the streets. As much as the Raelnans mourned, Merc mourned more deeply. The sorrow of Raella's people only served to remind him of his own sorrow. This is turn fueled his anger.

The bodies of curfew violators hung from every lamp post, pop-eyed and bloated and dripping with finely chopped sweet pickles. True to Nethershawn's command, they had been killed with relish by the heartless Maceketeers.

Rif left us to look up some of his contacts. Merc and I headed into Slumville, the poor northeast section of the city. Its ramshackle wooden buildings, all dangerous firetraps, stood in sorry contrast to the iridescent towers which made up the rest of the city. It was initially hard to understand how the misery and squalor of Slumville could exist amid the wealth and prosperity of Raelna.

It was, of course, an illusion. Slumville was maintained by royal decree as a reminder of the suffering and poverty which had beset Raelna in the past. Royal engineers studied actual slums as far away as the pirate city of Rancor and used their observations to make Slumville as realistic as possible. City workers labored long and hard to maintain its blighted appearance by breaking windows, scattering trash in the streets, releasing rats and stray dogs, and setting fires from time to time. The beggars, drunks, and dirty urchins roaming the streets were highly skilled actors who never broke character. The prostitutes and pickpockets were real, however. The authorities tolerated them since they provided authentic local color. Slumville was a popular tourist attraction. Raelnans came from all over the kingdom to experience the unfamiliar lifestyles of the poor and unknown.

We took a room in a cheap hotel called the Severed Arms. It was four stories tall and painted the color of dried vomit. Our room was on the top floor. It was barely wider than the narrow door frame. The bed was a pile of moldy straw with odd things squirming in it. The only other furnishings were some bits of wood and broken wine bottles. The place smelled of urine and rotted cabbage.

"This reminds me of Darnk," I said. "Except Darnk is real."

"I've seen worse."

I glanced out the window, which overlooked a narrow street full of dead dogs and decomposed potato peels. "Nice view. You know, I've been meaning to ask you how you met Rifkin."

"It was several years ago in Zastria. He was trying to find a stolen alchemical formula before Natalia Slash did. I was searching for a magic bracelet that Eufrosinia the Cruel also wanted. Thanks to a rogue elephant and a one-eyed werewolf, our paths crossed and we joined forces. That's the short version."

"Did you find what you were looking for?"

"Yes and no. To explain I'd have to tell you the long version, which we don't have time for."

"I'd like to hear it sometime."

"Maybe you will."

Rifkin arrived soon afterwards. He looked unhappy.

"Bad news?" I asked.

"Zaran struck last night in a village called Glymph, about thirty miles west of here."

"I know the place," said Merc. "What happened?"

"The usual mayhem. His forces burned, looted, raped, and pillaged before vanishing into the night."

"His boldness will be his undoing," said Merc coldly. "We will pursue him after we finish here. What news of Thule?"

"He has seized the Solar Palace and his storm troopers control several sections of the city. Most of the riots have ended since most of the citizens have fled the city, but Home Guard and regular army units are battling the Maceketeers for control of the streets."

"We didn't see any fighting on our way here," I said.

"Most of it is on the other side of town. Slumville is being ignored."

"This doesn't make much sense," I said. "How does Thule expect to hold the city, let alone the entire kingdom, with five thousand Maceketeers? The Army of the South alone outnumbers him two to one. If the other armies turn on him too, he's finished."

"Maybe he's expecting help from the Dark Magic Society," Merc suggested. "A few sorcerers could offset his numerical disadvantage."

"Yes, I suppose they could."

"That is the only explanation I can see," said Rif. "Without support from the army or the other nobles, the Dark Duke can't possibly back up his claims unless he relies on allies outside Raelna."

"Can we reach the Solar Palace?" asked Merc.

"It's heavily guarded, of course," Rif said. "And the dusk curfew is still in effect. That works for both sides, though Thule's men enforce it more harshly."

"It's almost dusk now," said Merc. "I guess we'll just have to break the curfew."

"What about Hotfur?" I asked.

"She was tortured, but she's still alive, at least according to one source. Possibly Thule wants to send her to Myrm Ironglove as a gesture of goodwill."

General Myrm Ironglove was the Imperator of Ganth and an ideological soul mate of Nethershawn. Vixen's father, Vulpinus Hotfur, remained loyal to Ganth's royal family when Ironglove staged his coup. Vulpinus was put to death by the dictator. Vixen swore to avenge her father, and the Ganthian regime viewed her as a threat. Ironglove dared not act against her while she was part of Raella's government. Now that she was in Thule's clutches, the Imperator might be eager to join forces with the Dark Duke in order to get his hands on her.

"Should we try to contact Highrider and Gerron?" I asked. Devra Highrider headed the Rae City Home Guard, responsible for policing the city. Colonel Gerron commanded the regular army garrison in the capital. Together they led the opposition to Thule in Rae City.

"No," said Merc. "I don't want any chance for betrayal or incompetence to hinder our plans. We'll slip into the palace tonight, free Hotfur, and kill Thule. No one knows we're here, and that's how we want to keep it until we strike."

I glanced out the window. "Ahem. Rif, you weren't followed by any chance?"

"Possible, but unlikely. Why?"

"Take a look."

At least two hundred Maceketeers lined the street below, facing the hotel.

Bobhe Skuldrudge shouted up at us. "Mercury Boltblaster! Jason Cosmo! You are under arrest by order of His Majesty! The building is surrounded! You will surrender at once!"

"Hmmm," said Rif. "Maybe I *was* followed."

"You don't say."

"This is embarrassing."

"Embarrassing?" I drew Overwhelm. "We're surrounded by hundreds of mercenaries and you're embarrassed?"

"I pride myself on my ability to sneak around without being followed. It's an important skill in my profession."

"You should give Jason some pointers," said Merc. "He's a little weak in the sneaking department."

"I'm not the one who led an entire army to our hideout."

"Whoever tailed me is good," mused Rif. "I didn't have a clue."

I watched another couple hundred storm troopers move into position. "Someone sure gave them a clue."

"Wait a minute!" said Rif. "How do we know it wasn't you and Merc who were followed? No one called my name."

"Why don't we just ask the Maceketeers when they get here?" said Merc irritably.

"Good idea," we said.

We heard the tromp of many boots upon the stairs.

6

The flimsy wooden door shattered when the first soldier struck it. Three Maceketeers fell to the floor in a tangle of bodies and weapons. The rest of their unit was right behind them. Merc vaulted over the fallen men and kicked a storm trooper in the chest, bowling him over and taking several more down with him. The others backed away. There was barely enough room in the passage for one man to wield a sword.

While Merc confronted the soldiers to the left, I stepped through the door and engaged a trio who had moved to the right. I swung Overwhelm in a wide arc. The enchanted blade passed through the confining walls as if they did not exist. With three strokes I shattered my opponents' swords and split their bucklers. They immediately fled to the end of the hall, but there was no exit in that direction. Rif drew a long dirk and smilingly stalked them while I turned to help Merc.

He didn't need it. Not even having the courtesy to draw his own saber, Merc demolished his foes with empty hands. Fresh opponents streamed up the stairway at the left end of the hall. Merc let the first soldier reach him and casually disarmed the man, broke his neck, and flung him to his fellows. The storm troopers fell back again.

"Shoot the dogs!" said one. A crossbowman stepped to the fore and took aim. Merc stopped the quarrel with telekinesis, spun it about, and sent it back into the crossbowman's heart. The remaining Maceketeers retreated down the stairs.

"We've discouraged them for now," said Merc, "but we're still surrounded."

"Shall we go to the roof?" suggested Rif. His three victims lay stacked at the far end of the hall.

"They have archers on the surrounding buildings," I said.

"Up is not the way to go," agreed Merc.

"Down doesn't look too promising either," said Rif, glancing out the window.

The soldiers had a mobile ack gun aimed at our floor. An ack is an automatic arbalest, a large mounted crossbow which cocks and loads itself after each shot. Belt-fed, it could shoot a stream of ten yard-long steel quarrels in as many seconds. The ack crew opened fire, raking the fourth floor with deadly missiles that punched through the thin walls like fork prongs through lettuce. The barrage forced us away from the street side of the building. A crowd of archers and crossbowmen in the narrow alley behind the hotel also fired at the fourth floor, though with less spectacular effect. Others shot from the neighboring rooftops.

"They're chewing the walls apart," I said. "They'll bring down the roof."

"That's probably the idea," said Merc.

A crossbow bolt shot up through the floor two feet to my left and stuck in the ceiling. Another nearly skewered Rif, who danced aside just in time. Quarrels from the room below pierced the floor at random. We dodged and shuffled to avoid messy impalement.

"Shoddy construction here," noted Rif.

"I think it's time to go," said Merc. "Stand back."

With an emphatic downward gesture, he sent an invisible beam of force through the floor. It punched a shaft all the way to ground level.

"Follow me," said the wizard, leaping into the hole.

"I hate this sort of thing," I said.

Rif shrugged in reply and we jumped. Merc cast a spell to smooth our descent. We drifted gently into the hotel lobby, which was filled with Maceketeers. Perhaps fifty soldiers armed with swords, maces, and halberds surrounded us. They were packed too closely together to use their weapons effectively. Furthermore, we had the advantage of surprise. I laid about me with Overwhelm, breaking weapons and splitting skulls. Merc and Rif used their martial arts skills. We soon routed our attackers, sending them scurrying out the front door.

"So we have the place to ourselves," I said. "Now what?"

"It's not ours yet," said Merc.

Another two dozen men, most cradling crossbows, charged down the stairs. We braced ourselves for their onslaught. But they swept right past us and out the door without so much as a parting shot.

"Do they know something we don't?" I asked.

From above we heard a thunderous cracking of timbers and the clatter of falling boards. It sounded as if the entire building was about to come down on top of us.

It did. The roof caved in on the fourth floor, which crushed the third, which smashed the second, which gave way and dropped the entire mess on our heads.

We did not stand idle as this happened. Mercury raised an umbrella of mystic force which sheltered the three of us from the shower of debris. In seconds we were huddled together within a small dome of open space beneath a very large woodpile.

"Perfect!" exulted Merc, igniting a pocket lantern.

"Perfect?" I echoed. "This is not my idea of perfect."

"They think we're buried in here. It will take hours for them to dig through and discover their mistake. By the time they do, we will be inside the Solar Palace."

"But Merc, we *are* buried in here!"

"Not for long. Hold the umbrella."

Merc pulled a wooden box about one foot long and four inches deep from within the endless folds of his cloak. He knelt and opened it while Rif and I looked on.

It contained a dozen glass and ceramic vials of various colors, each marked with a paper label.

"We have to get out quietly, and I don't know a spell that will do that. But I may have what we need here in my Acme Alchemical Sampler. I've never had much use for potions. They're too unreliable. But we have no choice."

"You inspire confidence," I said.

"Let's see. We have levitation, universal antidote, night vision, sex appeal—ah! Bodily evaporation." He lifted a pale yellow vial.

"What does it do?" I asked.

"It will turn your body and belongings into a cloud of invisible vapor for about a half-hour if it works properly. That will allow you to flow right out of here undetected."

"Me?"

Merc studied the label. " 'Do not mix with other potions without consulting your alchemist . . . Do not use during pregnancy . . . Keep away from small children too stupid to know they shouldn't drink out of strange bottles.' Should be safe for you to use, Jason. As safe as potions can be."

"What about you two?"

"Here's a possibility for Rif. A shrinking potion. Rif, if you were about three inches tall, could you climb out of here in less than an hour?"

"No problem."

"Then you take this one." He handed Rif a green bottle. "What else is here? This one allows transformation into a small animal. I could turn into a snake and get out of here in no time. Though I hate transformations. I'm always afraid I'll get stuck in another form." He lifted a red vial and put the box away.

"We could trade," I said. "I'll be a snake."

"No. Animal transformations are too tricky for an amateur. Without proper training, you can forget that you aren't really an animal. I don't want you to get sidetracked chasing mice. Or Rif."

"Let Mercury be the snake," Rif hastily agreed. "Could I see that sex appeal potion?"

Merc smiled. "Some other time. We'll meet at the

Royal Ashley Tower. Be sure to quaff the entire contents of your bottles."

Rif drank his potion first. He rapidly shrank, clothing and all, until he was roughly six inches tall.

"You're supposed to be smaller," said Merc. "The potion must be spoiling."

"This is just fine," said Rif. His voice was comically high and tinny. He jogged up a crack beam until he was on a level with Merc's head.

"Fine unless the potion wears off while you're in a tight spot. You'll be meat pie then. Get going. We'll be right behind you."

Rif waved and scampered into a black gap to begin his climb.

"You're next," said Merc. I handed him the umbrella and drank my potion. It fizzed and stung as it went down and I felt its effects instantly. I become lightheaded and saw my body, clothes, and weapons shimmer and vanish into thin air—which is what I had become. I tried to speak, but naturally could not. I had no lungs, no vocal cords, no mouth. Yet my senses continued to function. I received inputs of sight, sound, and sensation directly in my mind, which was reduced to pure psychic energy. I maintained a sense of self and location despite my insubstantial condition. It was a bizarre and thrilling experience.

"Either it worked or it disintegrated you," said Merc. He drank his potion. His form shimmered and twisted, and he became a deadly violet and indigo-striped Cyrillan deathadder. It was just like Mercury to choose a dangerous species in case he ran into trouble. The wizard slithered into the same hole Rif had used, abandoning the mystic umbrella.

I allowed myself to flow upward through the cracks. Movement was a matter of mental effort. I thought of the direction I wanted to go and my airy substance obeyed. I slipped through the smallest of spaces. Anywhere air could go, I could go. I circulated myself to the outside.

Dozens of storm troopers busily dug through the ruins of the collapsed building, dragging beams, posts, and planks away in an effort to confirm our deaths and recover the bodies of their companions. The archers on the surrounding rooftops eyed the scene with suspicious caution.

After a few minutes, Rifkin slipped out of the wreckage and past the crowd into a nearby alley. It would be a long hike to the Royal Ashley at his present height, and he would be endangered by any passing dog, rat, or cat. I expected him to get under cover and wait for the potion to wear off before heading for our rendezvous.

Mercury slithered out moments later and made for the same alley. He still had several yards to go when a storm trooper spotted him. The Maceketeer raised his mace to crush the snake's head.

I swooped down and blew a cloud of dirt and trash into the soldier's face. His blow missed Merc. Moreover, the startled warrior tripped and fell flat on his face. Merc struck, biting the unfortunate storm trooper on the neck and injecting a dose of lethal venom before making his escape. The soldier foamed at the mouth, convulsed, and died.

I intended to follow Merc and Rif so that we would be together when the effects of the potions wore off; but I was caught in a sudden gust of wind that slammed me into the side of a building across the street. My substance scattered in every direction and it took me a few seconds to pull myself together. An updraft caught me and lifted me in a tight spiral, upward and upward, until I was higher than even the pinnacle tower of the Solar Palace.

From this vantage point I could see the whole city and the surrounding countryside. Rae City was laid out in a series of concentric circles. In the center was the angular Solar Palace. Its upper surface was covered with mirrored reflectors, prisms, and skylights. Solar energy ran the air and water pumps that made life in the huge palace possible. The mirrors and crystals atop the palace gathered the bounty of Rae for these purposes, though not on dark days like this.

The palace was the focus of the city. Twelve circular avenues called "wheels" surrounded it. The First Wheel was the one nearest the palace. The Twelfth Wheel marked the inside of the city's outer wall. Twelve avenues radiated from the palace like spokes. The Avenue of Morning led east to the Dawn Chapel, located between the Eighth and Ninth Wheels. The west-running Afternoon Avenue led to the similarly located Dusk Chapel. The rest of the spokes ran all the way to the Twelfth Wheel. As a result, the city looked like a gigantic pie cut into sections. It was a pie with a diameter of about three miles. Of course, there were many side streets and alleys, but the wheels and spokes dictated their placement.

Slumville occupied a wedge of land in the northeast quadrant from the Tenth Wheel to the outer wall. A large detachment of Maceketeers from the Solar Palace headed into Slumville to aid in moving the hotel debris. From the west side of town, a force of Home Guards, distinguished by their crimson uniforms and feathered helmets, marched to engage the storm troopers. If the two forces met, storm troopers would be pulled away from digging out the rubble. That would delay discovery of our escape.

I headed for the Royal Ashley Tower. It was named for the legendary Queen Ashley, heroic wife of King Raemond the Quite Patient, a ruler in the seventh century A.H. "Lady Lively," as Ashley was known, was not one to sit around the castle and knit sweaters like other highborn women of her day. Instead, she traveled about fighting monsters, smiting evil-doers, dueling, jousting, and otherwise outshining most male warriors of her era. Stories about her were a favorite among Raelnan girls.

The tower named in her honor, a smooth spire of Ganthian bluestone, had suffered extensive damage during last spring's demonic invasion of Rae City. The upper levels were destroyed by the deadly light beams of the rampaging AMOK defense system. Repairs were still underway, as evidenced by the fragile scaffolding surmounting the half-built structure.

Night fell and so did I. I felt myself solidify as I whirled my way down through the girders. I still amounted to nothing more than a sudden breeze, but if I didn't reach the ground before my transformation back to human form was complete, I would become a sudden red splash. I crossed the plane of the high wooden fence which kept the public out of the construction area. But I was still twenty feet above the sidewalk when my body abruptly returned. Fortunately, my miraculum armor absorbed most of the shock. I dissipated the rest by rolling over and over. Luckily, no one noticed my sudden appearance in the area.

Observing no sign of Merc or Rif, I strolled down the sidewalk and turned onto the Seventh Spoke fronting the southeast side of the tower, intending to circle the building. If my half-hour was up, my companions had a while yet before their potions wore off. I was on my tenth circuit of the building and starting to feel conspicuous when Merc called to me from a shadowy alcove.

"Pssst! Jassson! In here."

His voice seemed unusually sibilant, and when I ducked into the shadows I saw why. Merc was more or less restored to his normal form, but he had serpentine eyes and scaly skin with pale violet and indigo stripes. When he smiled, I saw that he also retained a serpent's fangs and forked tongue.

"The damned potion hasss done thisss to me," he hissed. "I hate potionsss."

"Is this permanent?" I asked in horror.

"I sssertainly hope not. I exsspect thesse ssside-effectss will wear off sssoon. Have *you* notisssed any problemsss?"

"Not since I ssshifted, I mean shifted, back."

Merc nodded. "Good."

"Where is Rif?"

"Right here," came a voice at my waist. I looked down and saw that Rif was still only about three feet tall. "My potion is wearing off in fits and starts."

"No matter," said Merc. "We will go forward. Open that manhole, Jassson."

"This should give us access to the maintenance tunnels beneath the street," said Rif as I lifted the heavy metal lid. "We'll follow the network directly into the dungeon beneath the palace. Then we can do what we came here to do."

7 _____

The maintenance tunnel beneath the street, which workers used to gain access to water and sewer lines, was dark, damp, and narrow. Because of the pipes clustered all around us, we had to walk in single file. Merc led the way. We traversed perhaps two hundred yards, passing beneath the Royal Ashley and the First Wheel, to reach a door of plated steel that sealed the tunnel. A faint light globe hung above it. The words **High Security Area: Authorized Personnel Only** were stenciled across the door in bold black letters. I saw no apparent means of opening it.

"Rif?" Merc called.

The thief squirmed to the front and ran his sensitive fingers across the gleaming surface of the door. He probed the cracks where the door met its frame. "It drops from above," he announced. "The operating mechanism is on the other side. The slight discoloration of the metal shows that the door is a magisteel alloy."

"What's that?" Metallurgy was not one of my strong points.

Merc explained. "Because of their magnetic propertiesss, iron and ssssteel block sssome kindsss of magic by disrupting the arcane energy patterns." He coughed. "Ah, my natural tongue is back. Those extra *s*'s were getting to be a pain. As I was saying, the presence of a large enough quantity of iron can cause certain spells of misfire or fail altogether. Magicians call this the "iron effect." This problem was first overcome about three hundred years ago when Pondu, the father of modern alchemy, developed the synthetic mineral magist. Mixed with iron or steel, magist neutralizes the disruption effect without disturbing the other properties of the metal. The resulting mixture is called magiron or magisteel. It is much more expensive than ordinary steel."

I yawned. Merc ignored it.

"You can identify magisteel by the faint blue or green sheen in the metal," said Rif. "Of course, it takes a trained eye to spot it."

Merc continued: "Long-term spells cast directly onto an object—such as warding spells on doors—are particularly subject to the iron effect. It is next to impossible to enchant an ordinary steel sword or suit of armor. It has to be magisteel or some other metal like miraculum. That's why everyone you meet doesn't have a magic sword."

Rif took up the lecture again. "As Mercury suggests, the presence of magisteel in this door may indicate the presence of a warding spell, either a trap or an alarm. Or both."

"I wasn't expecting this," said Merc. "Raella must have installed these since the last time I was down here, which was several years ago. Ordinarily, I'd say it was a good idea. But normally I'd be on the other side of the door."

"The CIS blueprints don't show warded doors," said Rif. "Someone is slipping up on the job."

"Did we answer your question?" asked Merc.

"Quite. Remind me not to ask another one."

"Mercury, can you run a spell check?" inquired Rif.

"Stand back," said the wizard, pulling an oblong silver object from his cloak. It was about the size of a loaf of bread and resembled a giant metallic cockroach. The device had a pair of short antennae at one end, a small glass screen, and several dials.

"What is that?" asked Rif.

"The Magitronics Spellsniffer 2000. I bought it at a technomagic trade fair last month. This device contains a smart crystal capable of detecting and identifying over fifteen hundred spells and enchantments. It will even measure the strength of the spell and calculate how long ago it was cast. By using this, I conserve my personal energy for emergencies."

"I should get one of those," said Rif. "It could be useful in my work."

"Provided you have sufficient magical talent to learn

the activating spell," said Merc, flicking his fingers. The Spellsniffer hummed and glowed in response.

"Oh well," said Rif.

Merc aimed the device at the door and scanned it from top to bottom in a series of horizontal and vertical sweeps. The antennae quivered as the machine hummed and clicked softly. Merc studied the screen and adjusted the dials. After about five minutes, he switched off the device and hid it under his cloak.

"We've got a standard alarm and locking spell in the middle range of strength. It was cast about a year ago. I can neutralize the enchantment easily." He made several elaborate hand passes and muttered some incomprehensible magical babble. "Done."

"The door is still closed," I observed.

"That is because I have not yet cast a door-opening spell, which I am about to do." He pointed at the door and said, in a commanding voice, "Presto!"

The door slid open, and we entered a dank corridor. After walking fifty yards, we emerged into a large room dominated by four smelly, gurgling metal tanks at least thirty feet tall. Each had a pipe as thick as an ale barrel protruding from its top and disappearing into the shadows above. We could not see the ceiling due to the profusion of lesser pipes, ladders, and catwalks above us. A dozen poorly placed light globes in wire cages provided dim light. Malodorous puddles of unidentifiable liquid stained the floor. Dripping leaks from joints and spigots fed them.

"Every drain from every tub, sink, and toilet in the palace runs into these four tanks," said Merc. My nose agreed. "To the north are the steam and water pump rooms. East is the air pump system and the heavily guarded sunlight vat." The Raelnan military had a secret process for making liquid sunlight, which they stored in huge vats and used to power the AMOK system. "The cell block is beneath the center of the palace, northeast of our current location. Follow me."

Before we could take five steps, a rat bigger than a Ganthian shepherd dog rushed out and bit my leg. Its teeth penetrated the tough leather of my boots but did not reach my flesh. The animal's shoulder was as high as Rifkin's at the moment. Its damp fur was matted with filth. Foul yellow saliva dripped from its mouth. I gave the beast a swift kick that sent it sprawling across the floor. But it quickly regained its feet and charged again. Five more of its kind joined it. They came at us recklessly, spitting and drooling, their claws scuttling across the stone floor, their fleshy tails flicking from side to side.

"Scum rats!" said Rif. "Their diseased bite means certain death." He sent a knife through the lead rat's skull. The rest kept advancing. I drew Overwhelm and Merc produced his favorite saber to meet the attack. We each dispatched a rat. The two remaining rats leaped for our throats. Mercury neatly sidestepped his rat, which crashed into a cluster of pipes behind him. It was stunned when it hit the floor and Merc skewered it before it could recover.

My rat bit at my chest, hissing with pain as its fangs shattered against my armor. I sliced it in two before it hit the ground. The smell was sickening, but considering the diet of these creatures, one would not expect their innards to be rose-scented.

"Let's move before the rest arrive," said Merc. "These five are not the full pack."

"True," said Rif, who had grown a foot taller during the fray.

We killed another four rats before reaching the exit we sought, but heard many more hissing in the gloom. I slammed the steel hatch behind me as we exited the chamber of sewage.

"That should hold them," I said.

"At least until they find an alternate route," said Merc. "Scum rats are cunning and persistent. Though I think they'll be content to feast on their fallen brothers for now."

There were fewer pipes in this tunnel, all of them near the ceiling. The passage was wide enough for Merc and I to walk side-by-side, with Rif trailing behind. It was lit with dim light globes spaced just far enough apart that we could stand under one globe and barely make out the next one. We moved rapidly but cautiously, none of us fully convinced that the vicious scum rats had given up. Nor did we know what other denizens of the dark we might encounter.

After ten minutes, we entered a better-lit and more frequently traveled area, where we promptly encountered a pair of Maceketeers on patrol.

"Halt!" they commanded, lowering their pikes.

"Is there a problem?" I asked, raising my hands. They never got a chance to answer, because while I distracted them, Merc struck like a cobra, hitting both men with sufficient force to knock them unconscious. Rif made sure they wouldn't wake up. We continued down the tunnel until we came to an intersection.

"Around this corner and down a short stairway is the guard station," whispered Merc. "Beyond it is the gate to the cell block. There are twenty cells, ten on each side of a straight corridor. Each has a steel door. At the end of the corridor is the old torture chamber. Once we take out the guards, you will be the lookout, Rif. Jason and I will look for Hotfur. We have to hit hard and fast and be out of here before reinforcements arrive. Any questions? . . . Then let's do it."

We drew our weapons and rounded the corner. A steel-plated door barred out path.

"I forgot about this," said Merc. "It's usually open."

"Would it have a warding spell on it?" I asked.

"No, it's ordinary steel."

"Then I'll open it." I used Overwhelm to cut a six-foot hole in the door, and kicked the circle of steel and underlying oak through to the other side. It tumbled down the stairway with an enormous clang. I was right behind it, bellowing a fearsome war cry.

Ten startled Maceketeers awaited us. In my first rush, I beheaded one and amputated the sword arm of another. Both left scarlet trails in the air as they fell.

Merc and Rif entered the room before any of the other defenders could react. The wizard slashed with his saber, the spy with a long dirk. We took our opponents by complete surprise, not giving them any time to utilize their advantage of numbers.

"Stop that one!" cried Merc, but his warning came too late. One of the storm troopers yanked hard on a stout cord hanging from the ceiling. Elsewhere in the palace a bell rang, summoning reinforcements. The soldier continued to pull on the cord as I cut him down.

Only three of the enemy remained standing. I called on them to surrender, but they snarled defiance and attacked. Each of us engaged a trooper. The bodies hit the floor together.

"Jason! The door!" The gate to the cell block was identical to the door I had just sliced through. I gave this one the same treatment, and Merc and I rushed through.

We wasted no time inspecting the cells. I took the left side, slicing the locks out and kicking the doors open. Merc took the right side, shouting "Presto!" over and over.

All twenty cells were empty. That brought us to the torture chamber. This door was plated with ominous black iron. It made no difference to Overwelm.

The round room beyond was filled with tools of torture, including a rack, an iron maiden, a bed of nails, a fire pit, and large brass tubs. There were racks of knives, hooks, feather dusters, pliers, hammers, and saws. The room reeked of pain and suffering. The floor was dark with ancient blood stains.

With her arms tied behind her back, Vixen Hotfur hung by her ankles over a bed of hot coals. Her naked body, slick with sweat and criss-crossed with the fine white scars of many battle wounds, was a mass of purple welts and bruises. Blood trickled from her nose and mouth. Where her left eye had been, there remained only a ragged red hole.

The torturers were hiding, attempting an ambush. It was a futile effort. We knew they were there, and we knew they would never leave that room alive. One stood inside the door, his club raised to strike. It shattered on my helmet, doing no damage. I grabbed my attacker by the front of his black tunic and hurled him across the room. He landed on a bed of nails with a wet thud. A second man rushed me with a pike. I sliced the haft in two, then did the same to him.

Merc got the third man. It wasn't pretty. He fell in several different directions. A fourth jumped him from behind. The wizard flipped him through the air so that he landed in the hot coals. I put my sword through the torturer's heart, ending his screams, then used his smoking body as a foothold while I cut Hotfur free.

The stench of burning flesh drove us from the room. I set Vixen down gently in the corridor and Merc knelt to inspect her.

"Is she—"

"Alive?" groaned Hotfur. "Aye, lad." She peered at Merc with her remaining eye. "You look like a snake."

"And you look like Hell."

"I feel worse. Those cork-slurping syrup-slickers have been working on me since I got here." She spit a tooth. "Thule himself put my eye out with a hot poker."

"When was this?"

"How in damnation should I know? I've been hanging upside down in a dungeon since the wedding!"

"You should have seen the reception," I said.

"Move it back there!" yelled Rif. "I hear many boots headed our way."

"You're in worse shape than I expected," said Merc.

"You should talk, scale-face."

Merc produced his box of potions. "I've got a healing elixir here, General, which should restore you in short order if it works properly. But the side effects are unpredictable."

"I'll chance it."

Merc poured a thick pink liquid down her throat. She coughed and sneezed and shuddered and groaned and passed out.

"It must be potent," I said.

Merc withdrew buckskin breeches, boots, and a jacket from his cloak. "Let's get her dressed." We went to work.

"The party is about to start without you!" called Rif.

"I think I've got an eyepatch too." He rummaged around under his left armpit until he found it and strapped it in place aound her head. "Ouch!" he exclaimed.

"What?"

"I cut my tongue on these damned fangs."

We left Hotfur where she was and hustled back to the guard room. Through the door I saw a squad of Maceketeers rushing down the corridor with lowered pikes. We were trapped again.

8

"I've had enough of this," groused Merc. He wriggled his fingers, said something unpronounceable, and incinerated the onrushing Maceketeers with a sheet of golden flame.

"Wow," I said. "You should do that more often."

"No," said Merc. "A wizard who relies overmuch on his own magic becomes a dead wizard. I know that looked easy, but there is always a chance that your spell will fizzle, usually when you need it most. That's why I learned the arts of physical combat. I reserve my spells for those situations in which I have no alternative."

"Or lose your temper," noted Rif.

"That too. Let's check on—"

"Me?" said Vixen Hotfur, striding into the room. The cuts and bruises on her face were gone. Except for her missing eye, she showed no signs of her recent ordeal. The elixir did its work well.

"What a surprise," said Merc. "I thought my miracle cure had finished you off. You never know with potions."

She flexed her arms. "I feel as fit as ever. Just give me a sword and I'm ready to help you hang Thule's maggoty head on a pike."

"Take your pick," said Merc, indicating the litter of dead storm troopers in the guard room, none of whom would complain if Hotfur borrowed his weapons. "But I assure you I have nothing so gentle in mind for the Dark Duke."

"Suits me," said Hotfur, selecting a buckler and saber.

"So what is the next phase of your plan, Merc?" I asked.

"Now we go upstairs and find Thule."

"Inspired," said Rif. "Brilliant strategic thinking."

"Thank you."

We took an elevator to the throne-room level to begin our search. It stood to reason that if Thule fancied himself a king, he would want to do kingly things like sit on the Prism Throne and wave the golden scepter about while he issued royal decrees. Usurpers especially go in for that sort of thing.

The doors slid open and we stepped warily into an antechamber just off the grand corridor, which led to the throne room. We heard a crash and clamor of serious armed combat. Peeking cautiously around the corner, we saw a palace coup in progress. Or was it a counter-coup?

Whatever the appropriate terminology, if Thule Nethershawn was in the throne room, he was in trouble. About thirty Maceketeers defended a barricade of overturned furniture in front of the massive silver doors which sealed the entrance to the throne chamber. Their opponents were a force of Home Guards and regular army troops who outnumbered them two-to-one. A bronze-limbed woman with platinum blond hair plaited into war braids led the attack. She could only be Devra Highrider, daughter of a hill tribe chieftain and Captain-General of the Home Guard. Well, she could have been someone else, I suppose. It wasn't as if sword-slinging, bronze-limbed women with platinum blond hair weren't a common sight.

Merc smiled as we stepped into the corridor. "Well, well, well. It looks like Thule sent so many of his lackeys into Slumville that he left himself short-handed here. He's more afraid of us than I thought."

"You did quite a job on him the other day," I said. "And I *am* Jason Cosmo."

"I guess you're right. Well, it was clever of Captain Highrider to recognize Thule's error and get things started here. We'll have our dramatic throne room confrontation sooner than I thought."

"She's a good lass," agreed Hotfur. We drew our weapons and strode side by side toward the fray.

Before we could join the battle, more shouting and the ring of weapon on weapon broke out behind us. Fifty or so Maceketeers were driving back a dozen white-uniformed Palace Guards. The Guards, charged with protecting the Solar Palace and its inhabitants, looked half dead. They were gaunt and unshaven, their filthy uniforms in tatters, their shields battered, their bodies pierced with many wounds. Hotfur and I sprang to their aid while Merc and Rif continued toward the throne room.

"For Raella!" cried Hotfur, laying into the storm troopers with the fury of a Malravian rock tiger. And not just any Malravian rock tiger, but one which has been wounded by hunters' spears, seen its mate and cubs slaughtered, and gone without fresh meat for several days.

I echoed her cry and swung Overwhelm. I didn't quite muster the fury of a rock tiger, Malravian or otherwise, but then I hadn't been tortured by these guys for four days straight. The Maceketeers fell back.

"My General!" exclaimed the leader of the Guards as he recognized Hotfur. He was a swarthy Xornite with a thick bull neck. "We thought you dead!"

"Taurus, you old mud walrus! No, man, I was just relaxing in the dungeon. Why didn't you visit?"

Captain Taurus hung his head in shame. "We were taken unawares, my General. Most of my warriors were with me in the wedding parade when a thousand Maceketeers stormed the palace. For four days we have fought alongside the Home Guard against the rebels. Only this night have we regained the palace. Of my hundred fighters, only eleven remain."

"Chin up, man! We're soon to set things right. At them!"

Hotfur and I waded into the Maceketeers with Taurus and his brave Palace Guards right behind us, ready to fight until they dropped from sheer exhaustion. We drove our foes back down the corridor and through a cloak room into the state dining room. With much smashing of china and glassware and breaking of chairs, we pushed the Maceketeers on through to the grand ballroom. There the dance of death continued until only two storm troopers remained, then one, then none. They knew better than to surrender. There would be no quarter asked nor given in this fight.

"To the throne room!" I cried.

"Hold it!" said Hotfur. "I give the orders here, Cosmo."

"Sorry. I just got carried away."

"To the throne room!" cried Hotfur.

We retraced our steps to the great corridor. There was not much left of the storm troopers' barricade, nor for that matter the storm troopers themselves. The silver doors were ajar and weirdly colored flashes of spell light emanated from the gap. Merc was obviously venting his rage on those within.

We started for the throne room, but paused when a chime announced the arrival of an elevator. Did it bring friends or foes? We ranged ourselves before the elevator bank and waited to find out.

The doors slid open to reveal a car filled to the top with hissing, squirming scum rats. The cunning animals had followed my party's scent from the dark passages below and still thirsted for our blood! They piled out of the elevator and advanced, fangs bared.

"I'll handle this," I said. "The rest of you go on!"

"Nonsense, man!" cried Hotfur. "We can't leave you to face these vermin alone!"

There was no time for further debate, for the rats were upon us. As before, they jumped and bit and scratched. Even ordinary mail was proof against their needle-sharp teeth, but they were fast and vicious, striking at exposed flesh whenever they could. Two guards went down in the press and were quickly ripped apart. Several others suffered nasty bites which would soon fester with infection. Still, we put most of the beasts to death. A few survivors piled back into the elevator and escaped, but we didn't have time to chase them now.

I was the first to reach the throne room. I stepped warily through the doors, Overwhelm held high, to behold the ruins of a wonderland. Half the glass dome of the ceiling had collapsed, littering the carpeted floor with jagged crystal shards. Here and there lay huge chunks of white stone. Pools of boiling water from shattered fountains made the floor a swamp. Ragged holes had been blasted in the walls. Clouds of vividly colored smoke and pastel steam hung thickly in the air. The trees and bright flowers of the place were burnt, crushed, wilted, and otherwise damaged. Stunned parrots flopped on terraces. Dead soldiers lay everywhere in broken and grotesque postures.

On a high dais was the Prism Throne, carved from a single gigantic crystal. Thule Nethershawn sat there, laughing that contemptuous laugh that only the foulest villains can muster. A jeweled diadem adorned his brow. Weird spirals and globes of sorcerous light flashed and flickered around him and were sucked into the substance of the throne. Their source, of course, was Mercury, who stood in the midst of the devastation waving his hands, wriggling his fingers, saying strange words, hopping on one foot, flapping his elbows, and doing the other things wizards do to work their magic. I saw no immediate sign of Rif, Highrider, or the other soldiers.

"You are an obstinate fool, aren't you, Boltblaster?" said Thule. "You know as well as I that the Prism Throne is enchanted to protect its occupant from all harm, both magical and physical, yet you insist on hurling your entire arcane arsenal at me. All you are likely to accomplish is to bring the roof down upon yourself and your fellow rebels. I shall emerge unscathed." To punctuate his remark, a stray streamer of mauve fire rebounded off the far wall and nearly took my head off.

"I'd advise ducking for cover," said Rif from beneath a tent of rubble. "Merc isn't worrying much about bystanders." I joined him in his makeshift shelter. Hotfur and the others also dashed for sanctuary wherever they could find it.

"What did I miss?"

"Merc went through the Maceketeers like a whirlwind and led the way in here. He threatened to do many unpleasant things to Thule and vice versa. He cast a few ineffective spells. Thule laughed and made a few pompous remarks. Merc fired off a few more spells which bounced all over the place, the rest of us ran for cover, and that's about where you came in."

"This defiance is useless," said Thule. "My loyal Maceketeers outnumber the treacherous Home Guard by several thousand. Even though you have breached the gates of the palace, it will avail you naught. As soon as my men return from Slumville you will be overwhelmed and annihilated. I certainly fear no harm at your hands in the meantime. My place on the Prism Throne is quite secure—in more ways than one."

"Thule doesn't know it," said Rif, "but none of his men are coming back from Slumville. Colonel Gerron has them trapped. Or so Highrider tells me. This is all working out rather well, don't you think?"

"Well, serpent, have you anything to say?" demanded Thule.

"No," said Merc, sending a small but intense ice storm at the Dark Duke.

"Of course you realize," said Rif, "that none of this world have been possible if I hadn't been followed, thus drawing the Maceketeers into the trap."

"Congratulations," I said. "I knew you had something brilliant up your sleeve."

"What is the point of my vaunting and gloating if no one is to offer me a rejoinder?" said Thule. "Have you no sense of propriety whatsoever?"

"I'll give you a rejoinder," I said, popping up. "I think you overlook the approach of Feri Halehart and Monfort Corona when you boast of how secure you are. Their numbers far exceed your own."

"Ah! Cosmo. I am not unaware of their treacherous march on my capital or of their numerical advantage. But what I lack in numbers, I make up in other ways. You have surely deduced by now that I am allied with members of the Dark Magic Society. Their sorcerous succor will be more than enough to crush those traitors."

"What do you know?" said Rif. "We were right."

Thule only blinked as a Ray of Terrific Force fizzled out around him. "Really, Boltblaster, this grows most tiresome. Why don't you just give it up?"

Merc didn't answer. Nethershawn didn't seem to notice that the Prism Throne had taken on a faint orange glow. I glanced sidelong at Merc and guessed what he was up to. The crystal of the throne absorbed spell energy, but there was a limit to its capacity. Once that limit was passed, the magic of each new spell would heat the crystal. Eventually it would become so hot that Thule would have to abandon it. Then he was ours. We were already over the threshold. I kept Thule's attention while Merc started another spell.

"You won't have much left to rule, Thule, after you destroy the army, murder all the nobles, and burn down the city."

"New armies can be raised, new nobles created, new cities built. I will bring Raelna an age of glory such as it has never seen. We will conquer Orphalia, lay waste to our ancient Brythalian foes, and make even the Carathan lords tremble in their shining towers."

"How progressive," muttered Rif.

"Uh-huh." Whatever spell Merc was cooking up, it was elaborate. I had to keep Thule's attention. "Tell me, Nethershawn, who placed the crown on your head? I doubt it was the priests of Rae."

"Those blathering clerics refused to perform the rite, so I crowned myself. They will sing a different tune once I drag them from their cubicles and send them to the salt mines!"

"Raelna doesn't have any salt mines."

"An oversight we shall soon remedy. We will have salt mines so deep and foul that none will dare defy me for fear of being cast into them." The tyrant paused, his nose twitching. "Do I smell smoke?" He glanced at his smoldering tunic. "What is this? The throne—"

He didn't complete his statement of the obvious. Merc rolled a thirty-foot fireball up the stairs, overloading the spell-saturated throne and superheating it so that it flared red, blue, and white-hot in the space of a few seconds. Thule leaped to his feet, howling in anguish as the flames whirled around him. His body was just visible amid the holocaust. He stumbled on the stairs, fell to his knees, and tumbled down to land at Merc's feet as a charred, smoking skeleton.

Everyone was stunned. Rif, Hotfur, Highrider, and the others emerged from their hiding places slack-jawed. They gaped at the glowing throne. They gaped at the remains of the well-done Dark Duke. They gaped at Mercury and his power. There was a whole lot of gaping going on.

"Well," I said at length. "I guess he got the hot seat."

"Yes," said Rifkin. "Frankly, I was expecting him to get away this time and show up later for the big battle at the end. We're doing pretty well to have knocked off one of the main villains so early on."

By dawn, Rae City belonged to the loyalist forces, though it wasn't clear to anyone just who exactly they were loyal to. Perhaps Duke Corona. He wanted to be King, and was likely to be, but wasn't yet. Vixen Hotfur had the respect of all, but obviously wasn't a candidate to be Queen of Raelna, being neither royal nor Raelnan. Merc lacked a few unspoken ceremonial words of being a bereaved Prince Consort of the Realm. As it was, he was merely bereaved. Of course, he wasn't Raelnan either.

Thule's death took the fight out of his warriors. Regular and Home Guard forces trapped the bulk of the Maceketeers in Slumville and set fire to the area. Most of them managed to escape out the northeast gate, but hundreds perished. Once outside the city, the storm troopers had little hope of reentering. Nearly four thousand Maceketeers led by Bobhe Skuldrudge escaped into the countryside. They were sure to turn up somewhere, someday, but they were finished as a force in Raelna.

While the victors patrolled the newly reconquered streets, the leaders of the city convened in the chambers of the Royal Council to begin the process of restoring order. The meeting room smelled of age and power and tradition. It featured a round table of light gray marble surrounded by comfortable leather swivel chairs. Oil portraits of past Raelnan kings and queens hung on the paneled walls. They were a stern and noble-looking bunch. Most had those famous blue Shurbenholt eyes.

Vixen sat on one side of the table, with Colonel Gerron, Devra Highrider, and Captain Taurus to her right. Mercury sat at Hotfur's left. His snakish appearance made everyone uneasy. I sat beside Merc. Midway around the table from our group was Lotho Corona, Assistant Deputy High Priest of Rae. He was now the ranking official of the Church of Rae. He was also important because he was Duke Monfort's younger brother.

Opposite the military officers were the surviving members of the civilian government, Chancellor Vannevar and the Royal Treasurer, Penrhyn Teller. Teller, nearly ninety, slept in his chair and snored loudly.

Rifkin was not present, having no place in the councils of state. He was presumably amusing himself elsewhere in the palace. I was present in my capacity as the favored hero of the Goddess Rae.

"The royal army has regained control of Rae City," said Hotfur. "We will organize a pursuit of the Maceketeers and—"

Chancellor Lord Vannevar coughed discreetly. Over seventy, Margrave Vannevar had held his post since early in the reign of Raella's father. He had a crafty gleam in his eyes that reflected his love of and talent for political intrigue and verbal dispute. It was said that old Vannevar could convince a circle it was a square if given half a chance. He had used his considerable prestige and talent to help Raella enact her sweeping radical reforms despite his personal belief that they were really too sweeping and too radical. Bringing them to life against the implacable opposition to his fellow aristocrats was a challenge Vannevar couldn't resist.

"Yes, Lord Chancellor?" said Hotfur respectfully.

"I am certain that you shall apprehend Thule's thugs in good time, General. However, our immediate task is to order the royal chaos which Her Majesty's government has become. Thule's assassins have slaughtered all of the ministers save Lord Teller and myself, who were fortunate enough to find safety with Colonel Gerron. The military is divided, with General Crossmaster's loyalties and purposes unknown and General Halehart's all too clear. The Council of Nobles is a shambles and the House of Shurbenholt with it. At the moment there is no effective government in Raelna. This is a dangerous condition. It makes us a tempting target for the likes of the Brythalian monarch or the Imperator of Ganth. Until we identify and install our new monarch, we cannot form an official government. Typically, the Council of Nobles governs during an interregnum, but we find ourselves in unique circumstances. I propose the formation of a Provisional Council to govern the kingdom until such time as a King or Queen can be crowned."

"We should have a King in a day or two," said Lotho Corona. The priest was a balding, corpulent man who sweated profusely and frequently mopped his brow with a red silk handkerchief.

"You refer," said Vannevar, "to your able brother, Duke Monfort, who I am sure you will have no objections to anointing."

"Naturally not," said Corona. "The House of Corona is a cadet branch of the House of Shurbenholt. Our great-grandfather was King Raebert the Hatmaker."

"Be that as it may, the choice of a King is delegated by tradition to the Council of Nobles. And until that Council meets in full and elects a King, there is no King. The problem, thanks to Thule's assassins, is determining the membership of the Noble Council. The heirs of the slain cannot legally inherit, and thus take their rightful places in the Council, until confirmed by the monarch. But no monarch can be crowned until the Council sits and elects him or her. You see the dilemma."

"Yes," said Lotho hesitantly.

"And thus the need for a Provisional Council. Someone must make policy, keep the machinery of government going, and generally guide Raelna through this crisis while the Noble Council is restocked."

"And who will sit on this Provisional Council?" squeaked Lotho.

"Myself, naturally, and the soundly slumbering Lord Treasurer to represent the government. You to speak for the Church of Rae. General Hotfur to represent the military. And a representative member of the noble class."

"My brother perhaps?" said Lotho tentatively.

"Splendid suggestion! I can't think of a more suitable individual. When he arrives, why don't you put the idea to him when you explain why he can't be King yet? It might soften the blow."

"I'll do that," said Lotho, clearly not relishing the prospect.

"Very well, then," said Vannevar. "We four shall carry on for now. We must elect a chairman."

"You are the obvious choice," said Hotfur.

"Then if there is no objection, I accept," purred Vannevar. "I will now entertain a motion to appoint General Hotfur to be Regent Protector of the Realm, with a full grant of emergency powers."

"What is this?" asked Corona.

"I want to give General Hotfur full liberty to suppress rebellion and secure the realm against foreign invasion. I want her to have carte blanche to do whatever she deems necessary without having to constantly report back to the Council."

"Is this . . . wise?" asked Corona, mopping his brow and glancing sidelong at Hotfur.

"If by that you betray a fear that General Hotfur will abuse such authority, I must remind you of her background. She has a well-founded and deep-seated abhorrence of military dictatorship and a clear understanding of the army's proper role. Isn't that correct, General?"

"Damn straight."

"I am still waiting for a motion," said Vannevar pointedly, his gray eyes boring into Lotho Corona.

"I . . . move General Hotfur's appointment," said the priest.

"Is there objection?" asked Vannevar. "Hearing none, the appointment is made. General, you will deal with the military situation as you see fit. Leave the diplomatic and civil side of things to the rest of us."

"Gladly."

"You may begin by giving us your assessment of the current state of affairs."

"Actually, we aren't in such bad shape. We've had no word from General Ercan the Reaver of trouble on the Brythalian frontier as of yet. General Halehart will join us in Rae City soon and brings a sizable reserve which can be sent to any trouble area. General Crossmaster's action in Orphalia is unauthorized, but there may be wisdom in it. We don't want the Brythalians or Ganthians to use the civil war as an excuse to gain a stronghold there."

Vannevar narrowed his eyes to slits. "So in your esti-
mation, General Crossmaster took it upon himself to
gain one for Raelna first?"

"That may be his reasoning. It's what I would have
done."

"Indeed? How interesting. You don't doubt his loyalty?"

"The Army of the Longwash was my old command. I
wouldn't turn it over to anyone I didn't have complete
confidence in."

"Then what course do you propose to take?"

"I will ask Cull to explain his actions. Assuming his
explanation is satisfactory, as I'm sure it will be, I intend
to let him carry on."

"Very well," said Vannevar, apparently satisfied. I
noticed that Merc had an odd look on his face and gave
him a questioning glance. He ignored it. "And what of
you, Lord Boltblaster? You have done Raelna a great
service by slaying the Dark Duke. What will you do now?"

"Now we will find Zaran Zimzabar and do the whole
world a big service," said Merc. "We'll pick up his trail
in Glymph."

"I will give you as many men as you need," said
Hotfur.

"We have all we need," said Merc.

"I was afraid you would say that," I said.

My statement was followed by one of those odd and
awkward moments of silence which grip groups from
time to time. In Arden, it was believed such silences
meant bad news would soon arrive.

It did.

There was a commotion at the door. A young lieutenant in the Army of the North entered the room. He was
covered with grime and sweat, having ridden far and fast.
He saluted wearily. We waited expectantly.

"My lords, I bear ill tidings. Late yesterday there was
a massive invasion in the northeast sector of the Brythalian
front. General Ercan estimates he faces a force of seventy thousand."

"Seventy thousand!" exclaimed Hotfur. "King Rubric
must have armed every gravy-sucking man in his lice-
ridden kingdom to field an army that big!"

"He evidently hired the remnants of King Halogen's mercenary army from last spring, my General. General Ercan believes the Brythalian objective is Rae City. He is attempting to maintain his position, but urgently needs reinforcements."

"Then he shall have them!" said Hotfur. "The day hasn't dawned when a Brythalian army of any size can beat Raelna's finest!"

"Or so we all hope," said Vannevar.

9

"Out of the question!" I said.

"Be reasonable," said Mercury. "It's the fastest way to go."

"That's what I'm afraid of."

Merc and I argued in Raella's bedroom, a spacious chamber with gem-studded walls and a lifelike celestial scene painted on the ceiling. The wizard wanted to conjure up a flying carpet from the blue magic carpet grass covering the floor. When we left the Provisional Council, they were still discussing the best response to the Brythalian invasion. Merc was eager to begin our hunt for Zaran Zimzabar. So eager that he insisted we travel by air.

"We can reach Glymph in less than an hour on a carpet. It will take most of the day by horse. Every minute counts."

"You remember what happened the last time we flew."

"Yes. We arrived safely in Caratha."

"You weren't piloting then. I mean the time we went down in flames right in the middle of an enemy camp. Or the time before that, when the carpet dissolved into a floating threadball."

"We weren't on board at the time."

"What about the karmic balance and theme inversions and all that?"

"Plot inversions. I don't think that's a problem any

more. The event sequence has advanced to a suitable developmental stage such that aerial transport shouldn't interfere with overall dramatic balance now. If you want me to chart the fifth dimensional occurrence vectors to prove it, I will."

"Never mind. I don't want to fly. You and Rif fly and I'll catch up with you."

"Nonsense. We need you with us."

"I do not want to get on one of those flying door mats ever again."

"You are being a child."

"No I'm not."

"Yes you are."

"Am not!"

"You have no logical basis for this irrational fear of flying. You have not died in a flying accident, nor do you have direct knowledge of anyone who has. Is this not true?"

"Well . . . yes," I admitted reluctantly.

"Then it's settled. We'll fly." He waved his hands and a six by twelve-foot section of plush blue carpet rose into the air. "That should be large enough to carry the three of us."

"Speaking of three, how do we find Rif?"

"He finds you," said the thief, strolling into the room. He was back to his full height. "I've been poking around the palace, seeing what I could pick up." He pulled a long blond hair off his sleeve and tossed it away.

"How should I take that statement?" I asked.

"Anyway you like. I see that your skin tone is improving, mighty wizard."

Merc had lost his scales, but still had dry and colorful skin. He also retained his fangs and reptile eyes. "I hate potions."

"I didn't have any problems with mine," I said. "And whatever it was you gave Hotfur seems to have worked well."

"Nevertheless. Shall we go?"

"Maybe we left something in the council chamber," I said. "I should check."

"Quit stalling and come on."

*   *   *

The ruins of Glymph still smoked when we touched down. The tiny farming community had been burned to the ground, its pretty shops, barns, and cottages reduced to black mounds of ash. On the town green smoldered the remains of the communal pyre upon which the bodies of Glymph's thirty inhabitants had been placed.

We encountered a platoon of soldiers. Mercury hailed their leader.

"What happened here, Sergeant?"

"Who wants to know?" demanded the non-com.

"I am Lord Mercury Boltblaster."

The soldier eyed him speculatively. "The wizard what was going to marry the Queen? I didn't know you were a reptile man."

"Never mind that."

"Didn't you try and kill the Dark Duke a few days back?"

"Yes. And I finished the job last night."

"Really? Well, that's good news. Never much cared for him. I hear as how Monfort Corona is to be King now. A just man so I've heard, but a—"

"Sergeant, I asked you a question."

"Why, so you did, milord. I was coming around to it. As you can see, this place has been clean burnt up. The folk were all gutted and strung up on posts—crucified as it were. They even had the chickens hung on little sticks. It was a gruesome and ghastly sight, it was. We cut them all down at first light and set them on a pyre. Well, not the chickens, of course. Had to bring up our own chaplain to do the rites, seeing as how the local priest was killed along with the rest. No survivors, you know."

"How did you learn of the attack?"

"We're stationed at Castle Kirkwight, about eight miles south. It was two nights ago, it was, we saw fire on the horizon. The colonel sent Cap'n Fletcher with fifty men to investigate, but we came too late. We sent word of what we found back to base. My squad pulled burial detail. Not that it's properly a burial when you stack folks up and burn 'em, as is the custom here, but that's what we call it. Always have. Cremation detail just doesn't sound right."

"The report was that Zaran Zimzabar was responsible."

"That's so, and he's the same bastard what killed the Queen, you know. Well, I expect you do and I imagine you're hot to do him the same turn, as it were. He left a note pinned to one of the bodies saying how these poor folks had been executed in the name of the Gorgeous New Odor or some such rot. Didn't see anything gorgeous about it, but there was a heck of a stench. Also said, plain as you please, that he was riding west to do more of the same."

"Naturally, Captain Fletcher rode west in pursuit," said Merc.

"I expect so, seeing as this Zaran fellow was so kind as to direct him into that vicinity."

"To no good purpose, I'm sure."

"Come again?"

"Thank you, Sergeant. You have been very helpful."

We boarded the carpet and headed west.

We spotted Captain Fletcher and his men twenty minutes later. Their remains were scattered in a field fifteen miles west of Glymph. Scores of circling carrion birds pinpointed the location long before the stench was detectable. From the looks of it, the soldiers had been ambushed the same night as the attack on the village. Their bodies had been ripped apart by some incredible force. Armored limbs and torsos littered an area of over a hundred square yards, along with battered shields, broken weapons, and a dozen dead horses. We circled the scene of the carnage twice before going on.

"Barbarous," I said.

"CIS estimates Zaran is responsible for over a thousand deaths," said Rif. "That's the conservative count."

"Why has he never been stopped?"

"He's very elusive and very lucky."

"His luck ran out when he killed Raella," Merc said.

"Is someone keeping track of all these grim and threatening statements he's making?" asked Rif.

"Not me," I said.

The tracks from the ambush site led westward still. As we crossed into the lands of the Earl of Rosewhip, Zaran's objective became obvious.

"He's heading for the Bronze Tower," said Merc.

The Bronze Tower was built by one of Raelna's most eccentric rulers, Raedon the Unhinged. Readon had a lifelong fear that the Demon Lords were subverting the realm by causing invisible vapors to seep up through the ground and kill his subjects. He also believed that his beautiful daughter Raecella was destined to bear a child who would someday kill him, a common fear among mad kings. To prevent this occurrence, he ordered his wizards and engineers to design an escape-proof prison in which he could isolate her. The result was the Bronze Tower, a gleaming one hundred-foot spire designed to be entered but not exited. The lovely princess was shut away in the structure.

News of her plight naturally brought scores of bold and handsome young men to the Bronze Tower seeking to rescue Raecella and win her love. None succeeded. Raedon eventually killed himself. His son and successor, King Raeman the Great, freed his sister, who married a Cyrillan magnate and had eleven children.

Since then, the Bronze Tower had housed many dangerous and important prisoners of the state. Its current inhabitant was Halogen, son of Lanthanide, the deposed King of Orphalia. Even after Raella disavowed her forced betrothal to the Orphalian prince, he insisted that he had a claim on her. When his father died, he raised an army of mercenaries and invaded Raelna in the hope of forcing Raella to marry him. Due in part to the actions of Merc and myself, Vixen Hotfur captured him. The Orphalian nobles renounced their liege and elected Stron Astatine to replace him.

As King Stron was unwilling to ransom him, Halogen remained in Raelnan custody. It was considered poor taste to execute royal prisoners, so Raella sent him to the Bronze Tower for safekeeping. As we approached the structure, it became evident that Halogen was no longer safely kept.

Forty miles west of Glymph, the Bronze Tower was situated atop an unusually tall, rocky mound which looked as though it had been transplanted from rugged, rocky Malravia. In fact, it had been so transplanted. The base of the mound was surrounded by a thick barrier of bramblethorns planted to discourage visitors. The tower itself was thirty feet in diameter at the base and thinly coated with shiny bronze. It lacked doors and windows and was normally entered through a tunnel from a nearby blockhouse where a small garrison was stationed.

Zaran was evidently not happy with the normal mode of entry. A ragged gash marred the tower from base to tip, as if someone had taken a giant can opener to it. Indeed, there was a giant can opener lying at the tower's base. Furthermore, the oaken door of the blockhouse was smashed to splinters, and there were several large holes in its outer wall.

"He's been here," said Merc.

We flew near the tower and saw that the cell chamber was empty.

"Why would Zaran free Halogen? He hates royalty."

"Maybe he wanted to execute him," said Rif. "Zaran likes executing people."

"We can always hope," said Merc. "But I doubt it. There is more to this than meets the eye. After all, it was not in Zaran's professed interests to help Thule steal the throne. He is merely doing the bidding of his Society masters and their scheme obviously involves Halogen. Let's take a closer look.'"

Merc landed near the blockhouse and we disembarked.

"I'll check it out," I said, approaching the entrance cautiously with Overwhelm in my hand. The charnel smell of rotting meat assailed my nostrils. I glanced inside and saw the jailers' dismembered bodies scattered about the dimly lit room. The walls and floor were splattered with day-old blood. My stomach started to rebel, but I brought it to heel.

"It was Zaran," I said tightly. "No doubt about it."

There was a sudden movement in the shadows, and a gigantic fist filled my vision. It was instantly replaced by multicolored stars as I flew up and backwards like a well-punted football. I landed flat on my back a good twenty feet away. Fortunately, my magic armor absorbed most of the impact.

My attacker stepped into view, bringing a good bit of masonry with him. He was ten feet tall and a yard or more wide, with muscles that bunched and coiled like frolicking whales. His blockish face, pocked and scarred, was twisted into a permanent sneer. His baleful eyes were yellow, his jagged teeth brown, his cruel lips the sickly purple of a ruptured artery. His hide was a mottle of ghastly grays, his long hair blond and greasy. He wore only a black loincloth. I had met this monster before and thought him dead, drowned in the waters of the Longwash. His name was Yezgar. He was half man, half ogre. He served Zaran.

"Yezgar smash!" he bellowed.

I glanced up at Merc in surprise. "He talks?"

"Yezgar kill!"

"A three-word vocabulary. Most impressive." The wizard hurled a blue bolt of death at the monster while I regained my feet. Yezgar's chest glowed, sizzled, and smoked, but he showed no signs of dying soon. To the contrary, he charged.

I ran to meet him, ducking beneath his mighty fist and slashing at his belly. I made a cut an inch deep and a foot long, but it had no effect. His skin was one thick layer of knobby callus, tougher than boiled leather and harder than horn. The blood vessels were buried deep.

As I danced to the left, Yezgar stuck out his leg and tripped me. I fell heavily and was barely able to get my shield up in time to ward off his next blow. The shield absorbed most of the impact. Even so, my right arm went numb to the shoulder. I was momentarily helpless.

"Yezgar smash!"

Rif came to my rescue, vaulting up to kick Yezgar in the face. With alarming quickness, the ogre batted him aside. Rif landed on his feet several yards away. This monster was fast, strong, and cunning. A dangerous foe, even for dangerous men like us.

I stood and raised Overwhelm for another blow, this time intending to stab deeply and do some real damage. Yezgar's huge hand streaked out to grasp my sword arm with crushing force. I felt bones grind together as I involuntarily dropped Overwhelm and fell to my knees, only to be wrenched off the ground like an ill-treated doll.

"Yezgar kill!"

"Great, Jason," snarled Merc. "With you grandstanding I can't get a clear shot for another spell."

"Spell?" I said as Yezgar whirled me above his head. "Why didn't you say so?"

"It should have been obvious."

"We must learn to communicate better."

With that, Yezgar released me. My momentum slammed me into the second floor of the blockhouse wall. I fell heavily to the turf amid a rain of stone and mortar.

Standing his ground as Yezgar charged him, Merc uttered an incantation accompanied by an intricate series of gestures. As soon as the ogre was within reach, Merc struck him with an open hand. The monster's scream shook the ground and brought more mortar down upon me. Yezgar fell, senseless.

"What did you do?" I asked, standing and brushing myself off.

"As you know, ogres have thick skin and few nerve endings. They can therefore withstand great violence while suffering little damage and less pain. This makes physical combat with such brutes a foolish undertaking at best, as you have so aptly demonstrated."

"Are you going to tell me what you did to him or not?"

"An ogre is unused to feeling pain. Therefore, when he is truly hurt, he overreacts. I simply sent a massive shock to the pain center of his brain, overloading it and rendering Yezgar comatose. I could have done so sooner if you hadn't gotten in the way."

"I'm sorry. Very sorry." I glanced at the inert monster. "When will he wake up?"

"In a few hours."

"Why is he here alone?" asked Rif. "Zaran wouldn't leave his bodyguard behind just to ambush us."

"Maybe the ambush isn't over," said Merc.

I willed Overwhelm back into my grasp. "I should finish Yezgar while I've got the chance. I don't relish a rematch."

"Go ahead," said Merc.

I raised my sword in order to plunge it into the ogre's foul heart.

"Zaran!" cried Merc suddenly. Rif and I turned to see the terrorist leader standing atop the blockhouse. He held a sleek black crossbow. "He was hiding inside. Shield your eyes. I'm about to turn that building into a smoking crater."

"I do not think so, imperialist dog!" Zaran spat.

I heard two quiet thuds behind us and turned to see a pair of hissing metal cylinders lying on the grass nearby. The PANGO raiders who had hurled them were some distance away, holding what looked like deluxe sling-shots. The faint scent of raspberries told me that the cylinders contained the magical gas dormadose, which makes a man sleep for a day. That was my last coherent thought before my companions and I fell to the ground with Zaran's laughter ringing in our ears.

10

I woke with sunlight streaming on my face. The glare was hot and blinding. I raised a hand to shield my eyes.

"Rae? Goddess? Are you there?"

I remembered falling into Zaran's trap and deduced that I was dead. The brightness reminded me of the realm of the Sun Goddess, which seemed like a logical place for me to be if I was dead. Once more I called her name. "Rae?"

"No such luck," said Merc. "Just us mortals here."

I sat up and blinked. "Where are we?"

"Somewhere in southern Orphalia, I think."

Merc sat to my left, Rif to my right. The wizard's skin was its normal olive tone, but he still had snake eyes. We were in a clearing in a pine forest, seated on a carpet of pine needles. It was a hot, cloudless day and my naked body was damp with sweat. I held that thought for a moment, letting its significance dawn on me. I glanced at my companions.

"We don't have any clothes on."

"Perceptive of you to notice," said Merc.

"This doesn't make sense. We should be dead."

"I, for one, am not complaining," said Rif.

"Jason is right," said Merc. "Zaran should have killed us after we walked into that setup at the Bronze Tower. That he didn't is very disturbing."

"It doesn't disturb me," I said.

"It should. You know Zaran's handiwork. He's a madman who takes perverse pleasure in torture, butchery, and senseless slaughter. He should have sliced and diced us. Instead he stole our clothes and left us in the woods. That doesn't fit his pattern at all."

"Conclusion: he had orders to keep us alive," said Rif.

"Exactly. And those orders came from the mastermind who planned Raella's murder. We've been stripped of our weapons, equipment, food, and other supplies. You don't have Overwhelm, Jason. I don't have my cloak. Rif doesn't have whatever he usually has with him."

"A beautiful woman?" suggested Rif.

"We still have our innate powers and abilities, but our effectiveness will be severely hampered."

"We've been slowed but not stopped," I said. "Weakened, but not destroyed. By design."

"I know how these Dark Magic Society types think," said Merc. "They like to make people squirm before they squash them."

"Our mysterious mastermind must intend to confront us eventually," I said.

"Probably to explain his whole brilliant plan before he finishes us," said Merc. "The Bronze Tower ambush suggests we are under magical surveillance. I haven't sensed any scrying, but that means nothing. I haven't been concentrating on that particular threat, and there are spying devices too advanced to be detected by the subject. But there is no way Zaran could have known we would arrive at the Bronze Tower when we did unless scrying was used. We left Rae City only an hour or so earlier."

"Then I wasn't followed into Slumville!" said Rif. "Our hidden watcher must have told Thule where to find us. So what now, great wizard?"

"We continue to pursue Zaran while we wait for our nemesis to reveal himself. My guess is that Zaran will lead us to him. But first we need food, clothing, and weapons."

My stomach rumbled at the mention of food and I realized that I was ravenously hungry. "I don't suppose there is a Burgher Lord nearby."

"Not likely," said Mercury. "It's going to be nuts and berries for a while." He smiled, showing that he still had fangs. "Or maybe small rodents."

My stomach turned.

"I think we have a more immediate concern," said Rif, leaping to his feet and pointing.

I looked in the direction he indicated and saw a huge, slavering, four-legged, beady-eyed *thing*. It was ugliness incarnate. Standing six feet at the shoulder, it had hoofed feet and was covered with dirty red bristles. Its face resembled that of a boar, but in addition to its two wicked yellow tusks, it sported a pair of bull-like horns. Steam jetted from its flaring nostrils in sharp puffs, and flame flickered from its jowls. It grunted and snarled and pawed the ground as we stared open-mouthed.

"What is it?" I asked.

"A war boar," said Merc. "They were bred by the Imperial Agricultural Extension Service in the time of the Empire of Fear and used as shock troops in battle. I thought they were extinct."

"Shock troops?"

"The imperial scientists gave them human brains. They can reason and obey fairly complex commands."

"Great. Anything else we should know?"

"They are immune to direct magical attacks, so I can't just blast it."

"I don't like this one bit."

"Nor do I," said Rif. "But isn't it amazing the way the monster held off while Merc explained everything?"

The war boar delayed no longer, lowering its head and charging with a contemptuous snort. We scattered in three different directions. The beast chose to follow me. Naturally.

I sprinted through the forest, dodging and skipping between trees in the hope they would impede the boar's progress. They did not. The big pig never slowed, but trampled the smaller trees like tulips and broke the trunks of the large ones with its massive shoulders, leaving a broad swath of destruction in its wake.

I came to a curtain of thorny vines, but dared not slow my pace with the boar at my heels. I plunged into the hanging brambles, which punctured my flesh in a hundred places, and lost my footing on the ledge beyond. For an instant, the vines held me above the dank green pool below. Then my weight pulled the ropy plants from their moorings and I fell about twenty feet into the water. It was warm and foul.

The boar glared at me from the embankment, then turned with a grunt and disappeared from view. I assumed the cunning beast knew a way to reach the far edge of the pool before I could. Or maybe it couldn't swim. Or maybe, I thought, as I felt the first dozen or so latch on, it doesn't want to be eaten by six-inch leeches. The nasty bloodsuckers were all over my limbs and torso in a matter of seconds. The entangling vines slowed me, but I swam for the far side of the pool, relying on my supernatural strength to get me there and swallowing a good bit of stagnant water in the process.

The ground on the far side was soft and muddy. I dragged myself out of the water and struggled free of the wet vines. But before I could yank a single leech off my chest, the war boar burst through the brush with a triumphant squeal and exhaled hot steam in my face, blistering and blinding me. I had nowhere to flee except back into the leech-infested pool. Formerly leech-infested. I seemed to be carrying most of its inhabitants on my person. In any event, I was trapped.

"All right, you ugly hunk of bacon! You've got me! What are you going to do with me?"

The beast snarled and flattened its ears. It opened its mouth wide so that I could see the hot flames crackling at the back of its throat. Then it stamped the ground and lowered its tusks to gore me through.

I squatted as it charged and lunged upward to meet it, grasping a tusk in either hand and bending its great neck back. The pig shook its head furiously from side to side, but I held on, with my feet planted in the muck. The beast abruptly flicked its head up, tossing me into the air. I landed on its bony back, facing its tail. The monster bucked and I was aloft once more, this time landing flat on my back on the ground several yards away. The boar trotted over and, with a piggish sneer, delivered a rib-crushing kick with its front hoof. Then it pinned me in place and once more scalded me with hot steam. This did have the beneficial effect of burning several leeches off, but was otherwise unpleasant.

I raised a free hand and punched the hellish swine square on the end of its snout. It responded by stamping down hard on my belly, rupturing most of my innards and making me spit blood. This encounter was not going well.

"There he is!" I heard Merc shout. A moment later, a telekinetically hurled tree trunk knocked the war boar off me. I rolled my head and saw Merc and Rif standing where I had fallen into the leech pool. Three more broken tree trunks hovered above them.

"Don't move, Jason!" said Merc.

"Don't worry," I gasped.

He launched the second tree with a gesture. It hit the boar on the right flank, driving it further away from me. The monster breathed a stream of flame in Merc's direction, then fled before Merc could launch his final missiles. He let them fall into the pool.

Merc crossed the water with a single magic leap and

came to my side. "Sorry it took so long to catch up with you. You were moving pretty fast."

"Wouldn't you?" I replied. I was suddenly short of breath, and my vision blurred.

"By The Gods, you look rough. Second degree burns, multiple leech bites, three broken ribs, punctured intestines, copious bleeding, and assorted abrasions. Rif! Get over here!"

"How?"

Merc levitated the thief over the pool.

My eyes closed.

"He's going into shock. Get these leeches off. We need something to stanch the bleeding."

"Telekinetic pressure?" suggested Rif, plucking off a leech.

"Yes." I felt a firm pressure on all my wounds.

"What about the ribs?"

"We'll need bandages. See what you can—"

I heard a distant crashing and the war boar's snarl.

"Here it comes again!" Rif said.

I opened my eyes to see the war boar thundering through the underbrush with its head lowered and great clouds of steam billowing from its nostrils. I eased my eyes shut again. It wasn't my problem now. Either my friends would stop the beast or I would be trampled to death—but it was beyond my control.

Foul water dripped on me as one of Merc's levitated trees flew overhead. I heard a crash followed by Rif's exclamation of dismay.

"The swine dodged it!"

"I see that," said Merc.

I couldn't, but I opened my eyes in time to see the boar neatly sidestep Merc's next shot. Using telekinesis to hurl large, heavy objects is hard enough. Controlling their flight with more than rudimentary precision is a challenge for even the most skilled wizard. The porcine powerhouse was able to evade Merc's attacks and close in for the kill.

It was almost upon us when a slender, beautiful young woman clad in a short green dress stepped out of a nearby tree like a ghost emerging from a wall and placed herself in the pig's path. With her hands on her hips, she shouted, "Stop!"

The war boar skidded to a halt before her and lowered its head sheepishly.

"Willy, you bad pig!" she scolded, shaking a finger. "I have told you time and again not to hurt travelers in the wood, haven't I?"

The pig sniffled.

"What do you have to say for yourself?"

Willy the war boar knelt, whining, and rolled his eyes up at her forlornly.

"Oh, its very well to be sorry now, with that poor man over there bleeding to death. Go to your lair right now and don't come out until I call for you. I'll deal with you later."

The pig stood and shuffled away with drooping head and downcast eyes. Ignoring his display of remorse, the young woman hurried to crouch beside me. She had a pretty brown oval of a face, happy amber eyes, full emerald lips, and short green hair that resembled pine needles. She wore a badge on her breast that read FONDLE.

"I am Loblolly, the local dryad," she said as she inspected my injuries. "I apologize for this. I feel responsible. Willy serves as my protector. He is the last of his kind. I have been trying to break him of his mean streak, but he inherited it from his ancestors."

"And he nearly sent Jason to meet his," said Merc, unmollified.

Loblolly ignored his gibe. "I have salves and remedies that will heal these cuts and burns in short order. The ribs aren't going anywhere. But the abdominal wound is serious." She glanced up at Merc and Rif. "Which of you is the wizard who lifted the trees? We have to get him to my cave."

Merc scoffed. "Do you think we don't know what dryads do when they lure men into their caves?"

"What!"

"This is all too convenient to suit me, Miss Loblolly the friendly first-aid dryad. Your pet pig tries to kill us and then you happen along and save the day. Now we're supposed to just trot over to your cave so you can crank up the magic charm and turn us all into your adoring little playmates forever. We aren't falling for it."

Loblolly stood. She was slightly taller than the wizard and leaned over him as she spoke. "Listen, you chauvinistic clod! I'm not one of those stereotypical fluffy-headed bimbo nymphs who spend all their time preening and beguiling men. I take my job seriously. Your friend here is dying and I can help him. Now either levitate him to my cave or start digging his grave!"

"Dying?" I said.

"Quite possibly," snapped Loblolly.

"Do what she says, Merc," I whispered hoarsely before fading to black.

Her small and cozy cave, lit by large glowing pine cones, had pine wood walls, floors, and furnishings. Loblolly gave Merc and Rif simple tunics to wear, but denied them entry to her lair while she tended me. As promised, a soothing salve took the sting out of my burns and abrasions. An herbal poultice applied to my abdominal wound stopped the bleeding. Loblolly made the damaged tissue whole by laying her gentle hands upon me. Healing energies flowed from her fingertips and arranged my cells in their proper order. She sped the process along by forcing me to quaff a variety of bitter medicinal brews and tonics. I drifted in and out of consciousness, spending more time out than in.

She kept me abed for three full days. When I was not sleeping and she was not engaged in her dryadic duties, we talked. I told her about my friends and my adventures. She was most impressed by my affiliation with the Goddess Rae, who apparently had some authority over dryads by virtue of her connection with the process of photosynthesis. For my part, I was fascinated by Loblolly's description of her own work as a dryad.

"We dryads are the immortal caretakers of the woodlands, created by The Gods during the Age of Nature. We are under the supervision of the Goddess Silvana. Our task is to tend to injured animals and damaged trees, plant seedlings, prevent forest fires, fight pollution, and generally maintain the ecological balance. We are required to file an annual report with the Divine Nature Bureau, which in turn reports to the Holy Environmental Resources Commission. That board is composed of all the nature deities, including your Goddess Rae."

"Sounds complicated. Are there many dryads?"

"Not enough. A few dozen for all of Arden. We're spread too thinly to be effective. Our numbers were once greater, but many of my sisters perished during the Ages of War and Despair. Today many woodland areas are unmanaged because so few dryads remain. And The Gods refuse to create more."

"Why?"

"It's not part of the Divine Plan, they say."

"So you're overworked."

"Yes. These pine barrens cover almost three thousand square miles and I have to manage them alone, with little support from upstairs. That's one of the reasons I joined FONDLE." She tapped the badge on her breast.

"I've been meaning to ask you about that."

"The Federation of Oreads, Naiads, and Dryads for Labor Equity was founded to promote the interests of all nymphs. Dryads are just one variety of nymph, as you may know. There are oreads who tend the hills and mountains and naiads who are responsible for lakes and streams. We all face similar problems. The creation of more nymphs, including males, is at the top of our agenda."

"Male nymphs?"

"The reason so many of my sisters neglect their work and turn to seducing mortal men is that we lack suitable male companions of our own kind. It wasn't a problem when The Gods walked Arden freely. Nymph-god liaisons were common. But since the Holy/Unholy Non-Intervention Pact, gods are scarce and mortals have been the only suitable alternative. As a result, nymphs have gotten a bad reputation. FONDLE wants to change that."

"What else do you want?"

"Vacations. Rotating assignments. Improved support services. The list is a lengthy one."

"I see."

"As for you, favorite of Rae, you are now well enough to travel. You should take it easy for several days, if possible."

"I'll try. Thank you for saving my life."

"It's just part of my job. You were injured in my wood by one of my creatures. Furthermore, you are a favorite of the Sun Goddess. I was naturally obligated to aid you."

"Naturally."

"But I am not obligated to do this."

She leaned over and gave me a tender kiss. Her lips were pure softness. An electric tingle swept through my body.

"I thought you didn't go in for that sort of thing."

She smiled. "Dedicated and serious-minded I may be, Jason Cosmo, but I am still a nymph. And you are a most handsome mortal. Now get out of my cave. Your friends are eager to see you."

11

"Here he is, hale and whole as promised," said Loblolly as we emerged from her lair. Her cave was cut out of a hillside at one end of a small concealed glen. A tiny pool of crystal pure water rippled nearby.

Merc and Rif, looking like a pair of foresters in their green tunics, eyed me suspiciously. Willy the war boar lay on the ground close by, watching them with equal suspicion.

"Did you miss me?" I asked jokingly, stepping forward to clasp their hands. I felt a familiar surge of strength as the full light of the sun shone upon me.

"You seem to be all right," said Merc dubiously. He still had snake eyes.

"Of course I am! Loblolly took excellent care of me."

Rif raised one eyebrow sardonically. "Two days and

nights alone with a dryad. Yes, I would call that excellent care. Would that Willy had gored me instead of you."

"What's that supposed to mean?"

"Are you ready to leave now?" asked Merc, ignoring my question.

"Of course."

"Are you sure?"

"Why shouldn't I be?"

"You have to ask?" said Rif, glancing sidelong at Loblolly.

"I have not beguiled him," said Loblolly coldly. She turned to me. "Your friends still mistrust me and my motives."

"Really, fellows. Her intentions were strictly honorable."

"I should be so honored," said Rif.

"What was that?" said Loblolly. Willy snorted a little puff of steam.

"Nothing," said the thief. "Just clearing my throat."

"We can trust her," I said.

"Exactly what you would say if you were under her spell," said Merc. "I've seen it before."

"I'm not under a spell, Merc. Use your Spellsniffer."

"It's not handy."

"Oh, right."

"Enough. Your mind and will are still your own. My apologies for doubting you, dryad. I have a suspicious nature."

"I've noticed," said Loblolly.

"So whither are we bound?" I asked.

"North," said Merc.

"Indeed," said Loblolly. "Your enemies are approximately thirty miles north of here. They are thirty in number, plus the ogre."

"Half-ogre," said Merc.

"Half an ogre is bad enough. I have been monitoring their progress since they entered my domain."

"How?" I asked.

"The trees tell me much. How do you think I found you in the first place?"

"You talk to trees?" I asked. "You didn't mention that."

"Well, anyone can talk to trees. The significant point is that the trees talk to me."

Merc stroked his beard. "We can move much faster than a party of that size, even in this terrain. We should be able to overtake Zaran in a couple of days."

"I forbid it," said Loblolly.

"Excuse me?" said Merc.

"I want no further violence in my wood. Follow your enemies if you will, but do not attack them until they are out of the forest."

"Fair enough," I said. "We will honor your wishes. Right, guys?"

"Of course," said Rif gallantly. Merc merely nodded. He wanted to get his hands on Zaran as soon as possible.

"Very good," said Loblolly. "I have prepared provisions for you. Willy will show you the best path. May The Gods be with you."

"And with you," I said.

Accompanied by the giant pig, we set out once more on our interrupted quest for vengeance. By Merc's calculations, it was the last day of summer. If he was right, it had been five days since our battle at the Bronze Tower.

We made good time as Willy led us along game trails, down twisting ravines, and through sunny glades. Or at least the going was easy and we had the illusion of rapid progress. I suspected the boar of wasting time by leading us roundabout. Some of those glades and ravines looked pretty familiar the second or third time around. However, I did not voice my suspicions. Loblolly had evidently instructed her swinish servant to ensure that we did not catch up with Zaran and company within the confines of her woodlands. Nevertheless, we did see occasional signs of their passage, such as discarded PANGO political pamphlets and Yezgar-sized footprints.

Four days passed before we reached the northern fringe of the pine barrens, some thirty miles from Loblolly's cave. Willy poked his snout through an opening in the underbrush, grunted, glared at us, then turned and trotted back the way he had come.

"Thanks, Willy!" I called. "No hard feelings!"

We emerged from the forest and looked down across the settled and cultivated Orphalian central plain where most of the kingdom's half-million inhabitants lived. Orphalia faced Raelna across the River Longwash to the southeast. To the west and southwest, the Crownbolt defined its borders. Beyond was the military colossus Ganth. The Incredibly Dark Forest and the untamed Bitterspleen Hills marked the wild northern frontier. In the east, Orphalia shared a disputed border with Brythalia. The only city of any note was Voripol, the capital, which was roughly in the center of the kingdom.

Orphalia was a grim and cheerless land. Most Orphalians were serfs bound to the estates of knights and barons. They rarely traveled more than twenty miles from their place of birth, were forbidden to carry weapons, required their lord's permission to marry, paid heavy taxes, and had very few legal rights. But for all that, they were a step above the slaves, who had no rights at all. Both serfs and slaves spent most of their time being exploited and oppressed, the popular pursuits of the lower classes everywhere.

The nobles, living off the labor of their chattels, had much idle time on their hands and occupied themselves by killing one another in private wars fought for petty reasons. The staff of the *Orphalian Review of Martial Exploits* provided extensive coverage of their many battles and gave Orphalia's thousand or so knights prowess ratings based on cumulative victories and defeats in battle. The figures, updated monthly, were somewhat inflated, since most defeats were terminal and resulted in removal from the charts.

Orphalia lacked a strong central authority. The king, elected by the barons, was no more than first among equals. He had few formal powers, but got great discounts at the fairs and markets, could appoint his friends to high office, and presided at all state banquets. His chief function was to give Orphalia an excuse to call itself a kingdom rather than a collection of petty fiefdoms. This system did not tend to promote stability in government.

The late King Lanthanide was an exception. A shrewd

politician, he wielded great power by Orphalian standards and used it to further what he called the "Great Hypothesis." His goal was to stabilize his kingdom by creating a lasting dynasty. He had his son, Halogen, designated as king-elect before his own death. The hypothetical marriage of his heir to Raella Shurbenholt would have hypothetically cemented an alliance with the most long-lived royal house in the Eleven Kingdoms. Their hypothetical child would have inherited both kingdoms and, hypothetically, welded them into one united realm. This would bring Orphalia unprecedented hypothetical order, wealth, power, and prestige.

The "Great Hypothesis," however, proved to rest upon rather shaky assumptions. The marriage was not to be and Halogen was a miserable failure as King. His rejection in favor of Stron Astatine put an end to any thoughts of building a dynasty. And now Stron's death had precipitated the kind of civil war old Lanthanide had hoped to make a thing of the past. It just went to show that tradition was hard to overcome.

Baron Henrik Bismuth, a mighty warrior, dominated southern Orphalia. His personal holdings were extensive, and most of the lesser barons between his lands and Voripol supported his bid for the throne. His ancestral rival, with a power base in the north and west, was Baron Nulf Tungsten, also a doughty fighter. The third contestant, Baron Krawlar von Zinc, controlled the northeast. He was an obese man said to be overly fond of drink and gluttony, but a shrewd strategist. One of these men would be the next King of Orphalia.

Zaran's trail led across the countryside to an unpaved road leading northward. He helpfully marked the way by burning several small villages, slaughtering a troupe of itinerant actors, and leveling a castle. The typical Orphalian castle was a wooden house atop an earthen mound surrounded by a palisade and moat. They weren't that difficult to reduce if you had the help of an ogre. Or even a half-ogre.

"I would say this destruction dates from the day before

yesterday," said Rif as we stopped for lunch amid the ruins.

"Then we might catch him by nightfall tomorrow," said Merc. "We'd best arm ourselves."

We picked over the bodies of the fallen, which had already been looted once. Rif located a rusty knife and a bit of leather from which he made a sling. Merc found half a broken lance which would serve as a quarterstaff. I uncovered an open-faced helmet and a hefty oak cudgel.

We marched on diligently for the rest of the day, covering at least ten more miles before dusk. In the last moments of daylight, we were overtaken by six mounted knights bearing lances and shields. The leader sported plate armor and a great pot-shaped helm. His fellows wore chainmail and open helmets like mine. They were still a couple hundred yards away when we spotted them. We halted, and they spurred their horses into a canter.

Merc stroke his beard thoughtfully. "Horses. Just what we need."

"You aren't suggesting we rob these men, are you?" I said, aghast.

"Sure. Why not?"

"It's unheroic."

"We need the horses. We don't want Zaran to get away."

"Stealing is wrong."

"It is?" asked Rif, shocked.

"Orphalian knights are thugs," said Merc. "It's okay to steal their horses. They steal horses from one another all the time."

"Nevertheless. . . ."

Merc threw up his hands. "Why does this have to be a moral dilemma? Just do whatever has to be done, that's how I see it. You take this heroic honor bit too seriously, Jason."

"You have your ethics, I have mine."

"What if they attack us first?" Merc asked. "Then can we take their horses? To the victor belongs the spoils."

"That, of course, is a different matter," I said. "But only if they attack us first."

"Agreed," said Merc. He cupped his hands around his

mouth and shouted, "Ho there, you lice-ridden, maggot-loving, spit-swilling, smutty sons of harlots!"

"Do you think they'll attack?" asked Rif as the knights lowered their lances and spurred their horses to a gallop.

I rolled my eyes. "That was not quite fair."

"Two for each of us," said Merc. "How fair can you get?"

Rif loaded a rock in his sling and let it fly. The stone hit one of the approaching knights in the eye and knocked him from the saddle. Rif's second shot was equally accurate and brought similiar results.

"Well, there's my quota," he said.

The remaining knights were upon us. Merc and Rif, in unison, vaulted upward and turned midair flips which brought them down behind the knights. Not being so nimble, I simply dropped my club and grabbed the lance of the nearest warrior. Using my supernatural might, I levered him out of the saddle and flung him through the air. He landed hard in the ditch. With a little telekinetic help from Merc, two more knights flew backward off their horses and made equally bad landings. None of them would rise for at least half an hour. Their horses meandered off the road and started grazing.

The leader was the only one left. He swept past me and wheeled his horse about for another charge, pausing to ask, "What manner of knaves art thou to dispatch mine fellows so handily?"

"Do all knights talk like that?" I asked Merc.

"Yes, unfortunately. This one, incidentally, is all yours. I got my two."

"Thanks for saving me one."

"Don't mention it."

"I'm Jason Cosmo," I declared, recovering my club and waiting for him to cringe in terror.

"Indeed," said the knight. "I be Sir Simon de Sulfate, vassal to my Lord Bismuth."

"You've never heard of me?" I asked. "Jason Cosmo?"

"What was that name again?"

"Jason Cosmo," I said clearly.

"Nay. Should I have heard of thee, base varlet?"

"Scaring him with your reputation won't work," observed Merc. "Orphalian knights don't keep up with current events like they should."

"My friends and I just took out all five of your companions in less than ten seconds," I pointed out to the knight.

"And I shall smite thee for such impertinence," boasted the knight.

"In addition to being ill-informed, Orphalian knights are remarkably sure of themselves and have little sense of self-preservation," added Merc. "Quit talking and fight him."

Sir Sulfate charged. I side-stepped the point of his lance and swung my heavy club up into his armored chest, unhorsing him with a great clang. He landed on his back and was unable to rise due to the weight of his armor.

"Fie upon thee, villain! It were most unmanly of thee to avoid mine lance."

"That's just a matter of perspective," I said.

"My servants will happen this way soon," warned Sulfate. "They are numerous and brave."

"Good," said Merc. "We'll be gone when they arrive, but maybe now Jason won't feel so bad about leaving you lying in the road."

In addition to the six horses, the spoils of battle included armor, coin, and weapons. We rode on for a couple of hours past nightfall in order to put some distance between ourselves and our fallen foes. Sulfate's servants would find him soon enough and the knights were sure to seek revenge for their ignoble defeat.

By mid-morning the following day we reached Castle Bismuth, the seat of Henrik Bismuth's power. It was one of the few stone fortresses in Orphalia. Even so, it was not very impressive, consisting of a stone keep and sloping twelve-foot walls enclosing a small courtyard. It did, at least, have a dry moat and drawbridge.

As we topped a rise, we could see that the castle was not to be the focus of the day's events. Instead, preparations were underway for a pitched battle on the open field in front of the structure. Just outside the castle gate, Baron Bismuth's knights sharpened their swords, polished their armor, inspected their horses, and did limbering-up exercises amid billowing silk tents. Overhead, colorful banners snapped in the breeze. At the other end of the field stood the bright pavilions of Baron Tungsten's knights, who were likewise occupied. Roughly two hundred yards of open space separated the two armies.

Low wooden bleachers lined the sides of the battlefield. The noisy spectators included peasants, artisans, merchants, a sprinkling of fair damsels, reporters from the *Orphalian Review*, and a large group of grim-faced soldiers in black uniforms. Enterprising vendors worked the crowd, hawking small flags and pennons bearing the crests of Tungsten, Bismuth, and important knights in their service. Others sold beer, hot dogs, and candy. Bookmakers and their helpers shouted odds and collected bets. Musicians played fight songs. Rival squads of cheerleaders shook their hips and chanted taunts at each other. Signs proclaimed that this was a "Succession Slugfest" not to be missed.

"It looks like a carnival," I said.

"This is how the Orphalians wage war," said Merc. "We'll go around. I doubt Zaran came this way."

Rif pointed at the men in black. "That one in the middle, with the silver skull on his surcoat, is Myrm Ironglove."

"You're right," said Merc. "It seems the Imperator of Ganth is taking an interest in today's proceedings. All the more reason to go around. Ironglove has hated me since I helped defeat his last major invasion of Malravia."

"Really?" said Rif. "The last time I saw the Imperator he threatened to have me roasted slowly over an open flame."

"Why?" I asked.

"It involved either a violation of Ironglove's daughter or Ganthian national security," said Merc.

"Both," said Rif. "Well, there was also the matter of the Ganthian crown jewels."

"The Ganthian crown jewels disappeared during the coup," said Merc.

"They disappeared into Ironglove's private vault," said Rif. "That's where I found them. They are now in the hands of a private collector in Caratha."

"The Imperator sounds like a charming man," I said.

"He's not," said my companions.

"Nevertheless," boomed as amplified voice directly behind us, "General Ironglove would like you to join him in viewing today's event."

We all turned in the saddle. The speaker was a seven foot figure in silver and black plate armor. The suit appeared seamless, being a single unit rather than a collection of individual pieces strapped into place. It must have weighed several hundred pounds. The figure was surrounded by a faint purple nimbus.

"Dhrakol," said Merc. "How nice to see you again."

"I am certain you recognize the futility of resistance," boomed Dhrakol.

"Of course," said Merc.

"I'm confused," I said. "But I'm sure you'll explain."

"Naturally," said Merc. "Dhrakol is the only surviving member of the Knights of Dreadnought, an unholy order of evil warrior-mages who served the Emperors of Fear. There were thirteen originally. The other twelve were destroyed in the final battle with the Mighty Champion. Unfortunately, Dhrakol survived. Ironglove dredged him out of the Western Ocean, scraped off the barnacles, and made him his personal enforcer."

"How?" I asked.

"The Imperator spoke the Word of Command which I must obey," said Dhrakol. "Now come."

"I'll explain the rest later," said Merc. "For now we had better do as he says. He has the power to destroy us all quite easily."

12

A squad of Ganthian legionnaires disarmed us and escorted us to the stands, where the Imperator awaited us, a bag of popcorn in hand. Myrm Ironglove was about sixty. His dark brown hair was graying and his stern face had wrinkles, but his steely eyes were as cold and piercing as a knight's deadly lance. He looked at us in the same way one inspects a dead dog in the ditch.

"Boltblaster. Wildrogue. We meet again." His baritone was as clipped and precise as a fencing master's riposte.

"We heard you were in the neighborhood and just had to drop by," said Merc.

"Always a comic," said Ironglove.

"And how is your lovely daughter?" asked Rif. "Myra, I believe it was. Charming girl."

"Too free with her charms. I had her thrown into a well which was then filled with heavy stones."

"Such a devoted father," said Merc.

"You are both under a sentence of death. It will be carried out soon."

"Aren't we beyond your jurisdiction?" asked Merc.

"Where my sword reaches, there reaches my law also. Who is the third man?"

"I'm Jason Cosmo," I said.

Ironglove thoughtfully chewed a mouthful of popcorn and Dhrakol snapped his head up to glare at me. The legionnaires tensed and gripped their pikes more firmly.

"I doubt that," he said at length. "The real Jason Cosmo would not have surrendered so easily."

"Okay, if it makes you happy, I'm not Jason Cosmo."

"Having you drawn and quartered will make me happy. I don't like smart guys. All of you be seated. We will watch this pitiful excuse for a battle and conduct our business afterward."

We sat beside the dictator. Dhrakol stood behind us, arms akimbo.

"I didn't know you had time for recreation," said Merc. "It's a long way from Gandopolis."

"The Orphalians do not understand war," said Ironglove. "Like most Easterners, they think it is a sport, an activity reserved for the upper class. They don't understand that it is necessary to mobilize the entire society, the full resources of the nation, in order to truly wage war. There are no rules in true war, only victory and defeat."

"Spoken like a true Ganthian," said Merc.

"You scoff, but the Sons of Gan understand war. We live it. We breathe it. War is our friend. That is why we are masters of all the land from the Western Ocean to the Crownbolt, from the Gaede Range to the Blasted Land."

"Of course, most of that area is uninhabited," said Merc.

"Eventually, we shall conquer the petty kingdoms of the East. They do not comprehend that war and conquest are the highest and most glorious of all possible endeavors."

"You're right," said Merc. "That's beyond me."

"These petty lordlings have brought their full armed might, a mere five hundred knights between them, together at an appointed place and time in order to resolve their dispute. They give no thought to strategy. They make a circus of it, a picnic. War is no picnic."

"But maybe a circus," said Merc.

"Their King Halogen had a faint glimmering of what war should be. He fielded a massive force of mercenaries for his failed invasion of Raelna. They were ill-disciplined and poorly led, an unruly mob rather than an army, but at least Halogen recognized that a handful of knights was not adequate for his purpose."

"Especially when facing the She-Fox."

Ironglove nearly choked on a mouthful of popcorn, spewing wet kernels in every direction. In a voice thick with menace, he snarled, "Do not mention that traitor's daughter again, or I will dispense with these pleasantries and have you killed on the spot."

"Assuming I don't mention Vixen Hotfur again, just when and how do you plan to kill us?" asked Merc.

"Whatever the outcome of this battle, I shall be the true victor. While the Orphalian lordlings were busy arranging today's event, my Fifth Legion has occupied the western half of this kingdom. The fools don't realize that fact yet. I am ostensibly here as an observer, but the Second Legion is nearby, ready to do my bidding. After matters are properly arranged, I will have Wildrogue roasted, our false Cosmo drawn and quartered, and you will be executed by—how did I promise to kill you when last we met?"

"By pulling my intestines out through my nose," said Merc.

"Yes, that was it. I expect we'll be ready for all that just before the evening mess."

"It sounds like we're going to be the evening mess," I said.

"Indeed," said Ironglove. "I see that the Orphalians are ready to begin their charade. Would you care for any popcorn?"

"No thanks."

"Then let us watch."

From the castle wall, an announcer introduced the combatants, his voice amplified by a magic megaphone.

"Ladies and gentlemen, welcome to the Succession Slugfest, a clash of titans which will decide the fate of all Orphalia. The people of the Eleven Kingdoms, indeed the folk of all Arden, await with bated breath the outcome of today's colossal conflict. Two lords of the realm, princes among men, champions par excellence, will meet on the field of battle to determine who shall be the next King of Orphalia. Will it be bad boy Baron Bismuth, the Scourge of the South? Or will Nulf "Terminator" Tungsten claim the prize? You will be the first to know, because it's going to happen right before your eyes, right here, today. These warriors have never met in mortal combat before. Both are undefeated in over a hundred engagements each. The *Review* ranks them tied for first place in the rankings. The odds-makers say this one is too close to call. History is in the happening right here, right now, so let the battle for the destiny of a kingdom begin!"

"He talks as though Baron von Zinc doesn't even exist," I said.

"He doesn't," said Rif. "For now." He shrugged. "It's all hype."

The knights mounted their chargers and formed two opposing lines. Most wore chainmail, a few had plate mail. All bore lances and kite shields. The rival barons, Tungsten and Bismuth, positioned themselves in the front ranks of their respective forces. With a fanfare of trumpets, the knights lowered their lances and charged. The crowd roared with delight.

Dozens of knights fell as the lines met. Lances splintered, horses neighed, men shouted, armor clattered. Some of the fallen rose to their feet and drew swords to continue fighting. Others were unable to get up due to broken bones, unconsciousness, or armor that was too heavy. Those still mounted sought out rivals also still in the saddle while the warriors on the ground dueled one another. In mere moments, the combatants stirred up so much dust that it was impossible to see what was going on. Still, we could hear the ring of steel on steel, the shouted war cries, the exclamations of pain. This went on for about an hour. Then a halt was declared.

"Halftime," said Merc as squires and pages rushed onto the field to drag away the dead and wounded. Those knights still in action withdrew to their respective ends of the field and guzzled cold water, wine, or ale according to taste. Fifteen minutes later the official tally was announced. Tungsten had a hundred knights still fit for combat. Bismuth could field a hundred fifty. The survivors mounted up again with new lances and started all over again.

"How long does this go on?" I asked.

"Until one side or the other concedes," said Rif.

"Or until there is no one left to fight," said Merc.

"Be quiet," said Ironglove.

"Oh, let us talk," said Merc. "You're going to kill us soon anyway."

"Very well, but no discussion of escape."

"Escape?" said Rif. "Us?"

"I was just going to tell Jason here about Dhrakol," said Merc. "The Dreadnoughts were originally a group of powerful sorcerers attached to the court of the Evil Emperor. Being quite paranoid, he suspected them of plotting against him and so 'volunteered' them to undergo a magical process which bonded their souls to specially enchanted suits of armor. As part of the enchantment, the Dreadnoughts were subjected to a secret Word of Command known only to the Emperor. By this means, he compelled their absolute obedience. He used the Knights of Dreadnought as bodyguards, special enforcers, and commanders for his armies. Have I got this right, Dhrakol?"

"For the most part," the Dreadnought boomed.

"Then the Mighty Champion showed up and instigated the Great Rebellion. The Dreadnoughts were unable to defeat him. Eventually, of course, the Final Battle was fought in the imperial capital. The Mighty Champion slaughtered the Dreadnoughts, slew the Evil Emperor, and banished Asmodraxas to the Great Beyond. In the process, a large chunk of this continent sank, taking the capital with it. That area became the Sunken Land. Another big section was blasted to ruins."

"And is now known as the Blasted Land," I concluded.

"Correct. To make a long story short, an early Overmaster of the Dark Magic Society, one Arizol by name, made contact with the spirit of the dead Emperor and learned the Word of Command. He planned to reanimate the Dreadnoughts, but was assassinated before he could enact his scheme. Overmasters didn't last long in those days. His grimoire, containing the Word of Command, eventually came into the hands of our friend the Imperator. He mounted an expedition to the Sunken Land and came up with Dhrakol."

"I didn't think Ganthians put much store in things magical," I said.

"I utilize any available weapon so long as it is reliable," said Ironglove. "Dhrakol is totally reliable."

"Dhrakol has the might of an arcane master combined

with the prowess of a veteran warrior and augmented by the massive powers of his enchanted armor," said Merc.

"Keep that in mind," said Ironglove.

The Orphalian knights fought ferociously, neither asking quarter nor granting it. For centuries, warriors such as these dominated the battlefields of the Eleven Kingdoms, wreaking havoc with sword and lance, living and dying by the ancient code of chivalry. Only the pikes of the Ganthian legions could withstand those armored horsemen of old. They were the elite, the fighting class, feared and respected by king and peasant alike.

But the face of war changed over time. New weapons such as the crossbow pierced the once-invincible armor of the knights. Powerful siege engines reduced their castles to rubble. Innovative generals developed ruthless and unchivalrous tactics. Wizards devised powerful spells of destruction for use in war. Kings began to rely on standing armies of low-born mercenaries rather than their host of still-lordly but increasingly obsolete knights. Suddenly war wasn't fun anymore. Only in antiquated Orphalia did the knightly class cling to their privileged position. Unable to compete with the modern armies of the neighboring kingdoms, the Orphalians made war upon themselves in the old-fashioned manner. Ganth, Raelna, and Brythalia agreed not to interfere in Orphalian affairs, letting the kingdom stand as a harmless buffer between the three superpowers.

Halogen's invasion of Raelna, ineffectual as it was, changed the great powers' perception of Orphalia. It became a potential threat and hence a potential target. The chaos following the deaths of Stron and Raella provided an opportunity for conquest which Ganth and Brythalia could not pass up. Nor could Raelna, as Cull Crossmaster evidently understood. Bismuth and Tungsten fought today for the Orphalian crown, but it really didn't matter who won. Orphalia was destined to become a mere prize in a larger struggle. The victor might reign, but he would never rule.

At the moment, it looked as though that victor would be Baron Nulf Tungsten. Though outnumbered three to two at the start of the second round, his knights fought like demons. They soon made it an even fight, then gained the upper hand. Within twenty minutes, they had unhorsed all of Bismuth's men. As chivalry demanded, Tungsten's knights did not press their advantage, but dismounted to continue the battle on foot.

"Imbeciles!" snorted Ironglove, shaking his head in dismay. "Utter madness."

"Polite, though," I said.

Tungsten and Bismuth sought each other out amid the fray. As the two leaders closed and hurled challenges, their followers disengaged and fell back. The crowd went wild. This is what they had been waiting for. Tungsten and Bismuth would decide the outcome of the battle, and thus the fate of Orphalia, in single combat.

"Prepare to taste the keen edge of mine blade, thou base and fatherless vermin!" shouted Tungsten.

"Nay!" rejoined Bismuth. "It is thy blood which shall be spilt upon the grassy sward this day, boaster! And I shall make of thine empty head my wine goblet!"

"Thou art deep in thy cups already anon and so forth if thou truly believest thou shalt vanquish me, knave!"

"Braggart! White-livered beggar! Verily, I swear thou shalt rue taking up arms against me! I am the mightiest knight on life and thou art naught but a . . . but a . . ."

"Do thy addled wits fail thee, numbskull?"

"Nay! A chary-eyed noddy-noggin! That is what you are! I mean, that is what thou beith! Whatever."

"Oh, is this so, lout! Thou art a vile toad! A simpering salamander! An icky iguana!"

I nudged Merc. "Are they going to fight, or just shout each other to death?"

"This is all part of the show. They must exchange insults before they exchange blows."

"I see."

"Cry-baby!" shouted Bismuth.

"Sissy-boy!" yelled Tungsten.

"Die!" they chorused as they crossed swords. Being in full armor, they moved like lumbering giants, hefting their great swords at one another in what looked like slow motion. Most of their blows were true, but their armor was so heavy that they did little physical damage to each other.

"This could go on for quite a while," I observed.

"The crowd doesn't want a short fight," said Merc.

"It almost seems like this is a big put-on."

Merc gave me a warning look. "Don't say that so loudly! One sure way to get yourself lynched in Orphalia is to suggest that their warfare is fake. They take this very seriously."

"Like professional wrestling?"

"Exactly."

The crowd screamed curses and encouragement at the combatants. Ladies swooned with every telling blow against their favorite, recovering in time to cheer his counterattack. The rival bands joined forces to provide stirring martial background music. The cheerleaders jumped and strutted and shook their pom-poms. The vendors sold their refreshments and raked in the profits.

The duel lasted nearly an hour. Then Tungsten struck Bismuth's sword from his hand and rammed the defenseless man with his shield, knocking him to the ground. Planting his foot on his fallen foe's chest, Tungsten aimed his sword at Bismuth's throat.

"Yield!" roared Tungsten. "Or die!"

"I yield," gasped Bismuth. "Truly, Sir Nulf, you have bested me fairly."

"Then will you swear loyalty to my cause?"

"I so swear. I will fight for thee and under thy banner, though it lead me to the end of Arden and the Halls of Death."

"Then rise!" It took several men to hoist Bismuth to his feet. The rival barons removed their helmets and gauntlets and shook hands as the crowd roared its approval of the spectacle and its outcome.

"Good match, Henrik," said Tungsten, abandoning his flowery mode of speech as they exited the field. "You had me going for a while there."

"It just wasn't my day, Nulf. Maybe next time."

"Maybe so. But now we've got von Zinc to deal with."

"Later. Right now I just want to grab a hot babe and a cold brew."

"You said it."

The crowd rushed the field to begin the victory celebration, partisans of both sides joining forces to eat, drink, and be merry. The barons, meanwhile, approached Ironglove's party.

"Well, my Lord Imperator," said Tungsten, "what did you think?"

"Amusing," said Ironglove. "An entertaining theatrical diversion. I congratulate you, the next King of Orphalia."

"I've still got von Zinc to settle with," said Tungsten.

"Don't worry," said Ironglove. "We shall crush him easily."

"We? I don't need your help."

"Nonetheless, you shall have it. I have taken an interest in this succession struggle, and I have decided that you shall win."

"We will brook no Ganthian meddling in our affairs!" said Tungsten hotly.

"Aye!" agreed Bismuth.

"You have no choice, little man. My legions have already occupied your lands and those of your vassals. If you will look out across the countryside, you will see that the Second Legion has surrounded this gathering. I have but to give the command and they will slay you all. I prefer to avoid such unpleasantness and allow you to enjoy your festivities. But if you insist, I can give you a demonstration of true armed might which you are unlikely to forget. I offer you your heart's desire, Nulf Tungsten. You will be King of Orphalia. Your nation will enjoy the protection of the Ganthian legions, and all we ask in return is a small annual tribute of gold and slaves."

"This is intolerable!" said Tungsten, drawing his sword. "I should gut you now, you arrogant pig!"

"I do not recommend that course of action," said Ironglove.

Dhrakol pointed a glowing gauntlet at the furious baron. Tungsten saw the wisdom of Ironglove's warning and sheathed his weapon.

"Accept the inevitable gracefully," said the dictator

smoothly. "Yours is a small, weak land, easily preyed upon by your more powerful neighbors. You need protection. I will not interfere in your internal affairs. You may order the kingdom as you wish. You may continue to enjoy your quaint lifestyle. This alliance will be best for all concerned. Don't you agree?"

Tungsten remained stubbornly silent. Bismuth appeared equally grim.

"Or," said Ironglove. "I can level every castle, burn every town and village, sow your fields with salt, and take every inhabitant of this petty little land off to work in the copper mines of Karastan until they die of dehydration and heat exhaustion. Which will it be?"

Tungsten and Bismuth exchanged glances. Tungsten smiled wanly at Ironglove. "I . . . welcome your assistance, Lord Imperator."

"Good. I can see that you will be a wise king for your people. I now have a little something to add to this party." He indicated me and my companions. "These are enemies of the Ganthian state who have been sentenced to die interesting deaths. I hope that your men will enjoy watching."

"Yes," said Tungsten, giving us a cursory glance. "Nothing to get a party going like a few gruesome executions."

"Excellent," said Ironglove.

"That's our cue," said Merc. Rif and I each turned and grabbed one of Dhrakol's armored legs. We hoisted the Dreadnought backward off the bleachers. Merc meanwhile used his powers to snatch away the pikes of the legionnaires and turn them against their owners. Ironglove, recognizing his danger, dove off the back of the bleachers to join his fallen bodyguard. Merc sent a pike after him, but missed. Rif and I swung our fists, sending surprised Ganthians reeling back in every direction. We soon cleared the bleachers of foes. Dozens of legionnaires rushed toward the stands to punish us for assaulting their leader, but Merc held them at bay with the levitated pikes.

"What's your plan?" I asked Merc as I tossed a major over the edge.

"Plan? What plan? I don't think we can get out of this,

but I'm not going to let them pull my intestines out my nose without a fight."

"My sentiments exactly," said Rif.

Our section of the bleachers rose fifteen feet into the air and flew at tremendous speed toward the castle. I nearly lost my footing and fell off, but caught myself.

"Good idea, Merc! I hate flying, but I must admit levitating the bleachers away is brilliant." I waved gleefully at the frustrated legionnaires below.

"I'm not doing this!" said Merc. "It's Dhrakol! Jump!" The wizard leaped off the flying bleachers and landed amid the revelers below. Rif and I followed instantly. Seconds later, the bleachers smashed into the unyielding castle wall. I was glad not to be aboard.

I disentangled myself from a couple of stunned cheerleaders and grabbed Merc by the arm. The partygoers were in a panic, screaming and running in every direction.

"Where is Dhrakol? I don't see him!"

"Move!" said Merc, shoving me aside. A sizzling red bolt from the sky dug an eight-foot hole where we had just stood. I looked up. Twenty feet above us, Dhrakol walked through the air as if it were solid ground.

"He flies?" I dodged another blast from above. It vaporized a hapless knight.

"Obviously," said Merc. "I'll try to stop him. You handle the Ganthians."

"Right. Thanks."

The entire Second Legion advanced toward the battlefield with lowered pikes. They had us completely surrounded and they weren't stopping for anything. Tents, women, children, horses—they marched relentlessly through them all, impaling and trampling anyone in their way. They were going to kill the whole crowd, most of it unarmed, just to get the three of us. The only gap in the tightening ring of death was the open gate of the castle. The panicked crowd packed its way onto the drawbridge, shoving many unfortunates into the dry moat. Others jumped in on purpose to escape the merciless pikes of Ganth.

I didn't see Rifkin anywhere. Merc battered Dhrakol with the Emerald Beam of Ehrlibann, followed by a

Ruby Ray of Ruin, but even the two mighty spells in combination did not so much as dent the Dreadnought's armor. Dhrakol meanwhile hurled blast after blast of awesome sorcerous energy groundward, killing dozens and gouging up great gouts of turf.

"His aim is pretty bad," I noted.

"That depends on what he's trying to do," said Merc.

I then noticed that Dhrakol's blasts had carved a deep channel between the two of us and the castle, cutting off our most likely avenue of escape.

"He'll keep us busy until the troops can take us," said Merc. "I think Ironglove still wants to kill us slowly."

"You are correct," boomed Dhrakol. "Surrender now. You cannot harm me. You cannot escape. Resistance is—" He broke off suddenly and backed away, throwing his arms before his face.

"Yes?" I said. "Resistance is what?"

Merc tapped my shoulder. "Jason, turn around."

Legionnaires, knights, and peasants alike threw themselves to the ground all around us. I turned and looked to the sky.

"Oh my Gods!" I exclaimed.

13

Before me stretched a golden stairway of light, reaching all the way up to the disk of the sun. On it stood two lines of angelic women in white sun dresses, all of them blond, bronze-skinned, and wearing dark glasses. With two on each step as far up as I could see, there must have been over a hundred thousand of them, chorusing a beautiful song without words. I saw a lone, regal figure moving between the lines, descending from the sun. All eyes turned toward her, thoughts of fear and slaughter forgotten in the majesty of the moment.

"It must be the Goddess Rae," I said. "They told me I

would get special help in times of great need. But *this?* I didn't even have to ask."

"I'm impressed," Merc said.

As the tall, stunning woman got closer to the ground, however, I saw that it was not Rae. At least, it was not the incarnation of Rae I had encountered before. I knew the Sun Goddess as a beautiful woman with blue eyes, coppery brown skin, and long, reddish-gold hair. This divine figure was certainly beautiful, but her hair was short and black, her skin dark and dusky, and her violet eyes bright as the evening star. She wore a velvety black gown that seemed to be spun of twilight. In fact, she looked slightly out of place on that brilliant stairway, as if she were more at home in the cool, waning shadows at the end of a hot day.

"Jason Cosmo," she said as she reached the bottom of the stairway. "I'm Gloama Eventide, Goddess of the Dusk. I am one of the minor deities who assists the Goddess Rae." She held out her hand for me to kiss.

"I'm pleased to meet you, O Gloama. Where is Holy Rae?"

"Having her hair done."

It figured. "Well, I'm certainly glad to see you. We were in quite a jam until you got here."

The Dusk Goddess took in the scene. "So I see."

"How did you know I was in trouble?"

"I didn't. I came to give you this." She handed me a small yellow wafer about the size and shape of a playing card. It was made of a strange hard substance and had my picture in one corner. It bore the legend, "JASON COSMO, CHAMPION OF RAE."

"What is this?"

"Your credentials. This card identifies you as the Champion of Rae. Display it to any of her worshippers and they will render you whatever aid you require. It will also gain you admittance to any area of any temple of the Goddess. You should have received this months ago, but the paperwork got misdirected. Don't lose the card. Replacing these things is a nightmare."

"What is it made of?" I said, fingering the card.

"Plastic."

"What's that?"

"A substance concocted by Mita the Maker, Goddess of Technology. We have much of it in Paradise. But enough prattle. My mission is accomplished. Goodbye and good luck, favored mortal."

"What? You're not going to rescue us?"

"You know about the Non-Intervention Pact. The Sunshine Girls and I could easily destroy your enemies, but we are forbidden to interfere in worldly events."

I waved the card. "But I'm the Champion of Rae! Doesn't that rate a little divine intervention now and then?"

"Perhaps, but I don't have the authority to help you. Only Rae herself can authorize such action and she would only do so in the most dire circumstances."

"This is pretty dire. I'm sure she would approve."

"She would have to tell me so herself. She will return from the hairdresser in a couple of hours. If you can hold on until then I might be able to help you out."

"A couple of hours!"

"I am sorry I can do nothing for you, Jason Cosmo. You are on your own." The stairway receded at the speed of light, whirling back up to the sun in the blink of an eye.

"Let's go!" said Merc. Everyone else was still on their knees, not realizing that the divine visitation was over. We sprinted over the prostrate bodies of the awestruck Orphalians, hoping to make it through the Ganthian lines before events resumed their normal course. A mighty blast of power from Dhrakol thwarted our plan. He hovered above us.

"I could not bear the presence of that goddess—but she has abandoned you. You *are* Jason Cosmo! I knew your face was familiar, even after a thousand years!"

"That's quite a memory you've got."

"*You* were the Mighty Champion! *You* were the one who destroyed the Empire and condemned me to centuries of watery oblivion at the bottom of the sea! Now I shall have my revenge!"

"It wasn't me!" I yelled, dodging a deadly bolt of green lightning. "You've got the wrong man!"

"Nay, Cosmo, I know you now! You were the one! And you will die for it!"

The Ganthians rose up and continued their interrupted advance. They probably took the divine visitation as a sure sign that The Gods favored their cause. That was how the jingoistic Ganthians thought. We were right back in the same situation we had been in before Gloama arrived. If anything, we were worse off. Dhrakol was now making a serious effort to exterminate us.

"Stand still!" said Merc. "I'll put a protective spell around us."

We stood together and Merc surrounded us with a bubble of blue light. It withstood all of Dhrakol's polychromatic pyrotechnics. Up to a point.

"That will not shield you from my wrath for long!" said the Dreadnought. "I summon the Crimson Claws of Chaos!"

"Uh-oh," said Merc. "I'd better come up with a good counterspell fast."

The Crimson Claws shredded our defensive envelope and snatched me into the air. "A little faster please, Merc!"

"I'm thinking. Ah! Dynamora's Deadly Discharge should do some damage!"

"I'm immune to it," said Dhrakol, making a fist. "In fact, I slew the great Dynamora myself."

"Merc, do something!" The Claws tightened. I felt as though my ribs were imploding.

"He is powerless to save you, Cosmo," said Dhrakol. He placed his fists together, one atop the other, and twisted them in opposite directions. The Claws mimicked his action, turning my lower body one way, my upper body the other. I strained against them, but it was futile. The Claws would rip me in two.

Merc gestured and a gigantic yellow ruler appeared and rapped the Claws soundly. The phantom hands dissolved into red vapor, and I fell to the ground. The giant ruler vanished. I lay on my back and groaned.

"I had fogotten that I even knew the Didactic Ruler spell," said Merc. "It's one of the few counters to the Crimson Claws."

"Counter this," said Dhrakol. *"Horns of Fontyr and Dark River's flood, let unholy flames sear the spells from his blood!"*

"Noooooooooo!" cried Merc, clutching his head. Dark blue smoke boiled out of his ears. He fell to his knees, pitched forward, and lay still.

"What did you do? Broil his brain?"

"I eradicated his magical ability with an ancient spell of magic ability eradication unknown to modern magi. He is thus irrevocably rendered as incapable of casting spells as you are. And now, Jason Cosmo, we have a very old score to settle."

He raised his gauntleted hand to strike. I steeled myself for the blow. Dhrakol would have his revenge for my ancient ancestor's deeds.

"That will be enough, Dhrakol," Ironglove interjected. "You have done well."

I stared up into a faceful of pikes. The Second Legion was all around me, their gory lances dripping blood. Myrm Ironglove stood over me. Dhrakol landed beside him.

"You should allow me to kill this one immediately," said the Dreadnought. "He is the most dangerous of the lot."

"I give the commands here. Or have you forgotten?" Ironglove snapped. He extended his hand to me. "So you truly are Jason Cosmo and, moreover, you have traffic with The Gods. You fought bravely, warrior. There is a place for a man like you in my army."

"No thanks," I said, ignoring his hand and standing up on my own.

"I will give you an officer's commission and place you on my personal staff. That is a rare honor for a foreigner, but you impress me."

"I'm not interested in licking your boots, dictator." The legionnaires grumbled at that.

His tone grew frosty. "I suggest you choose your words more carefully, Cosmo. It is not wise to insult me before my men. Now decide quickly. Either accept my offer or die."

"Not the old 'Join me or die' routine," said Merc,

sitting up. No less than five pikes pressed against his back and an equal number against his chest.

"Slay them both now," urged Dhrakol.

"You forget yourself, Dreadnought," warned Ironglove. "Seek not to advise me again. What is it to be, Cosmo?"

"Go to hell."

"Kill him," he told Dhrakol.

"Gladly." The Dreadnought caught me by the throat with one hand and lifted me off the ground. His metal-clad fingers contracted until I was barely able to breathe. I clawed at them, trying to break his grip, but the Dreadnought was far stronger than I, even in full sunlight.

"Ironglove!" said Merc.

Savoring my execution, the Imperator half-turned, just in time to see Merc launch himself from the ground faster than the legionnaires could react. The wizard flew at Ironglove and sank his viper's fangs into the dictator's exposed throat, injecting a lethal dose of venom. Foaming at the mouth, Ironglove lost his balance. Several of his men caught him. He writhed in agony. The end would come in mere seconds.

"Dhrakol! Save me!" gasped the dying dictator. Forced to obey Ironglove's every command, Dhrakol dropped me and enveloped his master in a stasis field which would block the action of the poison until it could be purged from his body. The Dreadnought took the Imperator in his arms and flew him to safety, leaving us to the tender mercies of the Second Legion.

Merc fought like a madman. He was unarmed, stripped of his power, and weak from his battle with Dhrakol. He still managed to kill seventeen men before he went down. The legionnaires were in no hurry to kill him. They pinned his arms and legs to the ground with pikes and then took turns kicking him and dancing the Ganthian polka on his face.

I was also unarmed and weary. The sun's rays gave me the strength of many men, but strength alone was not enough against such overwhelming numbers. It didn't take the Ganthians long to bring me to the ground also. Thankfully, they didn't feel the need to skewer me with pikes. They just kicked me. Amid hot flashes of pain, images of Sapphrina flashed in my mind. I hoped she was safe. I hoped Rif would get away to carry on with our quest. I hoped I wouldn't have to spend my eternity in Paradise listening to the Goddess Rae chatter.

The Goddess! "Rae! *Ufff*! Help . . . *argh*!. . . me!" That was all I got out before a soldier's boot got stuck in my mouth. I hoped someone up there heard me. I hoped Rae was back from the hairdresser. I was doing a lot of hoping in my final moments of life.

I suddenly felt the ground tremble beneath me. The barrage of kicks stopped and the sky grew black. The legionnaires looked up in fear as the ground shook again, this time so violently that they lost their footing. It was an earthquake. Even as I realized this, a gigantic fissure opened up beneath Castle Bismuth, plunging it into an abyss. The fissure streaked across the field, swallowing hundreds of legionnaires, but somehow missing me. Thunderbolts rained from the sky, incinerating a dozen Ganthians at a time. The Second Legion, all ten thousand warriors, scattered in every direction, fleeing what could only be the wrath of The Gods.

"Thank you, Blessed Rae," I gasped.

"Your Sun Goddess didn't save you," said a muffled voice. "I did."

"Who?" I wiped the blood out of my swollen eyes. I was no longer lying on the battlefield. Now I was in the midst of an endless desert of burning white sand. Merc lay nearby, pinned to the sand by six pikes. He was badly beaten, but still alive. The speaker stood beside him, a tall figure completely shrouded in crimson robes and a hood the same shade as the Claws of Chaos.

"Who are you?" I said. I was too weak to rise.

"The one you seek," said the figure, pulling one of the pikes out of Merc's leg and tossing it aside. "I am the illusionist. I am the one who freed Zaran Zimzabar and helped him enter and exit Rae City. I am the one who promised Thule Nethershawn the Raelnan throne if he would aid me." He extracted another pike. "I am the one who watched every move you heroes made. I am the mastermind. I am the prime mover." He pulled yet another pike free.

"Are you Phantasm?"

"Perhaps."

"Mirrorsmoke?"

"Perhaps. And perhaps I am Acheron. And perhaps I am one you know nothing about." He plucked out a fourth pike. Mercury stirred. "You shall learn my identity in due time. Just before I kill you both."

"Where am I?" said Merc. He turned his head toward me. "The *desert*? Jason?"

"It is good that you are awake, Boltblaster," said the masked illusionist. "I was just explaining that I am, in a sense, the one who killed Raella Shurbenholt and that I intend to kill the two of you. That is why I had to save you from the Ganthians. It is not yet time for you to die. That is for me and me alone to decide."

"You!" said Merc, with more venom in his voice than he had injected into Ironglove. "Who are you? Show your face!"

"In due time, Boltblaster. At the moment you are in no condition to confront me. Three leagues north of you is a Temple of Healing. I suggest you visit it. Once you are whole you must continue to pursue Zaran Zimzabar. You will find him in Voripol."

"A trap," I said.

"Yes. But for him, not you. He has served his purpose. He killed Queen Raella at my command. He led you on a merry chase, giving me time to bring my plans to fruition."

"And he freed Halogen," I said. "Is that part of your plan?"

"Perhaps. In any event, Zaran is no longer useful to me. You may avenge yourselves upon him, as you have done with Thule Nethershawn. Enjoy it, because you won't have the satisfaction of killing me. Still, two out of three isn't bad."

"I'm going for the full count," said Merc.

"No. You will catch Zimzabar. I will see to that. The trip to Voripol will take him longer than he intends, so take all the time you need to rest up."

"Forget Zaran. I want to kill you," said Merc, straining against the two pikes which still held him fast. *"You!"*

"After you eliminate Zaran, I will reveal myself to you and then we will meet face-to-face. Do be more careful from now on. I'm a busy individual. I can't be constantly saving you from your own mistakes." He pulled up the last two pikes. "Farewell. I'll be in touch."

The members of the Blessed and Charitable Order of Healers Divine, Surgeons Sacred, Physicians Ordinary, and Nurses Attendant—known colloquially as the Medics— were the doctors of Arden. At least, they were the official doctors. There were, unfortunately, a large number of renegade herbalists, apothecaries, wise women, gypsies, holistics, chiropractors, witch doctors, and others running about curing people of sickness without any kind of formal sanction or supervision at all. To most sufferers it made little difference who cured them or how, so long as it was done, but the Medics took a different view of the matter.

They were, after all, not merely healers, but also ordained priests of Ama, Goddess of Health, Healing, and Medicine. From the lowliest novice-orderly to the Grand High Koop himself, the Medics were carefully screened and highly trained professionals. They took it as an affront bordering on blasphemy that anyone outside their order would presume to treat or, even worse, cure a patient.

There was little excuse for anyone in need not to visit a physician-priest. The Medics maintained Temples of Healing, also called hospitals, in all major cities and many lesser ones. There were even a few out in the middle of nowhere to serve the overwhelmingly rural population of the Eleven Kingdoms. Most towns and villages of any note had a solo Medic or two, and itinerant physician-priests wandered the countryside to take up any slack as best they could.

Their ministrations did not come cheaply, but then, as the Divine Ama said, health was certainly more important than wealth. Acting upon this precept, the Medics sought to improve the overall state of their patients by giving them as much health and relieving them of as much wealth as they possibly could. The ungrateful wretches often frustrated these efforts to purify their souls as well as their bodies by consulting unqualified quacks willing to dispense dubious cures for no more than a hot meal or a couple of chickens rather than cold, hard cash. Such miscreants were clearly in league with the devils. So too those who suggested that the Medics should provide free care to all, as if people were somehow entitled to it just by virtue of living and breathing. That kind of madness had demonic plot written all over it.

The next thing I remembered after our little chat with the illusionist was waking up in a private room in the St. Hematogen Memorial Regional Healing Temple of South Orphalia. Rifkin sat at my bedside.

"Easy there, Jason. You took quite a beating. Don't try to sit up."

"Why would I want to do that?" My body felt like one big bruise, which in fact it was. I wore no clothes, but wasn't quite naked, being wrapped like a mummy in several yards of bandage. "What—"

"Let me see if I can answer your questions before you ask them. After we jumped from the bleachers, I made a run for Castle Bismuth. Dhrakol caught you and Merc, then everything stopped when some gorgeous goddess appeared and gave you something."

"That was Gloama Eventide."

"You'll have to introduce me sometime. After she vanished, it looked like you were losing, but I couldn't reach you. Not that I would have been much help. Then Dhrakol flew away carrying Ironglove and the two of you went down in the press. I thought you finished."

"So did I."

"However, for some odd reason the entire Ganthian Second Legion took a notion to run off in every direction screaming as if all the demons of all the Hells were hot on their heels. From what Merc tells me about your interview with the illusionist, I gather they saw something unpleasant. I took advantage of the confusion to steal a wagon, scoop you up, and rush you to this healing place. Of course, the concerned Medics didn't want to treat you until they saw the gleam of good gold, which I shortly procured from their own treasure room. This stay is on the house, unless they have an audit soon."

"You spoke to Merc? How is he?"

"Physically, he's fine, or will be. He lost much blood, but the physicians say he will pull through. His wizardly recuperative power is the only thing that saved him."

"And his magic?"

"Gone. Dhrakol put a powerful curse on him. Merc says the part of his mind that 'partakes of the ambient magical energy field of this world,' as he puts it, has been shut down. He remembers all his spells, he says, but he can't cast them."

"You mean he has some kind of mental block?"

"It goes deeper than that, I think, though I admit I don't understand half of what he told me. Whatever it is about him, in his blood or genes, that allowed him to work magic has been turned off. His arcane potential is gone and without it his magical training and knowledge are useless."

"He's become a mere mortal then."

"As close to it as he'll ever get. He still has his secondary powers. In any event, it looks as though we will be here a good many days. Which is all right with me. We've kept an active pace since leaving Caratha. It's good to stay put for a while."

"Meaning you've found a pretty Medic you like."

Rif shrugged. "I thought it wise to take a physical examination. One thing led to another. You know how it goes."

I laughed carefully, respectful of my bruised ribs. "I'll take my time at mending then. Wouldn't want to cut short your romantic interlude."

"Thoughtful of you. You won't get the same tender care here that you got in Loblolly's cave, but the healers are proficient. You'll be swinging a sword again in no time."

Our stay at the Temple of Healing lasted twelve days. The damage Mercury and I had sustained would have kept us abed many weeks more had this particular temple not offered the services of two Healers Divine, the highest rank of Medic. Surgeons Sacred and Physicians Ordinary relied on casts, scalpels, sutures, poultices, medicines, and the like for results. Healers Divine, on the other hand, were able to excise tumors, eradicate infections, and restore damaged flesh by an exercise of will and magic. Their efforts were similar to Loblolly's laying on of hands. Though they were slower and less efficient than the dryad, they were faster than the lesser doctors. They were also more expensive, making up for our shorter stay in the hospital by charging higher fees. This presented no problem, as Rif provided a steady stream of heisted coin to fund our care.

By the end of our convalescence, events were getting ripe for a denouement. In Raelna, Hotfur and General Halehart joined with Ercan the Reaver to halt the advance of the gargantuan Brythalian invasion force and drive King Rubric's mercenaries back across the border. The might of well-trained Raelnan regulars combined with the tactical genius of the She-Fox was just enough to overcome the two-to-one Brythalian advantage of numbers. Sunfare, Glint, and many lesser settlements burned to the ground. The border marches and the north reaches of Duchy of Whitwood were all but laid waste. Many thousands of brave men lost their lives. But the Brythalian juggernaut was turned back and the vengeful Raelnan troika of generals carried the fight into Rubric's realm.

The fourth Raelnan general, meanwhile, found himself in different straits. Cull Crossmaster's advance on Voripol went smoothly, his battalions easily overcoming the antiquated Orphalian knights. But once he got there, he faced a different kind of enemy. The army King Rubric hurled against ancient foe Raelna was not the sum of his might, for the Brythalian liege personally led over twenty-five thousand warriors to Voripol to support the claim of his client and ally, Baron Krawlar von Zinc.

Imperator Myrm Ironglove further confused the picture. Apparently saved from a venomous death by Dhrakol's sorcery, he showed up with two legions in tow to advance the cause of his unwilling puppet, Baron Tungsten. Voripol was not a healthy place to be this time of year anyway, what with the Orphalian flu virus and other deadly germs holding their annual convention there. The arrival of three hostile armies made it even less safe. Crossmaster's true motives were still unknown, but one sure winner in this mess would be Death himself.

Merc, Rif, and I strode out of St. Hematogen's together, the chief healer preceding us backward and attempting to shoo us back inside. He urged us to prolong our stay a few more days "just to be on the safe side." He had not yet caught on to Rif's deception and was eager tack a few more crowns onto our bill.

"We've had enough healing for now," said Merc, shooting the physician-priest a glance dark enough to blot out suns. He had his own human eyes back now, but even those could be frightening. "Get out of our way before you have to heal thyself, physician."

Realizing Merc was deathly serious, the healer paled and scurried back into the hospital.

Rif had procured fresh horses, clothing, weapons, and supplies for us, all generously if unknowingly provided by the Medics. Merc mounted a black stallion, Rif a roan courser, and I bestrode a white destrier. A pair of sturdy pack horses carried our belongings.

We looked boldly northward. There were hills on the horizon and nestled among them was our goal.

"To Voripol," said Merc.

14

There was debate in anthropological circles on whether Voripol could properly be called a civilized place. The city looked as if it had been built by unscrupulous contractors competing for a prize in shoddy workmanship. The royal palace and city wall were made of stone, or at least a moldy material that resembled stone. That seemed to have exhausted every available quarry.

Dark, narrow lines snaked between dilapidated wooden structures with sagging thatch roofs. The unpaved streets were muddy quagmires when it rained and swirls of hot, irritating dust when it didn't. The whole place was tucked away in a small valley between five hills that hid it from view. This prevented anyone from wandering into the city by accident.

The population of Voripol hovered around six thousand in good years, but births were having a hard time keeping up with deaths. Disease was not only rampant here, it was militant. The inhabitants had no concept of sanitation. They threw their refuse, including their dead, right out into the street where it festered and decayed and served as a breeding ground for creatures too loathsome to describe. Other leading causes of death were fire, murder, and—not at all surprisingly—suicide. Furthermore, packs of wild dogs roamed the alleys and took down a few unwary pedestrians each week. Even they gave a wide berth to the rats of the place, who had been known to forcibly evict entire families from their tenements. No self-respecting cat would come within a hundred miles of Voripol.

The night we arrived, the city was in flames. All in all, this was probably not a bad thing.

"How are we going to find Zaran in all this?" I asked.

"We'll find him," said Merc.

Most of its denizens had long since fled the city, content to let the foreign invaders fight over it and come back when the dust settled. From a bluff southwest of the shattered city gates we watched as thousands of Ganthian, Raelnan, and Brythalian soldiers skirmished in the valley by the light of the burning city. The knights of Orphalia were not in evidence. They could only stand by as the three superpowers decided their fates for them. This was not the kind of war they understood.

"Do you think he's there?" Rif asked. "In the middle of all that?"

"I don't know," Merc said. "His trail has long grown

cold. All we have to go on is what the illusionist told us, and he is scarcely one to put our trust in."

With a blast of sulphurous smoke, a disembodied head shrouded in a crimson cowl appeared in the air before us. "Zaran is in the city," it snarled. "You will find him in the palace. The magic amulet which previously protected him is inoperable. Go! You will not be seen." The head burst into flame and vanished.

"I suppose that answers one question," I said. "Here's another. Do you suppose the illusionist is nearby?"

"That's what I was wondering," said Merc. "Normally, illusion spells have a limited range. The caster must be able to see the area or subject he intends to affect. But there are devices that can be used to transmit spells over a distance. To pull the stunt he pulled back at Castle Bismuth, our man—or woman—must have used such a device, and a powerful one. We know he's been watching us with some scrying device. Perhaps the two are one and the same—a magic mirror, an enchanted pool, or a big crystal ball. No, I doubt our illusionist is in the neighborhood. Likely he hasn't stirred from his hiding place since this all began." He spurred his horse forward. "Be that as it may, let's see about Zaran."

True to the evil illusionist's words, none of the warring soldiers took any notice of us, though we walked openly through the corpse-choked streets. The horses refused to come near the flames, so we left them tied on the bluff. We reached the palace by an indirect route, avoiding the inferno in the south part of the city. The heat was brutal, and we were drenched with sweat by the time we strode into the deserted palace courtyard, our weapons at ready. I held a spear. Rif had a long knife. Merc carried a saber.

The palace was perched unsteadily on a low mound in the center of town, which meant it had been the main target for the catapults of all three sides. It was laid out in a square, with watchtowers at three corners and the fourth being swollen into a donjon. There were gaping holes in the outer wall and two of the three towers were smashed. The donjon had wisely become a large pile of rubble to avoid further damage. The courtyard was littered with stinking corpses. Twisting fire shadows danced on their dead faces, giving them horrible expressions that made me think of tormented souls in the Deep Places of Hell. The only living things were a few scraggly dogs who ran off whimpering when we arrived.

"I wish it was daylight," I said nervously. "I'd be at full strength."

"Tonight we must rely on stealth," said Rif. "Stay here and let me scout ahead. I'll find them if they're here."

"Never mind!" hissed Merc, pointing across the courtyard. We hid behind a mound of rubble. The hulking figure emerging from a shattered doorway was unmistakable. It was Yezgar. Zaran stepped into view a moment later. They were accompanied by six terrorists.

"The rest of his band must be outside the city," whispered Merc. "Even so, we're outnumbered."

"Especially since Yezgar counts eight or nine times," noted Rif.

"We'll wait until they get close, then take them by surprise," said Merc. "Concentrate on killing Zaran. I'd like to take him myself, but as long as we get him I'll be happy. There won't be any time for speeches. Once he's down, we've got to run for it or Yezgar will tear us apart. No spells this time."

We hunkered down and prepared to spring upon the unwitting terrorist as he passed our hiding place. Zaran's group was still ten yards away when Yezgar stopped, sniffing the air suspiciously. The half-ogre pointed at the rubble pile and growled. Zaran and his men reached for their weapons.

"Uh-oh," said Merc. "I forgot about that ogre's sensitive nose."

"Half-ogre," I reminded him.

"Whatever."

"I suppose it's safe to say the illusionist is no longer shielding us from detection."

With a roar, Yezgar leaped atop the mound of rubble and bellowed down at us, "Yezgar kill!"

We scattered. Merc went straight for Zaran, cutting down two terrorists to reach him, only to have his saber shatter against Zaran's weapon. The terrorist had my sword—Overwhelm!

"Boltblaster!" snarled the PANGO leader. "This time I will finish you!"

Merc made no reply but gave way.

Rifkin wisely scrambled up the wall behind us, melding into the shadows on the battlements until he saw an opportunity to strike decisively. That left me, as usual, to face Yezgar. I braced the butt of my spear against the ground as he pounced, hoping that by his weight and momentum the ogre would impale himself.

"Yezgar smash!"

The angle was wrong, and the spear snapped, leaving me weaponless, but only for an instant. I reached out with my will, and Overwhelm flew to my hand, pulling Zaran off balance as it left his grasp. I raised the blade just in time to ward off a blow from Yezgar and counter by severing his right hand at the wrist. Green blood spurted from the stump and Yezgar reeled back in disbelief. Then the pain hit and the ogre bellowed even louder than at the Bronze Tower. His cry rebounded off the distant hillsides. The ground trembled, and more of the weakened castle walls collapsed. His eyes blazing with hatred, Yezgar came at me again, spraying green gore from his injured arm and curling his good hand into a massive fist.

Rif, meanwhile, leaped from his perch and knifed a terrorist in the back. Two others threw themselves at Mercury to protect their momentarily defenseless leader. The third follower came at Rif with a scimitar slick with contact poison. Rif backed away from her slashing attack, one step, two steps, then dropped to the ground like falling lightning and kicked her feet from under her. His knife was in her heart the instant she hit the ground.

Yezgar came at me with unstoppable fury. He waved his injured arm at me, spraying blood in my face. Temporarily blind, I stumbled and fell, luckily avoiding a crushing roundhouse punch. Unfortunately, I was in perfect position for Yezgar to kick me across the courtyard, which is what he did. I hit the side of the remaining tower and stuck for an instant before sliding down. I lost Overwhelm during my short flight.

"Yezgar kill!" screamed the ogre, coming my way again. I scooped up a handful of sand, scrambled to my feet, and wiped his blood out of my eyes. He was close and getting closer. I summoned Overwhelm.

The sword came to me by the most direct path, which took it through Yezgar. Overwhelm entered his back and exploded from his abdomen to streak to my waiting hand.

When Yezgar was mere feet from me, I flung the sand into his eyes and dove to the right. The enraged, wounded, blinded monster barreled straight into the wall. The shock wave from Yezgar's impact toppled the tower. Hundreds of tons of stone rained down on him like a shower of meteors, burying him completely. I just barely escaped the deadly collapse myself.

Merc and Rif, meanwhile, put Zaran in a tight spot.

"You and me, Zaran," said Merc as he disabled one of the two remaining raiders. "Just you and me." He ducked inside the wild swing of the last one's club and broke his neck with a precisely delivered blow.

Zaran scrambled to his feet and drew a long, curved knife dipped in poison from the deadly stinger of the Sanskaaran hellscorpion. "It is your time to die, wizard! I do not fear you."

"More the fool you," said Merc, stalking him carefully.

"I am invincible!"

"Your protective amulet doesn't work now, or haven't you noticed? Your sorcerous ally has betrayed you."

A look of consternation crossed Zaran's face as the truth of Mercury's words sank in. "You are right," he said, puzzled. "You should not be able to strike me." Then he sneered and snatched the amulet from its chain around his neck and hurled it to the ground. "No matter! I can still defeat the likes of you!"

Rif edged his way behind Zaran, but Merc waved him off. "This is between him and me."

"Royalist swine!" spat Zaran, cutting the air. "I will kill you just as I did that witch of a Queen!"

"Is that so?" said Merc, feigning an attack. Zaran countered with a knife thrust, and Merc knocked the weapon from his hand. It skittered across the flagstones and disappeared into darkness. "Can you kill me all by yourself? Without your army of fanatics? Without your coward's weapons?"

"You speak to me of cowardice, you who fight with tricks and spells?" Zaran retreated as Merc advanced, but Rif controlled his avenue of escape. He couldn't go far.

"I don't need spells and tricks for you," said Merc.

"Come no closer!" warned Zaran suddenly, holding up his right hand. On his third finger was the Ring of Raxx, its purple amethyst gleaming oddly in the firelight. "I shall blast you all to oblivion!"

"With that ring?" I scoffed, barely restraining my laughter. "I doubt it."

"I can do it!" said Zaran stridently. "I have discovered this ring's secret."

"You've been talking to squirrels?"

"If you can blast us, then go ahead and do it," said Merc, spreading his hands. "Atomize me. Annihilate me. Vaporize me. Whatever suits your twisted fancy."

Zaran swallowed hard and lowered his hand. "I am in a merciful mood. Some other time perhaps." He turned to run. Rif nonchalantly tripped him, and he skidded across the flagstones. Merc pounced on the terrorist and yanked him up by the front of his tunic.

"I surrender," squeaked Zaran. "There is obviously a temporary downturn in the rising tide of history."

"No kidding," said Merc, smashing him in the face and knocking out several teeth.

"Mercy, wizard!" whined Zaran. "I will tell you everything! Don't kill me! Please don't kill me!"

Merc snorted. "What do you know about mercy, butcher? How many hundreds of innocents begged you for mercy? How many got it?"

"None, but that is beside the point. I beg of you Boltblaster, show mercy. You are a wise man."

"True," said Merc, pummeling him again.

"If you kill me, you will be no better than I!"

"Do you really believe that?"

"Well, no actually."

"Neither do I." Merc twisted Zaran's arm behind his back and slammed his face against the ground. Kneeling on the small of his back, he removed the Ring of Raxx and tossed it to me, then pulled the terror lord's head up by his hair. "But since you've offered to tell me everything, go ahead."

"Do you promise not to kill me, great wizard?"

Merc rapped Zaran's face sharply against the flagstones, breaking his nose. "I never make promises I don't intend to keep. Talk. Name the wizard you served."

"I serve none but PANGO and the cause of universal liberation from absolutism and decadent imperalistic colonalism."

"Skip the propaganda and get to the point. The name."

"I do not know my benefactor's name. He never revealed it to me and always appeared hooded in crimson. He said he was a great lord of the Dark Magic Society. He rescued me from a band of crude mercenaries who were taking me to martyrdom at the hands of the bloated Prince of Caratha. He promised me much money, magic, and weaponry for PANGO if I would aid him in a great scheme. He said I would have a chance to kill many royalist maggots." Merc slammed his face against the ground again. "I am telling the truth! What was that for?"

"Punctuation. Go on."

"He gave me the amulet of protection and a magic arrow which I was to use against your Queen. He gave us advanced crossbows. My valiant cadres trained for the mission in lands of Thule Nethershawn. Though a fascist himself, he cooperated with the sorcerer to serve his own ambitions. One of the guiding principles of PANGO is that the contraditions of royalism will bring it down. The cannibalistic aristocracy feeds upon itself, and PANGO does what it can to accelerate the inevitable."

"In other words, you have no moral objections to working with the likes of Nethershawn if it serves your own purposes," sneered Merc. "And why should you? You're just alike."

"The sorcerer got my men in and out of Rae City with his illusion magic. Then he told me to go to the Bronze Tower and free Halogen. I was to leave a clear trail and wait for you to arrive. I was not to kill you, but to strip you of your goods and abandon you in the wilderness. Then I was to bring Halogen unharmed to Voripol."

"Where is he now? Halogen, I mean."

"Just before your attack, we locked him in a cellar as instructed. The journey here took much longer than it should have. We were lost for days, utterly unable to find our way."

"Your former benefactor bewildered you with illusions so we could catch up to you," said Merc. "He wants you dead. How did he give you orders?"

"He projected images to tell me where you were and what must be done. He said that once I reached Voripol I was finished. Here I was to collect my reward."

"Guess what?" said Merc. "You will."

"What about my armor?" I said. "And your cloak, Merc. Where are they?"

"Well?" said Merc.

"In the cellar with Halogen. I was to leave the sword and ring as well, but I decided to keep them."

"Does anyone have more questions before I end his miserable existence?" asked Merc.

"Which cellar?" I said.

"Good point," said Merc, pulling Zaran to his feet. "Take us to Halogen and our belongings."

"Of course," said Zaran, spitting blood. "I'll be glad to."

With Merc still pinning his arm, Zaran led us across the courtyard and into the passage from which he had emerged a few minutes ago. We descended down a narrow stairway to a stone chamber about ten feet square. It had three doors, all closed and barred shut.

"The center door," said Zaran. "Halogen and your goods are beyond it."

I lifted the bar and opened the door. The air within was cool and dry. The room beyond was filled with moldy sacks of meal and flour.

"I don't see him," I said.

"On the far side of the room is a hidden door. Halogen is in a small room beyond it."

"Check it out, Rif," said Merc. The experienced thief crossed the room like a cat and examined the far wall. "I don't see anything," he reported after searching for several minutes.

"We covered the door with sacks of flour. There in the corner," said Zaran.

"I'll help you move them," I said, joining Rif in the cellar. Before I hefted the first sack, I heard a scuffle and Zaran shouted in pain. Rif and I hurried to the door to see Merc hustle to his feet and charge up the stairs. Zaran was already gone. We followed Merc to the courtyard. Zaran had vanished.

"Damn!" said the wizard. "He escaped again."

"How did he break your grip?"

"By letting me break his arm. Almost any hold can be broken if you're willing to sacrifice a few bones."

"Shall we go after him?" I asked.

"I will," said Merc. "The two of you keep looking for Halogen and our things. Zaran was doing something down in those cellars."

Merc ran out of the courtyard. Rif and I explored all three cellars and eventually found a secret room off the chamber to the right. The room was empty, though we saw signs that someone had been there recently. We did not find Merc's cloak or my armor anywhere. Disappointed not to recover our property and angry that we had let Zaran escape, we returned to the courtyard.

By now it was filled with skirmishing Raclnan and Brythalian soldiers. Rif and I watched from the shadows as they battled. It was an even flight until more Raelnans arrived and the Brythalians fled. The Raelnans gave chase.

Soon after they departed, Merc returned. I saw in his face that he had failed to find the terrorist.

15

Angry and dejected that Zaran had escaped us, we exited the burning city and returned to the bluff where we had left the horses. We found a cavalry squadron scouting the area. Their captain and four troopers waited near our steeds. We watched from under cover as the officer ordered his men to find the owners of the horses.

"What do you want to do?" I asked. "They're Raelnan."

Merc thought for a moment, then made a decision. "You two stay here." He walked out of the brush and hailed the captain. The soldiers wheeled their horse about and drew their sabers.

"Who goes there?" demanded the captain.

"Mercury Boltblaster."

"Lord Boltblaster?" said the captain, confused. "What are you doing—I mean, milord!" He saluted and his men followed suit. "Captain Nikla Kellman, at your service."

"I see you've taken good care of my horses."

"These are yours? Good. We though they might belong to enemy scouts. Allow me to recall my men."

"Hold off on that just a moment."

"Milord?"

"You serve under General Crossmaster, do you not?"

"Indeed, milord. I don't see—"

"And whom does Crossmaster serve?"

"I don't understand milord's question. He commands Her Majesty's Army of the Longwash."

"*Her* Majesty. Very good. But the Queen is dead."

"Yes, milord. 'Tis but a figure of speech. We fight for Raelna."

"I hope so." He raised his voice. "Jason! You can come out now!" We took that as a sign that Rif was to stay under cover.

"Who are you?" said Kellman as I appeared.

"Jason Cosmo." I flashed my ID. "Champion of Rae."

"I think, milords, that General Crossmaster will want to see you both at once."

"I imagine that he will," said Merc, "but he can wait. Zaran Zimzabar is somewhere in the area. We must find him."

"Milord, my orders are to scout this area and report back to General Crossmaster by midnight."

"Fine," said Merc, glancing up at the moon as he swung into the saddle. "That gives us a couple of hours, doesn't it?"

Our search was fruitless. The darkness, the rough terrain, and the dueling armies all combined to frustrate our efforts. Zaran could have fled in any direction, rejoined the rest of his band, and be miles away by now. The illusionist was not forthcoming with any suggestions, not that we wanted his help. It nonetheless struck me as odd that he would be so eager to have us fight Zaran, then forget all about us. Surely with his scrying device he observed the encounter and its aftermath. Surely he saw which way Zaran fled.

It was nearly dawn when we rode into the Raelnan encampment in the heights southeast of Voripol. Kellman, long overdue, was apprehensive about facing his commander, though he had sent a messenger back to explain the situation.

General Crossmaster received us before his field tent. He was a tall, rugged man with salt-and-pepper hair and a full beard. His eyes were brown and piercing, his uniform stained with mud and gore. Like the She-Fox, Cull Crossmaster liked to take an active part in any battle. A native Raelnan, the son of a mule skinner, he had fought under the Sunburst Banner all his adult life, rising through the ranks on the basis of his skill, courage, and unflagging loyalty. He was Hotfur's second when she held the Longwash command and was the clear choice to replace her when she became Supreme Commander.

He saluted. "Lord Boltblaster. Master Cosmo. Good of you to drop by." He turned to Kellman. "You are

dismissed, Captain. You may make your report later."
He held open his tent flap. "Come in, sirs, and tell me
what I can do for you."

"Many have wondered what you're doing here," said
Merc once we were seated on camp stools.

"Aye," said Crossmaster with a brief chuckle. "But
I've sent messages to the She-Fox explaining all. I saw
that Orphalia was about to boil over and my spies reported a Brythalian force ready to move it when it did. It
was my judgment that a preemptive strike was necessary
to secure Raelnan interests. General Hotfur has con-
curred. And, of course, events have borne out my decision. Had I not acted when I did, Rubric and Ironglove
would be dividing this pie with not a slice for Raelna."

An aide served us goblets of mulled wine and discreetly withdrew. Merc sipped his drink. "I see the wisdom of that. It is indeed fortuitous that you acted when
you did, striking before news of King Stron's death in
Rae City could reach Orphalia and touch off the civil
war. Or even before the news could reach you. One
wonders why you did not seek authorization for such a
grave undertaking, but perhaps you knew there would be
no one to grant it."

Crossmaster's face darkened. "What are you saying,
milord?"

"Your reasons for your invasion are sound, but they
depend upon you having information you could not have
had when you launched your attack, unless you have
become precognitive or have been consulting a very good
oracle. Or unless you knew in advance that Stron Astatine and all your superiors were going to be dead. Orphalia
may have boiled, but the barons would not rebel against
their king. They don't take the kingship that seriously
here. You had to know something they didn't to attack
when you did. And an officer as *loyal* as yourself would
certainly clear an invasion with his higher-ups if he truly
felt it necessary for the defense of the realm. But I think
your motives were less pure, weren't they?"

Crossmaster's face colored with hot shame. "I acted
only for the good of Raelna," he said hotly. "For Raelna!"

"You knew there would be a massacre at the wedding. You sold out to Thule Nethershawn."

"No!"

"No? You knew in advance that there would be an attack, did you not?"

"Yes, but—"

"And you learned of it from Thule, correct?"

"Yes, confound you! But I never—"

"From those admissions the conclusion is obvious. You are a traitor. Can you deny it?"

"Yes! If you will give me a chance!"

"Go on," said Merc coldly. "This should be fascinating."

"I knew there would be an attempt on King Stron, but I never suspected a general massacre. I never dreamed that Her Majesty would be killed. You must believe me!"

"I don't," said Merc.

"Even if what you say is true," I said, stunned by this revelation, "why didn't you report it to the Queen?"

"I had been urging Her Majesty to take a more assertive stance in Orphalia. It was only a matter of time before the Ganthians and Brythalians moved in, and Raelna needed to be here first to safeguard our northern border. General Hotfur agreed with me, but we could not convince the Queen. Then, a month ago, I learned from an unknown source that there would be an attempt on the life of King Stron at the wedding. My first reaction was to report this to the High Command, but then I thought better of it."

"So Hotfur didn't know?" said Merc.

"No. She would have told the Queen. If I let the plot go forward, the civil war following Stron's death would give me a pretext to cross the Longwash. I could present the Queen with a *fait accompli*. With Raelnan troops already in combat, she would have no choice but to sanction my actions."

"You took it upon yourself to overrule the Queen and enact your own policy," said Merc. "That alone makes you a traitor."

"I acted for the Raelnan national interest," protested Crossmaster. "Even the She-Fox agreed with me inasmuch as she knew my plans. The Queen didn't understand the military realities. She didn't realize the danger. This had to be done, don't you see that?"

"No," said Merc.

"You could have prevented many deaths if you had reported what you knew," I said.

"Do you think I don't know that?" cried Crossmaster in anguish. "When the news of what had happened reached me, I was shocked. I didn't want to believe it. But Her Majesty's death made my mission all the more urgent. I pushed on toward Voripol. Then I received a messenger from Thule. 'King Thule,' he called himself. He said that he had been the unknown source of my information, that he had known what I would do even before I did, that my actions had facilitated his takeover by getting the Army of the Longwash out of his way. He commanded me to complete the conquest of Orphalia. I could name any reward, he said. I was enraged! I wanted to march back to Rae City and rip out his black heart, but then thought that would be futile. I decided to take Orphalia and make it a haven of resistance to him. I thought him stronger than he proved to be, for a few days later came word that he was dead at your hands and a Provisional Council installed. Hotfur was alive and she directed me to stay the course. So I fight on."

"Well that's just inspirational," snarled Merc. "We'll have to see about getting a medal struck for you."

"I never meant for this to happen!" said Crossmaster in tears. "I never meant for my Queen to die! I only wanted to make her see the danger, to listen—"

Merc struck so quickly that Crossmaster was flat on his back with a bruised jaw before I realized the wizard had moved. "Don't ever refer to Raella as *your* Queen again! You haven't the right, you miserable traitor! You caused her death with your pathetic scheming!"

Crossmaster broke down completely. "I know. I know. And the guilt of it rends my soul. Finish me, wizard. I have wronged you, betrayed Queen and country, brought ruin upon us all, but I lack the courage to take my own life. I beg you to kill me, milord, and let justice be done."

"If you kill him," I said, "we'll be lucky to get out of this camp alive."

"If I kill him," said Merc, "he'll get off far too easily. No, Crossmaster, I want you to live for a very long time, and I want you to spend every minute thinking about what you've done. That is the best justice I can devise." He turned his back on the weeping general. "Come on, Jason. I need some fresh air."

Rifkin rejoined us about a mile beyond the camp as another day of warfare began. We retreated into a forested area between the hills to eat our breakfast and avoid being caught up in the bloodshed.

"When did you realize the truth about Crossmaster?" I asked Merc.

"As soon as I learned about his invasion."

"You never said anything."

"There wasn't any point, and, as it turns out, I didn't have the story straight anyway. I thought he was an active ally of Thule, not a dupe."

"If you thought that, why did we go into the camp?"

"To see if I was right."

"A big risk just to satisfy your curiosity."

Merc shrugged. "I think the easy part is over. If Zaran goes underground, he'll be next to impossible to find. And our hooded illusionist can play games with us for a long time before we get a clue to his location."

"What are you saying, Merc?"

"The two of you have aided me greatly and I appreciate it, but I think it is time we separated. I will dedicate the rest of my life to tracking down and punishing Raella's killers. I've got nothing else to do. Not so for you, my friends. You've got your own lives to lead. I thought we could end this quickly, but it's obviously going to be a long-term thing now. I don't expect you to stick it out. I can go on alone from here."

"Without your magic?" I said.

"Like I told you earlier, I've never relied too much on magic. It's undependable, as we see. There is more to Mercury Boltblaster than fancy spells."

"That's not what I meant, Merc. I'm not going to abandon you. I owe you too much."

"Those debts are cancelled," said Merc.

"I'm still with you," I said. "Right to the end."

Merc clasped my hand. "Thank you, Jason. And what of you, Rif?"

"Mercury, you know how Queen Raella spared my life when I was caught spying in the Solar Palace. I should have hung, but she pardoned me because, she said, I had a spark that shouldn't be extinguished. She saw nobility and goodness in my aura. I—a thief, a liar, a swindler—noble! Good!" He gave a wry smile. "I fear I have not lived up to the potential the good Queen saw in me. I remain a dissolute, incorrigible rogue. But perhaps I can repay my debt and merit the mercy she showed by helping you avenge her. I will remain."

"Inspirational," said the illusionist's head, appearing before us. "But foolish. My quarrel is with Cosmo and Boltblaster, my 'noble' rogue. I advise you part with them now unless you are ready to die with them."

Rif shrugged. "If it comes to that."

"Where have you been?" said Merc sourly.

"Some guests arrived. I was unable to observe your failure with Zimzabar. However, you will get another chance. He has turned south again with the remainder of his band. There is a PANGO training camp in the hills beyond the Crownbolt, several leagues east of Stive. That is his objective. However, I shall maze him once again and guide you to him. And since you are obviously incapable of handling him alone, I will confound his party with illusions when you attack."

"We don't need your help," said Merc. "Why don't you drop the masks and melodrama and reveal yourself? Are you afraid of me?"

"Certainly not."

"Then come and face me. Or tell me where you are and I will come to you. Let's not play games anymore."

"Destroy Zaran Zimzabar. Then I will reveal my self."

"If you want Zaran destroyed, you destroy him. I knew where to find him now. He'll keep. I want you, sorcerer. You started this. Now let's finish it!"

The image was silent for a minute, as if considering how to respond to Mercury's challenge. Then it fixed him with a baleful glare. "Very well, Boltblaster. I am ready for you." Gloved hands appeared to remove the floating head's mask, revealing a handsome, dark-haired man with crimson eyes. "I am Rom Acheron, Master of Visions, a lord of the Dark Magic Society, and soon to be its Overmaster. If you are so eager to die, you will find me in Castle Bloodthorn. Come if you dare. I await you."

The image flickered and vanished.

16

They say you can judge a man by the company he keeps. This is also true of geographical features, for the Bitterspleen Hills were exactly what you would expect of highlands consorting with the likes of the thoroughly disreputable Incredibly Dark Forest, which lay at their western terminus. (Actually, the hills went right into the Forest and marched through it all the way to the mountains of the Gaede Range. But, by an injustice of cartography, all that area was considered part of the Forest, not the Bitterspleens. This insult made the remaining hills all the meaner.) The Bitterspleens were high and craggy and bleak and swept by winds so wicked they were banned from blowing in decent places. Tangled brush and barbed briars grew on their slopes, along with leaning, twisted trees. Here were the lairs of gryphons, bully beetles, shocknockers, grumpsnorts, axe birds, horngrims, warp wasps, lonesharks, and other nasty creatures that only an environmentalist could love.

Somewhere in this unpleasant region was Castle Bloodthorn. It wasn't on any map, because no survey party was so curious as to brave the dangers of the hills just to pinpoint its location. Since Bloodthorn wasn't on many itineraries anyway, this suited most people just fine.

Bloodthorn was of demonic origin. This is to say that it

was designed by demonic architects, constructed by demonic workers, decorated by demonic decorators, and inhabited by demonic inhabitants. Like most evil fortresses, it dated to the time of the Empire of Fear. The Evil Emperors were closely allied with the Demon Lords who, among other things, sent demon warriors to fight in their armies. The Emperors appreciated this, since demons make fierce warriors. What they do not make is good neighbors. The tastes and personal habits of the average demon are too disgusting even for the likes of Evil Emperors. So the Demon Lords had citadels like Bloodthorn built to house their troops stationed in Arden. Most of these castles were destroyed during the Great Rebellion, but there were still a few standing here and there as the dictates of fate and plot demanded.

Of course, we did not merely stroll out of Crossmaster's camp and find ourselves at the illusionist's front gate. It was an arduous journey of many days from Voripol to Bloodthorn. We first had to traverse the nearly uninhabited northern reaches of Orphalia. The farming was bad there, in part because of the soil, in part because monsters from the Incredibly Dark Forest and the Bitterspleens liked to roam about the countryside trampling crops and eating farmers. We passed a few small, isolated and heavily fortified settlements, but no one would talk to us or let us in. Hospitality was an alien concept in this area.

We encountered a band of brigands, desperate men for a desperate land. Desperate and stupid, apparently not realizing that there would be no rich caravans or wealthy wayfarers for them to rob around there. The terrain was excellent for skulking about and setting up ambushes, but without anyone to ambush, there really wasn't much point. They were obviously out of practice, setting off a rockslide that buried half of their own number rather than us. We graciously gave the rest of the band a permanent cure for their stupidity.

After five or six days, we arrived in the near vicinity of the Bitterspleens. There was a narrow, grassy valley between the last of the ordinary nameless hills of north Orphalia and the Bitterspleens proper. As we led our horses from a line of tree cover, the scent of decayed flesh assailed our nostrils. This, combined with the buzzing of flies and the flying of buzzards, led us to a pack of dead wolves, though whether dead wolves can still constitute a pack is an open question. Fifteen of the animals were sprawled about over a small area, their furry bodies torn to shreds.

"What could have done this?" I asked.

"Oh, any number of things," said Merc. "Dragons, ogres, claw devils, a gorgoratops, a flock of—"

"Never mind," I said, loosening Overwhelm in its scabbard. "Let's just keep our eyes open."

Keeping our eyes open, we soon noticed a flock of gray sheep contentedly munching grass on a nearby stone-dotted slope. They cocked their ears and stopped their grazing to watch our approach with sheepish interest.

"This is odd," I said. "I wouldn't expect to find a flock of gentle, harmless sheep so near a pack of dead wolves."

"Assuming, of course, that a bunch of dead wolves can properly be called a pack," said Rif.

"Of course."

As we mounted the slope, the sheep gathered around us, their red eyes shining. The animals pressed so close against us that it was almost impossible to walk. We halted.

"Friendly animals," I said.

"Kind of quiet though," said Rif. "Aren't sheep supposed to bleat?"

"I don't like the way they're staring at us," said Merc.

"I know what you mean," I said, surveying a silent circle of upturned fuzzy faces. There was something odd about their eyes, a kind of hungry gleam not usually associated with herbivorous grazing animals.

"Maybe they're just curious," said Rif.

"Yes, curious," I echoed.

"And notice that the horses aren't with us," said Merc. "They're standing back there. They gave us the slip so carefully we didn't notice."

"Wise animals, horses," said Rif. "They can sense danger."

"Danger," I repeated, tentatively reaching out to scratch

a nearby sheep's head. I nearly lost my hand to its snapping fangs.

"Sheep don't have fangs," I said, reaching for Overwhelm. "Especially not steel fangs."

"These do," said Merc, as the entire flock bared their sharply curved teeth and hissed like a chorus of lisping cats. They looked a lot less gentle and harmless.

"I think we know what happened to the wolves now," said Rif. "And it's about to happen to us, too."

"Not if I can help it!" I said, drawing Overwhelm and beheading the nearest two sheep all in one fluid motion. My companions drew their own weapons and joined the fight, hacking away at the animals and trying to avoid their deadly teeth.

"Their wool is like chainmail," said Merc.

"I hadn't noticed," I said.

"That's because you've got a magic sword that cuts through granite like it was wet cardboard," said Rif. "Of course you wouldn't notice."

We fought our way up the hill. I cleared a path through the flock with Overwhelm and my divinely augmented strength. Rif and Merc covered my back. Along the way I noticed that many of the "stones" on the slope were actually mossy bones. Not an encouraging sign.

We gained the summit, leaving several hundred pounds of malign mutton in our wake. The other side sloped gently into the aforementioned valley, which was about a mile wide, with a narrow river flowing through it. On our side was a carefully cultivated field of vegetables. A herd of large cattle grazed on the far side.

"Well, do we stand and fight here or make a run for it?" I asked.

"The horses have already chosen to run," Rif observed. Indeed, our clever mounts had gone around the hill and now charged across the valley toward the river.

"Then let's catch them," said Merc.

We dashed down the incline with two dozen steel-jawed sheep nipping at our heels and followed our horses through the planted field.

The vegetables weren't any friendlier than the sheep. The plants had a slow reaction time; but there was just enough of a gap between the passage of the horses, who stirred them up, and our arrival for the equines to go unmolested while we bore the full brunt of the horticultural onslaught. Razor-sharp leaves slashed our skin. Sharpshooting pods shot lead peas at us. Spiky carrots rose from the ground and lunged at our ankles. Acidic tomatoes flew from the vine to burst against and burn whatever they hit.

The vicious veggies attacked the sheep as well, and many of the enraged animals forgot about us and turned to uprooting their new enemies. We had fewer pursuers when we finally emerged from the hellish garden. That was just as well, for we ran full tilt into a flock of chickens the size of beer barrels. Naturally, these were most unnatural chickens. Each had a beak and claws of a different metal—bronze, steel, brass, gold, nickel, lead, aluminum, etc. Their lord was a miraculum rooster. The chickens had been engaged in pecking their feed of coins, ore, and bits of scrap metal. When we burst into their midst, they became enraged and promptly attacked. We just kept running and let the chickens and the sheep fight it out.

"This is like some kind of crazy farm," I said.

"If so, I do not want to meet the farmer," said Rif.

"Fellows, I think we just did," said Merc.

I skidded to a halt and looked up. Way up. He was at least thirty feet tall, with legs like oak trees and a chest like a cliff. He wore muddy boots, denim overalls, and a wide-brimmed straw hat. His face was like a craggy mountain top. In his hands was a pitchfork big enough to sink a galleon. Two woolly mammoths, their shoulders at his waist, flanked him. They seemed to be growling.

"WHAT'S GOING ON HERE?" he boomed. The sound of his voice knocked all three of us off our feet. The pitchfork came down in our midst, touching off a minor earthquake. "SPEAK, ERE I SET MY DOGS ON YOU!"

The mammoths definitely growled.

"No need to shout!" said Merc, cupping his hands around his mouth to shout up at the giant. "We aren't deaf!"

"At least not yet," I added.

"WHO'S SHOUTING? WHAT'S THE VERY IDEA, TRESPASSING ON MY FARM, TRAMPLING MY GARDEN, UPSETTING MY ANIMALS?"

"Your animals attacked us," said Merc, ignoring the part about trespassing.

"ATTACKED YOU? PFAUGH! THESE ANIMALS ARE TAME."

"I'm glad we didn't meet any wild ones," Rif said.

"YOU STILL HAVEN'T TOLD ME WHAT YOU'RE DOING HERE," the giant said.

"We are travelers bound north," Merc answered. "We came upon your farm by accident. It was not our intent to cause a disturbance, but we had to defend ourselves. Now tone it down, will you?"

"WHAT'S WRONG WITH A NORMAL CONVERSATIONAL TONE?"

"It's rattling my brain pan, that's what!"

"Oh, very well," said the giant in a whisper that echoed off the far hills. "How's this?"

"Better."

"GOOD! NOW STAY PUT WHILE I STRAIGHTEN OUT THE MESS YOU'VE MADE. SHEP! LADY! WATCH THEM!" The two mammoths sat and eyed us vigilantly. "GOOD DOGS!" The angry giant patted them on the head and stepped over us, shooing chickens and scooping up sheep. He carried his squirming burden up the far hill and deposited them on its crest, pausing for several minutes to look down the far side. He was even angrier when he returned.

"THERE'S A DOZEN OF MY PRIZE SHEEP LYING DEAD BACK THERE! WHAT HAVE YOU DONE?"

"That should be obvious," said Merc. "I told you we were attacked. You shouldn't let your animals roam where they can assault innocent wayfarers. You're lucky we weren't seriously hurt or you'd have a giant lawsuit on your hands, giant."

"YOU HAVE THE NERVE TO THREATEN ME AFTER WHAT YOU'VE DONE? I'M OF A MIND TO SQUASH YOU WHERE YOU STAND!"

"Really?" said Merc belligerently. "You'll not find that so—What is it, Jason?"

"Merc, look at the size of him."

"So?"

"We don't really want to fight him. And it's pretty clear now that we're in the wrong. We damaged his flock and his crops. I was a farmer myself back in Lower Hicksnittle, I understand these things."

"So what do you suggest we do?"

"Apologize."

"Apologize?"

"Sounds good to me," said Rif, glancing nervously at Shep and Lady. They were growling again.

"If you must," said Merc.

"Squire Giant!" I said. "We regret the damage we have done to your property. It was purely in self-defense, but we apologize nevertheless."

"NOT GOOD ENOUGH!" said the giant. "I DEMAND RESTITUTION."

"What will satisfy you?" I asked.

"You must serve me without pay for a year and a day."

"No way," said Merc.

"Friend giant, that we cannot do. We are on a quest to avenge my friend's murdered wife and many others. Perhaps you could name some other price?"

"I CARE NOTHING FOR YOUR QUEST, BUT I WILL ACCEPT YOUR HORSES AS PAYMENT." He pointed toward the river, where the animals drank. His arm blotted out the sun.

"Our horses?" I said.

"Go ahead, Mr. Fairplay," said Merc. "They'll be useless in the hills anyway."

"Sir Giant, please accept the horses as compensation for the injury we have done you."

"YOU MUST ALSO HELP ME COLLECT MY SLAUGHTERED SHEEP."

"Of course."

"DONE THEN. NEVER LET IT BE SAID THAT OLDE MACDOUNAGHALD DOESN'T DEAL FAIRLY WITH EVERY MAN." He lowered his voice to a more tolerable level. "And now, strangers, join me for a meal and tell me more of yourselves and your quest."

"We would be honored."

"Good." He scooped us up and carried us across the water, his elephant dogs splashing playfully after him. Looking down at his fierce cattle—which had horns like pole arms and collars of bone around their necks—I was glad to be cradled in the giant's arms.

"I have to keep my mookows on this side of the river," MacDounaghald said. "Otherwise the sheep might hurt them."

"What keeps them from wading across?"

"The ducks."

"Ducks?"

A freshwater plesiosaurus stuck its long neck out of the water and quacked, showing a mouthful of teeth as long as my forearm. "BACK, NESSIE," said the farmer. "THESE MORSELS ARE NOT FOR YOU." I noticed the horses wisely retreating from the river's edge. I didn't think they would be very happy here.

Olde MacDounaghald's farmhouse was carved out of one of the hills across the river. He set us down on his doorstep and tossed a tree trunk big enough to serve as ship's mainmast back toward the river. The mammoths charged after it, trumpeting joyously. "My doggies love to play fetch," said the giant. The animals reached the tree at about the same time, wrapped their trunks around it, and growled ferociously as they fought for possession. "Tug-of-war, too."

He rolled a side of the hill away and we followed him into a great cavern. It looked like the interior of a human cottage, only bigger. He seated us on his mesa-like table and began mixing a salad.

"I'm a vegetarian," he explained. "I hope you don't mind the absence of meat."

"Around here, I'd be a vegetarian too," I said.

"I make a robust salad though."

"Yes, we've seen how robust your vegetables are," Rif said.

"It's the fertilizer that does it." MacDounaghald chuckled. I feared his laughter would bring the roof down on us.

"It's a fine farm you have," I said.

"Thank you. It's a living. I get a good price for the steel wool and, of course, my ore chickens lay eggs of the purest quality. I store away the gold, silver, and platinum and sell the other. The miraculum market is a bit flat this year, but stainless steel is doing well."

"And the mookows?" I asked.

"Their milk is much prized among my people. You shall have mookow cheese with your meal."

"What of your people?" I asked. "Is it true there is a kingdom of the giants far to the north?"

"A kingdom? There aren't enough of us for a kingdom. It's a village we have. Giant Centre, we call it."

"And is your village in the north?"

"You are in my village now," MacDounaghald said. "You are always in it. We giants have a saying that 'The world is our village.' And that's the truth of it. We like lots of elbow room, so we have to spread out a bit. Giant Centre is everywhere."

"I think the lords of the Eleven Kingdoms might take exception to that idea," noted Rif.

"We don't pay much attention to human notions of property, nor they to ours, as you have demonstrated today."

"Point well taken," I said.

"Now tell me of your quest."

I did most of the talking, briefly relating the events which had brought us to Olde MacDounaghald's farm. The giant listened with interest, not interrupting except for an occasional grunt or shake of his head.

"A sad tale," he said, setting before us a salad that resembled a small jungle. "The evil you humans do to one another never ceases to amaze me, though I will admit there are evil giants as well. Your cause seems a just one to me, so I will help you a bit. I cross the hills from time to time when calling on my neighbors. I know where this Castle Bloodthorn is to be found. I can't leave the farm to take you there, but I'll give you directions. I can also warn you off from the lairs of some of the beasties which might give you trouble."

"We would greatly appreciate that," I said.

"Well then, eat up. You'll spend the balance of the day helping me clean up your mess. You may sleep here tonight and tomorrow I'll see you on your way."

17

We were lost. We started out well enough, waving cheerily as we left Old MacDounaghald's farm with our bellies full and our bodies not fully rested but certainly less weary. We spent a hard day hiking in the hills, looking for the landmarks the giant told us to seek. We found the lightning-split tree. We found the forked gully. We avoided the lairs of the arc-welder worm and the gruffasaurus. I think it was the hilltop shaped like a pig's head that threw us. We veered left at what we thought was the right place. It was only several frustrating hours later that we realized the giant's idea of a "pig" might be radically different than our notion of the animal. After making what we hoped was a course correction and forging boldly ahead for two more days, we were thoroughly astray.

The weather was turning cold. We were already several days into the Eightmonth and thus near the middle of autumn. The leaves were turning and falling. The sharp highland winds whistled through the canyons, bounced off the cliffs, and knifed through our cloaks. Our breath misted and a few early snowflakes danced in the air.

"We must go northeast," said Merc, studying the lay of the land from atop an outcropping of crumbly brown rock. "That should take us to the lake with the shape of a mashed banana. From there he said it is half a day's walk due north."

"Which means about three days for us," said Rif, massaging his sore feet at the base of the rock.

"I'm sure we've passed the lake, Merc. We need to go west a bit," I said, standing beside him and pointing.

"We're too far to the west already."

"And too far north," said Rif. "I think southeast would be better, Mercury."

"I *know* we haven't gone too far north," said Merc.

"How do you know that?" I asked.

"I'm a wizard. We know these things."

"Then why don't you know where we are?"

"I do. And I know we need to go northeast."

"If your wizardly sense of direction is so great, why are we lost in the first place?" said Rif.

Merc shrugged. "We aren't lost."

"I told you that wasn't a pig," said Rif.

"It looked like a pig to me," I said.

"Ah," said Rif. "It's your fault we're lost."

"It's no one's fault," I said. "Maybe we should backtrack."

"No," said Merc. "We can't afford to lose the time."

"We're losing time now," I said.

"It is better to lose time going forward than going backward."

"Yes," said Rif. "But we're going in circles."

"No, we aren't," said Merc.

"Really? Well that hill over there looks familiar. The one that looks like a pair of upended female mud wrestlers."

"I don't see the resemblance," said Merc. "We haven't been here before."

"Well, you can't tell me those weren't our footprints we came across this morning."

"I can and I will. They were similar, but not ours. There are three other wanderers roaming these hills."

"And their boots have the same cuts and scratches in the soles as ours," said Rif. "Remarkable."

"It's not impossible."

"Just unlikely."

I spotted a little black squirrel watching us curiously from edge of a grove of gnarled lance oaks. Rif followed my gaze. "Say, wizard, why don't we just ask that squirrel for directions? We can't do much worse than we are."

"Good idea," I said, regarding the Ring of Raxx upon my hand. "It must know the area." I crouched and slowly approached the squirrel, making what I hoped were soothing clicks.

"I was joking," said Rif.

"I'm not," I said.

"Since when can you talk with squirrels?" said Merc.

"It is a power of my ring. Valence from the League discovered it."

"Then by all means, ask the squirrel."

"Hi there, little fellow! Nice day, isn't it?"

The squirrel cocked its head and furrowed its brow. Its tail flickered and its nose quivered, but it made no move to flee. I concentrated on the ring, willing it to make my words intelligible to the animal.

"I'm Jason. My friends and I are lost and we wondered if you might be able to help us."

"Lost," said the squirrel. I glanced back at my companions.

"Can you understand it?" Merc asked.

"Yes."

"Can it help us?"

"I'm getting to that. Can you help us, kind squirrel?"

"Lost," said the squirrel.

"Yes. We're lost. We need directions. We're looking for a lake."

"Lost."

"Yes," I said patiently. "Lost."

"You seem to have established the problem," said Merc.

"Lake," I said. "Where is the lake?"

"Lake," echoed the squirrel.

"Right. Where is it?"

"Lake."

"Yes. A lake. Do you know where the lake is?"

"Is this conversation going anywhere?" Rif asked.

"Yes! Be quiet."

"Time to gather nuts," said the squirrel, turning to leave.

"Wait!" I said. "Please help us."

"Time to gather nuts," said the squirrel, shaking its head. "Winter comes."

"Yes, of course," I said. "Winter comes and it is time to gather nuts."

"Must have food," said the squirrel. "Winter comes."

"Food? You want food? How about some nice bread crusts?"

"Nuts!"

"I don't have any nuts. I can give you yummy bread crusts. Rif! Bring me those delicious bread crusts left over from lunch."

"Look, pal," said the squirrel, "I don't want your crummy leftovers. Just because I'm an unsophisticated creature of the forest doesn't mean I'm going to shell out something for nothing. If you want to know where the lake is, then you and your buddies had better get off your butts and start gathering me some nuts. Lots of nuts. It's going to be a tough winter and I've got to squirrel away plenty of provisions. So if you want anything out of me, hop to it!"

One hour of bending, stooping, and gathering later, we presented the squirrel with a blanket full of several thousand acorns. The hard-bargaining creature directed us to pour this bounty into a hole in the side of an oak, then climbed to a high branch to give us the directions we sought.

"The lake is to the northeast," said the squirrel. "You must cross three hills to get there, but you can't miss it."

I reported this to my companions.

"Northeast!" Merc exclaimed. "We spent an hour collecting acorns just to find out that I was right in the first place? You and your talking to squirrels!"

"Well, at least we confirmed your hunch," I said weakly.

"I *knew* I was right," said Merc. "Next time you'll listen to me."

We found the lake easily enough once we knew where to look. It was a popular watering hole for the locals. In the grass by the shore lounged a squadron of manticora, strange beasts with the bodies of lions, the wings of bats, and the heads of men. Two of them were playing bridge with a pair of winsome lamias, who had the upper bodies of attractive women and the lower bodies of sharp-clawed, four-legged beasts. All were sipping from goblets of fermented blood.

Red and yellow dragonets, none more than a foot long, wheeled and soared over the water, chasing insects and each other. A pearly-eyed horngrim, all spikes, ridges, and teeth, gnawed on an unidentifiable bone. Some trolls played water polo in the lake, much to the annoyance of a very vocal demonette of pale lime hue attempting to sunbathe on a drifting float. On the far shore, a chimera—a three-headed blend of dragon, goat, and lion—wrestled playfully with some sort of one-eyed, one-horned purple thing with wings.

Thankfully, we had already reached our quota of deadly wilderness encounters for this trip and none of the monsters paid us much attention. We filled our water skins, confirmed our route to Bloodthorn with the card players, and continued on our way.

By late afternoon, we were five miles closer to our goal, working our way up a steep gully. The wind had picked up and the sky was black with clouds blowing in from the north like a flock of large and misshapen ravens. Thunder rumbled and lightning flickered. Though sunset was an hour away, it would be just a formality today, for the sun was already blotted out.

"I hope the Great Whoosh keeps a leash on that until we reach higher ground," I said.

"Don't bet on it," Merc said. At that instant the downpour began.

The sides of the trench were too steep to climb where we were, so we forged ahead with the raindrops blowing into our faces and stinging our skin like a million tiny arrows. Within minutes we were up to our ankles in churning brown water and desperately surveying the barely visible embankment walls for some means of egress. None was evident, and it was soon too late—a ten-foot wall of water rolled down the ravine, snatched us up, and took us on a wild ride down the hill.

The flood swept us apart. I tried, with little success, to keep my head above the surface. I expected a convenient log to come by so that I could cling to it for survival the way heroes did in the stories. True to tradition, it showed up. It wasn't very familiar with its proper function, however, for it smacked me in the head and went on its way before I could grab hold. Nor did I come near any protruding roots, limbs, or boulders I could clutch for safety.

After a few minutes of bobbing madly along, I was washed over a cliff and fell fifty or sixty feet into a deep basin. The water at the base of the impromptu waterfall churned and boiled and tried to suck me under, but I caught up with the errant log and put it to its appointed use. Merc soon joined me. We waited patiently until the water level was high enough for us to clamber onto a shelf of rock. There we lay, gasping and panting, as the storm line blew over to vent the rest of its fury farther south. The waters began to drain away.

Rifkin was nowhere to be found. We shouted his name, but could do little else until the waters subsided sufficiently to allow a search. Even then, we hadn't the time to comb the whole of the Bitterspleens for our hapless companion.

Merc shook his head sadly. "He's either drowned or been carried by the flood to some point several miles from here where, half dead, he will be rescued and nursed back to health by a stunningly beautiful mountain nymph named Nyrene under whose spell he will remain for months or even years before escaping, resuming his roguish career, and turning up unexpectedly during the course of some future adventure of ours."

"Then it looks like it's down to just you and me again."

"Yes."

"We must be getting close to the end."

Three days later we reached Castle Bloodthorn. Poised on a bald mound of obsidian upthrust from the bowels of the underworld, it was like a brooding crown of iron thorns placed around a spike that pierced the sky. Each thorn in the crown was a metal tower a hundred feet high. The central spire, which had once housed a Demon Lord and his entourage, was five times as tall. The whole was discolored with ancient rust, making the thorns seem truly composed of dried blood. We got no further than the deep granite bed of what had once been a lake of boiling magma surrounding the mound. Large carnivorous lizards sunned themselves there. They would find no prey in that pit, suggesting that the denizens of the castle provided their meals. There was no bridge or ramp or other means of crossing the gulf, no evident way of scaling those walls of smooth volcanic glass.

Rom Acheron's leering head appeared in the air before us. "I see that you have reached my abode, minus your supernumerary sidekick. The next test, you simpering fools, is gaining entrance to my lair. My guests and I await you in the great hall."

"Come out here and face us, coward!" said Merc.

"I think not. Your struggles to arrive here have entertained us all, and we do not want to deprive ourselves of the grand finale. With your former powers you might have entered this castle easily, Boltblaster, but alas you have been metaphysically castrated. Now we shall see the extent of your vaunted determination and resourcefulness. Be thankful all is not as it was in the old days." In a flash, the dry lake was full of fire again. Hot hissing lava lapped at its shores, smoking and bubbling as it exhaled noxious gases. The lizards presumably died at once. Acheron laughed.

"Who are these guests he keeps talking about?" I said.

Acheron heard. "They are ones who would see you both dead," crowed the illusion master. "I have invited them here to watch your final struggles, your demise at my hands. Haven't you figured it out yet? The massacre at Rae City was the Society's revenge for the massacre at Fortress Marn, but only part of the blood payment we demand. You, Cosmo and Boltblaster, destroyed our headquarters and killed many of our associates on the Ruling Conclave. Did you think such effrontery would go unanswered for long? I was there when ancient Marn came crashing around our heads! We survivors thank you for opening the way to our own advancement, but you must pay for your defiance. You must suffer before I snuff you out. And for now it amuses me to let you howl impotently at my gates. There *is* a way in if you have the wit to find it. But do hurry. The party is starting without you."

An image of Sapphrina and Rubis chained in a dark dungeon appeared before me. Hideous demonic torturers stood over them with sharp, cruel implements, cackling with sadistic mirth as the helpless girls strained against their bonds. "Jason!" they cried. "Help us!"

I drew Overwhelm and charged forward, but my feet stuck to the floor. Furious, I put all my might into advancing. I bellowed with outrage, but could not take a single step. Paralyzed, I was forced to watch as the gleeful demons performed their horrible vivisection of the twins. My eyes wouldn't close. My head wouldn't turn. And through it all they screamed in agony and begged me to save them. When it ended, there was nothing left of two beautiful women but a pile of shattered bones and rended flesh.

"Take the remains to the kitchen," said Acheron from behind me. "They will make a sweet addition to the soup pot." As the demons smacked their chops and bent to obey, I turned. There stood the evil sorcerer.

"Acheron!" I said. "I'll kill you!" Now that it was too late to save them, I could move. I lunged and swung. He gave ground, but I pursued him relentlessly, Overwhelm whistling a song of vengeance as it cut the air.

"You cannot kill what you cannot catch."

"Die, sorcerer! Die!"

He was fast and agile, but he couldn't evade me forever. He sprang away to the left. I turned to face him, but he was suddenly behind me, deftly striking my shoulders and paralyzing both my arms. Overwhelm dropped from my numb fingers, and before I could will it back to my hand I was flat on my back with the triumphant wizard crouching over me.

"What a pathetic effort, you miserable worm! Is that the best you can do in the name of those you claim to love?"

Yet at the same time he also seemed to say, "Jason! It's Mercury! Snap out of it! I'm not Acheron. It's just an illusion!" The voices were superimposed, interfering with each other. So too the images, shifting between my friend

Merc and my enemy Acheron. Both seemed real, yet both unreal, I couldn't tell which was true, which false. Then I heard Acheron's laughter ringing all about me. It was suddenly clear that I was not in the dungeon, but still outside with Merc. But we were in Acheron's reality now.

18

"Sorry about that, Merc. I was a little disoriented."

"Well, you nearly reoriented my head with that sword of yours! From here on in, I suggest adopting a healthy skepticism. Make an effort not to believe everything you see and experience. If you don't believe in an illusion then it has no power to harm you. Or me."

"But it was so real."

"That's why we call it an illusion. If it *looked* fake it wouldn't fool anyone."

"Then how do I know what to believe and what not to believe?"

"You don't. So disbelieve everything."

"Does that include you? You might not be real."

"True."

"How do we know we've even reached Bloodthorn? That might be an ordinary hill over there. Or a two-hundred-foot cliff we're about to walk off of."

"Now you're getting the hang of it."

I looked around nervously. "Those rocks could be ogres. Those trees could be trolls. That cloud could be a swooping dragon. An attack could come from any direction and we'd never know what hit us."

"Exactly."

"This is making me paranoid."

"Oh, really?"

"Yes," I said, darting nervous glances in all directions.

"Good. Then we're ready to continue. Let's start by not believing in that lake of magma. It wasn't there when we got here, so it must be an illusion."

"Unless, of course, the dry bed was the illusion and this is the reality," I said.

"Hmmmm. I hadn't thought of that."

"Can't you feel the heat? It must be real."

"Real or not, we must cross."

"Uh-huh. How exactly does this disbelieving work?"

"Well, say we dive into the lake. We will probably think that we have been instantly incinerated, but we must instead cling to the notion that we have not and are in fact crossing a bed of hardened granite and fighting off large, carnivorous lizards we can neither see nor hear because we will appear to be submerged in lava."

"How can we be submerged and incinerated at the same time?"

"Good question. Illusions aren't my field, so I'm not fully conversant with the fine points."

"Did you just admit to a gap in your expertise? I begin to suspect it isn't really you."

"Well, I'll explain it if you like."

"Don't threaten me. As I see it we can either jump in the lake and believe we're incinerated or try to climb down a wall we can't see and fight lizards we can't see. Am I right?"

"You are."

"Why can't we just disbelieve the lava altogether rather than merely disbelieve its effects?"

"It doesn't work that way. An illusion is a false reality, but partially real nonetheless. It masks what would normally be there, but can't entirely replace it. Conversely, the illusion cannot be fully dispelled except by the will of its creator."

"But our wills can alter it?"

"To an extent."

"Well, could we believe it to be something else? If that illusory magma cooled we would have a level field of granite to walk across—no climbing, no lizards, no heat. That would be a much more practical thing to believe in. Can we do that?"

"Interesting idea. I'm not sure it's possible, but I don't know that it isn't, so it just may work. Let's try it."

We attempted to delude ourselves into believing that

the imaginary magma had cooled to form imaginary stone which we could walk across. Soon I had convinced myself, and Merc acknowledged with a nod that he was fooled too. We took a tentative first step onto the former lake of fire and neither fell nor burned. We took a few more steps, then strode rapidly and confidently toward the castle, specifically not thinking about the fact that we were actually walking on air. We had turned Acheron's spell to our own purposes.

Halfway there, the stone turned to water. Unperturbed, we swam onward. We hadn't really expected the illusionist to let us get away with our little stunt, but it was worth a shot. I ignored the impossible presence of the great white shark which chomped off both my legs, blithely swimming on without them. The huge fish swallowed Merc whole, but the wizard remained steadfastly oblivious to this fact, pushing on toward his goal in spite of the fact that he seemed to be in the stomach of a shark swimming in the opposite direction.

As we swam, the water level dropped. By the time we reached the obsidian mound which supported Bloodthorn, we were flopping on the old lake bottom. A gaggle of hungry lizards watched us curiously, not certain they wanted to eat such odd creatures. We looked as though we would cause severe indigestion.

"Not bad, Jason! Not bad at all!" said Merc. "It was a crazy idea, but it worked. Now do something about those lizards."

"What are *you* going to do?"

"Watch you. You're the Mighty Champion, remember?"

"I am *not* the Mighty Champion, just a distant relative."

Even so, I made short work of the reptiles despite the bewildering array of weird and terrible things they turned into during the course of the fight. Splattered with stinking lizard guts, I turned to Merc.

"Okay, I dealt with the lizards. Happy?"

"Not until we get inside. What do you know about glass walls?" He studied the smooth obsidian wall before us. It curved upward many feet to meet the iron base of the castle itself.

"Well, I know if you live in a house with glass walls

you should not throw rocks or play indoor soccer. Also, I've heard the old story of the princess imprisoned atop the glass mountain and the prince who comes and rescues her."

"Yes, that's what I was thinking of. How did he do it?"

"I'm not sure. I think it had something to do with being pure of heart."

"Oh, I see. Well, forget that."

"I could hack out handholds with Overwhelm!" I said.

"Handholds? Make a stairway."

What I ended up with was a crude ladder. Sharp and durable though Overwhelm was, it wasn't exactly a chisel. You can only achieve so much finesse hacking at the side of a mountain with a yard-long sword. The volcanic glass was slippery, and we took some good falls—thirty-four to be precise—before we succeeded in reaching the narrow lip of rock fringing the castle proper. By now, most of the day was gone, and the Disk of Rae was on the verge of slipping below the Wall of the West. Though sweaty and tired, with glass slivers in our palms, we could not pass the night on this precarious perch. I drove Overwhelm into the iron wall. My intention was to cut away an opening. I had no idea how thick the wall was or how long it would take to reach the inside, but there seemed to be no alternative course of action available.

"This worries me," said Merc. "We've had too easy a time of it."

"Easy!" I said, trying to keep my balance on the smooth rock as I put my waning strength into slicing away fillets of iron.

"Yes. Acheron hasn't thrown any serious illusions at us. That bit with the lava and the seawater was more help than hindrance."

"The thing with Sapphrina and Rubis was serious enough."

"Yes, but I'd expect more of the same. I'd expect him to throw the whole arsenal at us, play with our minds, turn the world inside out, rant and rave and taunt us. That's what evil wizards do when you assail their lairs."

"Maybe he didn't read his evil wizard handbook."

"Or maybe he *wants* us to get inside. That's where the real danger is."

"If that's the case, we're about to find out." I heaved aside the final iron ingot, sending it crashing down the slope with a tremendous clang. Cool air, rank with demon scent, oozed out of the opening I had made. It utterly failed to refresh me. "After you."

Merc squeezed through, the darkness swallowing him like a predator gobbling its prey. I followed, willing Overwhelm to cast its pale pink light.

"You should have gone first," said Merc.

"Why?"

"Take a look."

A goon squad of demons awaited us in the chamber beyond. They were a motley assortment representing the lowest dregs of the Assorted Hells. Some had tentacles. Others sported claws, pincers, or hooks. One had a head like a leprous ape, another like a burnt sponge. Still others resembled dogs, vultures, regurgitated turkeys, and melted candlesticks. They were armed with pole axes, whips, swords, clubs, flails, and innumerable other weapons.

"How many of these do you suppose are real?" I asked Merc.

"Let's find out."

We didn't waste any more time talking, but took the offensive. The demons spat, hissed, squished, buzzed, growled, clicked, and roared as they fought. Some vanished into puffs of smoke as soon as I struck them. Others were more substantial and had to be chopped to bits before giving up the fight.

"Say, Merc, have you given any thought to what we're going to do when we reach Acheron?" I gutted a dog-demon.

"What do you mean? We're going to kill him, of course." He hopped over a cantaloupe-demon and skewered a hyena-thing.

"I know, but if he has a bunch of his fellow Dark Society wizards up there, it could be difficult, you being bereft of your magic." I banished a mule-man, ducked under a hellish wolverine's slashing claws, backhanded a jackal-thing, and engaged an infernal eggplant.

"We'll worry about that at the appropriate time." Merc struck a rhinoceros-grasshopper hybrid with a spinning back-kick, cut a few tentacles off a slimy whatsit, skipped between two ape-boars, and evaded the grasp of a rotten peach with six arms.

"Which will be?" I gutted a rabid centaur and dodged a blast of fiery breath from a dragon-headed mongoose.

"When we get there. Behind you."

"Thanks." I narrowly evaded the axe of a traditional green demon with horns. "You know, you take a rather casual attitude toward all this. We're probably going to die here. The odds against us are—"

"No worse than we've faced before."

We cleared the press of our foes and broke into a run.

"When you've been in this business as long as I have," Merc said, "you learn that the odds are meaningless. You live or you die and that's that. A simple truth I try to keep in mind at all times."

We left the demonic menagerie behind and stumbled into a measureless cavern filled with gold and gems. An enormous black dragon stood atop a small mountain of treasure. It regarded us balefully with malicious green eyes.

"This can't be real, can it?" I asked.

"The cave is bigger than the whole castle. Ignore it."

"I'll try."

The dragon belched a spreading cone of fire at us. The heat melted the gold around and behind us into slag, but did not affect Merc and me because we refused to believe in it.

"By the way," said Merc. "You've gotten pretty handy with a sword."

"With *this* sword it's easy." Overwhelm's enchantment adapted my fighting style to match and beat any foe. "But back in Caratha I made a point of spending a couple hours each day working out with ordinary swords and other weapons—axe, bow, spear, staff, knife, javelin. Unarmed combat, too. I could always find willing partners down at the Mercenary's Union so long as I didn't tell them my real name. Most were able to give me good pointers, and I learned a few dirty tricks as well."

"A wise use of your time."

We strolled into a field of red poppies. A green city shimmered on the distant horizon. The air was thick with the flowers' sweet perfume, and I suddenly felt very weary. It would be nice to lie down and rest there, just for a little while. To rest, to sleep, perchance to—

"Snap out of it!" said Merc.

"Sorry." The poppies faded into nothingness. "What was I saying?"

"You practiced with weapons in Caratha."

"Aye. The investment has served me well on this venture. I've been without Overwhelm more often than not."

"Did you ever learn the Roquetti maneuver?"

We stood in the middle of a lamplit stone bridge over a gurgling black river. The buildings of an unknown city lined both shores. A full moon shone in a velvet purple sky. At one end of the bridge was a crowd of a hundred or more ruffians. At the other end was a single man with a rapier. He wore flashy clothes and a prominent nose. The ruffians charged and Merc demonstrated the Roquetti maneuver—an intricate and deadly bit of swordplay—on the first to reach us.

"How did that go again?" I relied on the basic hack-and-slash approach. Merc repeated his demonstration. I tried it.

"You've got to twist it more. Like this." He demonstrated a third time.

I tried again. "I think I've got it now."

"Yes, I think so. I learned that from Roquetti herself."

He waded into the mob, cutting a bloody swath through their ranks.

"You trained under Fulvia Roquetti? No wonder you're so handy with a sword!"

The bridge and surrounding scenery vanished and we fell through empty space to land lightly on an alien plain of red dust. A trio of ten-foot tall green men with four arms apiece attacked us. They carried swords as long as I was tall.

"Arden hasn't seen Roquetti's equal since she was poisoned by the assassin Ariminus Tolwar," Merc said, engaging one of the monsters.

I took on the other two.

"That's the rub, isn't it?" I said. "No matter how good a fighter you are, they can always get you with poison." The force of gravity was lighter here, so I took a leaf out of Merc's playbook and bounded over my opponents' heads, cutting one down from behind before the other could turn around.

"Or cut your throat while you sleep," Merc leaped up and stabbed his enemy in the throat. "Of course, killing Roquetti wasn't the best career move Ariminus ever made. Many of her former students were rather fond of her—Natalia Slash, Dolman Sureblade, Fearless Freya, and myself, among others. There wasn't much left of Ariminus once we found him."

"And his employer?" I finished up with the remaining alien warrior. The setting shifted, and we found ourselves in free fall. We were high above the clouds, which resembled a puffy white field of cotton. A rapidly approaching puffy white field of cotton.

"King Megaron of Cyrilla. Wanted Roquetti's exclusive services. She wouldn't work for him alone, so he decided she'd work for none of his enemies. Cyrilla got a new king soon thereafter."

"You, of course, had nothing to do with it."

"Of course not."

We plummeted into the clouds, where nothing was visible but white, white wetness.

"And where did you learn unarmed combat?" I asked. "You're like a harnessed cyclone."

We broke through the cloud cover. All of Arden was spread out beneath us. We seemed to be somewhere above the Incredibly Dark Forest, which spread out beneath us like a lumpy green carpet. I fought hard to contain my panic and continue the conversation in a normal fashion. I hated flying, but falling was worse.

"Hmph. The idea is to unleash the cyclone. I sought out the Martial Monks of Mhyrr in their stronghold on the cliffs of Becai overlooking the Scarlet Waves."

"Impressive. I've heard they take very few students." Just as we reached the tips of the trees, the scene shifted yet again and we landed in a snowdrift. Harsh arctic winds raked us with metaphorical claws. An unfriendly polar bear tried to rake us with more substantial ones.

"The only way to get an interveiw is to scale the cliff to reach their monastery, survive an encounter with one of the Nine Masters, answer the Sacred Riddle, perform Three Impossible Tasks, and enter the Cave of the Hungry Dragon."

"And that's just to get an interview?" While evading the polar bear, we slipped down a steep slope which appeared for just that purpose, becoming entrapped in an ever-expanding ball of snow that rolled down the incline with ever-increasing speed.

"Yes. There is also an essay question. If you pass these tests, the Nine Masters will consider your plea to become one of their disciples. You then have to pay your tuition by performing a dangerous quest, which might take a year or two. After all that, the training begins. Of the forty-six degrees of mastery, I only reached the third."

"As good as you are, you only reached the third degree?"

"The higher degrees are mostly esoteric—contemplating the sound of one hand clapping, seeking inner harmony, eating bean sprouts, and the like."

The snowball hit a brick wall and shattered. The wall collapsed and we sprawled on a hard stone floor amid a great deal of loose snow and broken bricks.

"We seem to have arrived," Merc observed.

Indeed we had. The great hall of Castle Bloodthorn was shaped like the inside of an upturned funnel. Thirteen high arched doorways of dull bronze led to the chamber, each embossed with demonic symbols. Frayed and faded tapestries depicting scenes of slaughter and torment adorned the walls. The floor was of black marble veined with red gold. Filmy light came from no apparent source, but was even throughout the room.

In the center of the hall was a raised basin of red gold decorated with devil heads of green jade. The pool was filled with a black liquid—either ink, oil, or dyed water. At the far side, facing the illusory brick wall through which we had entered, stood Rom Acheron. Behind him was a curtained-off area. At his right was the Apothecarian, a dark genius of alchemy with rheumy eyes and papery skin. To the right of him was a thin woman with cruel eyes, milky skin, and lavender hair. She wore silver bangles, a wisp of green silk, and no more. This was the evil enchantress Vrilya. Nearby, sprawled on a divan that sagged under his weight, was a loathsome mound of flesh and depravity that was known as Poskav the Slug. These were the Dark Society masters known to be in Acheron's camp.

Beside Poskav stood a handsome man with thick brown hair, blue eyes, and an arrogant set to his mouth. He was clad in green samite and wore a golden crown. He was Halogen, the former King of Orphalia and one of the people Merc most despised. The feeling was mutual.

Along the left side of the pool, as we viewed it, were those undecided sorcerers Acheron hoped to win to his banner. I easily recognized a pale woman with long black hair and steel-studded garments as Eufrosinia the Cruel. She had captured me in Fortress Marn months ago. If she was pale, the woman beside her was utterly colorless, her albino skin nearly translucent, her hair the color of fine ash. Her eyes were hidden by dark glasses. She was Thecia the Wan, the notorious Thessalan witch and cattle curser. Next to her was a mysterious figure in azure robes and hood whom I assumed to be the Blue Fear. He lured ships to destruction on the rocks of his enchanted isle off the Xornos coast. Beside the Blue Fear was the master of air magic and evil winds called Last Gasp. Finally, standing apart from the others, there was the haughty, bull-headed thaumaturge Chossos Idmeondies of Pylarum.

On the other side of the pool were three men and a woman of radically foreign appearance. They were evidently mages of great power, but their dress and looks bespoke the strange nations of the southern continent, not the Eleven Kingdoms. What exotic evils they represented I could not fathom.

We stood and dusted ourselves off.

"Welcome," said Acheron. "I trust you enjoyed your little trip."

"Not really," said Merc. "Your illusions were detailed,

but hardly creative. You didn't have enough variety. There were too many combat settings and the exceptions were uninspired. I thought—"

"Enough! I didn't ask for a critique."

"You didn't? I distinctly heard you say—"

"Perhaps you fail to realize the gravity of your situation, Boltblaster! You face nine arcane masters of the Dark Magic Society plus four other evil magi of the first rank. You are alone in my inner sanctum. You—"

"Alone?" I said. "I'm here too!"

"I meant the plural *you*."

"You are addressing Merc."

"I address you both."

"Well, you weren't very clear about that. Why don't you start over?"

"Cease this babble! You should be quaking with abject fear! Your lives are in my hands. You are mine to destroy whenever I choose."

"That's nice to know," I said. "What if we destroy you first? That *is* what we came for."

"Don't make me laugh! You are utterly incapable of harming me. You have only reached this chamber because I allowed you to. Did you really think that stunt of walking across the lava lake would have worked without my acquiescence? Do you really believe that the illusions you faced inside my castle were the worst I could do?"

"That I'll believe," said Merc. "The polar scene was too warm, the mix-and-match animal demons were fuzzy at the edges—second-rate magic all the way through."

"Yes. The seams showed." I said. "Furthermore, the whole sequence served no dramatic purpose whatsoever. If you had just opened the front door and let us stroll in we'd be much farther along and, quite frankly, would have missed nothing."

"Imbeciles! I'll soon put an end to your gibes! My illusions are the greatest ever conceived! With my Pool of Visions I can project them anywhere in Arden, as you know from experience! I did not grant you this confrontation, Boltblaster, to hear you hurl insults. Though perhaps since you can no longer hurl spells, that is all you are capable of." The evil wizards all laughed at his joke.

Merc's expression turned ugly. "Actually, I was just stalling while I assessed the situation here. Yes, you have us outnumbered. Yes, you have the magical firepower to blow us away. I figure Jason and I are dead men, but we'll take some of you with us. And you'll be the first one to go. If I can accomplish that, I don't care what else happens."

"You pathetic little worm, your cares don't matter. Your strategems are pointless. I am in complete control here!"

He snapped his fingers.

The universe turned inside out, did a triple backflip, exploded into space-time confetti, then faded to gray static.

19

"Wake up, Cosmo!" barked Acheron harshly. "You've slept for long enough."

I opened my eyes. I lay on my back on an uneven stone floor. The air was cool and moist and dark. I got the impression that I was alone in a vast cave, probably far beneath Bloodthorn.

"Where am I?" My voice echoed off the distant walls of the cavern.

"Alone in a vast cave far beneath Bloodthorn," said Acheron. His voice came from everywhere and nowhere and had no echo, so I assumed he wasn't actually in the cave with me, but was addressing me by magical means. "It will probably become your tomb, so get used to it."

I stood up and looked around, which was fairly futile, considering the absolute darkness that surrounded me. I was clad in naught but a dirty cotton loincloth. For some reason, bad guys liked to dress me in loincloths when they captured me. Even villains have some small sense of decency, I suppose. Of course, Zaran did leave us all naked in the pine barrens.

"Where is Merc?"

"Don't worry about your friend. But watch your step. You don't want to fall into a bottomless pit."

"How would you know?"

"Well, most sensible people like to avoid bottomless pits. I'd advise you to just sit still for now."

"Okay."

"I thought to spare you such melodramatic nonsense as saying that I have cast you now into the Caverns of Doom or the Tunnels of Terror or whatever. I will speak plainly. The caverns beneath Bloodthorn are extensive and dangerous. In addition to the natural hazards of such an environment, I have stocked the area with many unsavory life forms. The ratio of predators to prey is severely out of balance. You will find that you share the caves with several fearsome, fangsome, and famished monsters. One already has your scent and is moving toward you as we speak."

"And what is the point of this elaborate production? Why didn't you just slit my throat and be done with it?"

"That's not how things are done. You heroes have certain standards and so do we villians. I cannot kill you in any mundane fashion if I expect to maintain the respect of my peers. Furthermore, I have guests to entertain. Your struggles will amuse them. There is already a betting pool going on how long you will last and what the manner of your death will be."

"Well, I hope they enjoy the show. Especially the part where I come up there and wring your worthless neck."

"Dispense with the idle boasting. You will be far too busy saving your own neck to worry about mine."

"You're giving me no weapons? No light?"

"You have your wits, dull as they may be. Nothing more. Incidentally, the bottomless pit is to your left."

"Thanks."

"Don't mention it. Farewell. Or not so well."

I took a step to the right and nearly lost my balance when the floor wasn't there. Flapping my arms wildly, I pulled myself back from the brink.

Acheron laughed. "Oh well, I lost my bet."

"That wasn't funny."

Acheron didn't answer. Instead, I heard a weird, trilling cry that bounced off the walls and made my nape hairs stiffen. The call originated from a point in front of me, so I turned around and carefully shuffled along in the opposite direction. I went ten steps and encountered a sharp drop, which I quickly determined was a ledge or cliff. There was no escape that way. I moved to the left, slowly sliding my feet across the rocky floor just in case there was a bottomless pit in this direction too.

The strange cry sounded again, this time only fifty yards or so away. I heard small rocks and pebbles getting out of the way of something quite large.

Rocks and pebbles. I scooped up a handful and continued my torturously slow flight. They wouldn't be much defense against whatever it was stalking me in the darkness, but it made me feel a little better to have something solid and heavy in my hands.

The monster called again, this time so close and loud that I dropped my load of rocks in startlement, soundly mashing all my toes. I felt sudden movement and reflexively jumped back, the move saving me from the huge jaws that smacked noisily together above me.

Above me because my jump took me over the brink of the cliff. I fell a scant eight or ten feet and landed on a narrow ledge. I couldn't see that it was narrow, of course, but my frantic feeling about told me all I needed to know. It was about a yard and a half wide where I was, tapering off to nothing within five feet in either direction.

"The odds are twenty-to-one against you surviving the Grokorian cave lizard," announced Acheron.

"Is that what it is? I thought it was a subterranean elephant or something."

"I wasn't able to find one of those."

A questing paw of the lizard swished the air above my head, missing my scalp by inches. I couldn't stay here for long.

I didn't. A slimy, spongy tentacle reached up from below, snared my legs, and pulled me off the ledge without so much as a how-do-you-do. I didn't so much fall as ride down to the tentacled monster's lair.

"Congratulations," said Acheron. "You seem to have escaped the grok. Quite cleverly too."

"I'm nothing if not resourceful," I said as the tentacle dragged my lower body through a hole in the cliff face. I clung to the edges of the opening, resisting with all my might the inexorable pull of whatever it was at the other end.

"I didn't even know about the gastral grabber," Acheron said. "It must have crawled in recently. It's a simple-minded beast. Actually it has no mind at all, just an ample mouth, a large, acid-filled stomach and a very strong tentacle, as you see."

"No, I don't see. How can you see me?"

"Infrared scrying. One of the Society's many magical advances. The current bet is on whether the grabber will dislodge you and devour you whole or tear you in two and eat you in sections."

"What are you betting on?"

"Sections."

I let go and the grabber pulled me slowly down a narrow tunnel toward its gurgling maw. The rough stone grated my skin like cheese. I pawed madly about but didn't resist the tentacle's relentless pull until I found what I sought, a sharp wedge of stone. Clutching it tightly, I twisted about and hammered at the tentacle, tearing the gummy flesh. The thick goo within was highly acidic and seared the flesh of my hands and legs; but I kept pounding until I severed the cable-thick member. Then I clambered painfully back up the tunnel, my legs raw with agony.

"Outstanding," said Acheron. "A bold performance. Of course, the pseudopod will regenerate in a day or two and you will still be right where you are. Unless you think you're going to—I see that you are. It's a tricky climb in the dark, Cosmo, and the Grokorian lizard is still waiting for you."

"Well why don't you place a large bet on the lizard then?"

"I don't think you'll make it that far."

He was right. I climbed about twenty feet, then misjudged a foothold and fell, plummeting The Gods only know how far before hitting the icy waters of an underground lake. It felt as if my every bone had shattered on impact. They hadn't, but it felt that way. I plunged well beneath the surface, then bobbed back to the top.

"Are you alive, Cosmo? Cosmo?"

I couldn't have answered if I had wanted to. All I was aware of was the stinging cold and the tremendous mass of pain that had replaced my body.

"If you aren't dead, Cosmo, I regret to inform you that a twenty-foot albino bass is about to devour you."

The bass struck, its fishy mouth closing around my torso and yanking me underwater.

"Cosmo?" His voice was not distorted at all by the water. "Well, that's it then," he said, sounding peeved. "I expected more of him. Did anyone bet on the bass? No? Well, we will turn our attention to Boltblaster now. He should provide more sport."

The bass took me down, down, down. I fought to hold my breath, which wasn't easy with that massive mouth crushing my chest. I felt the fish's head with my hands, located its eyes, and jammed my thumbs through the clammy orbs.

The bass went wild, doing a lot of frenzied thrashing, hysterical twisting, panicked flopping, and so forth. I pushed my hands in further and must have found the right nerve, for the bass's mouth snapped open.

I swam for the surface, willing myself to stay conscious, to keep moving when my muscles refused to function. I made it to the top alive, but could only gulp air and drift. There was a slight current in the lake that carried me slowly along as I floated on my back, trailing blood.

The blinded, maddened bass struck several yards to my right, then to my left, then far enough away so that I didn't care. I had escaped one hungry fish, but I would soon be food for others. Eventually I would start to sink and there was not a thing in the world I could do about it. I was utterly spent.

*　　*　　*

"Well, is it alive or no?"

"Maybe. Maybe not."

"Who cares?"

"Throw it back."

"Be careful!"

"Oh, don't be such a worrywart."

"Duh."

The voices hovered above me in a circle. I opened my eyes and saw seven pairs of bright gray eyes peering down at me through a forest of white, brown, and black beards. Above each face was a bright nimbus of light. The combined effect made me squint.

"It's awake," said a white-bearded face. All of the faces were ruddy and lined with deep folds and creases, but this one was more wrinkled than the others.

Groggy, I sat up, partially shielding my eyes until they adjusted to the glare. The faces backed away. I looked around. I was surrounded by seven little old men, each about four feet tall. They wore work boots, light blue overalls, and yellow hard hats with little lanterns attached to the front. They were armed with picks and hammers, raised defensively. One was sopping wet, as was I. We were on a ledge beside an underground river which evidently flowed out of the lake I had fallen into earlier.

"Hi," I said.

"Hallo yourself, big fellow," said the white bearded one. "Nice day for a swim, eh?"

I glanced at the river. "That wasn't really planned," I said.

"I should think not," said the little man. "If Reckless hadn't dived in to pull you out, you'd be fish food now, you know?"

"The thought crossed my mind. Thank you for saving me, though."

"Well, he pulled you out, so that's that. Don't give it another thought, right, Reckless? My name's Marley, by the way, in case you didn't notice the name tag." He thumped his chest.

I didn't, but now quickly glanced at the labels on the others. Most of them had adjectives for names. Evasive. Cranky. Spiteful. Cautious. Reckless. And Dimwit.

"We're seven dwarfs," said Marley.

"The Seven Dwarfs?"

"Not *the* Seven Dwarfs, we're just seven dwarfs. We're a geological survey team for Roxxaco Interdimensional." He turned around so that I could see the Roxxaco logo patch on his back. It looked like a four-sided squashed orange triangle with an inside-out purple *R* in the middle, only the middle wasn't in the middle, but a little to the right of down. It hurt my eyes to look at it.

"It's very pretty in 4-D space, but kind of loses something in this continuum," said Marley.

"That it does. So how is it that you happen to be here? I thought dwarves were a fable. Imaginary folk."

"Hrmph!" said Cranky. "*Dwarfs*! Get it right!"

"We are and we aren't," said Evasive. "It depends."

"What he means," said Marley, "is that you find dwarfs in some places, dwarves in others, and in some places you don't find anything at all. I suppose it's fair to reason that none of our cousins are native to your world."

"My *world*? You mean you're from another world?"

"Like I said, we're with Roxxaco Interdimensional. We operate on many worlds. My team here is surveying this one for petroleum."

"What's that?"

Marley tugged at his beard thoughtfully. "Well, it's a kind of black goo that forms when decayed plant matter and dead dinosaurs and so forth are sealed underground for millions and millions of years. We pump it up out of wells and refine it into various kinds of fuel and so forth. Valuable stuff on some worlds, but getting scarce. Haven't found any signs of it around here, in fact."

"Did you say millions and millions of years?" I asked.

"That's right."

"Arden was only made about five thousand years ago."

"Well, tarnation and dagnabitall! I told you fellows the rocks around here seemed mighty young! They ain't natural."

"Upstairs will love this," said Spiteful.

"Duh," said Dimwit.

"Oh, shaddup!" said Cranky. "No one asked you."

"Pipe down!" said Marley. "This is why they send survey teams out in the first place, to find out where there's petro and where there ain't."

"Yeah," said Cranky. "Well, now we know there ain't, so what do we do until they send the boat back for us? Wait for more stupid big folk to come bobbing down the river?"

"We can explore," said Reckless. "We're sure to find some kind of valuable deposits."

"Should we be discussing all this in front of a native?" said Cautious.

"You're right," said Marley. "We don't even know this big fellow's name."

"Sorry," I said. "I'm—"

"Well, we're pleased to meet you, Sorry," said Marley. "Good thing for you we happened along when we did. You ought not be swimming down here in the dark alone, though. Always go with a buddy. Remember that in the future, son. Well, come on, men. We've got work to do."

Before I could ask them for a bit of food, or a weapon, or a light, the seven dwarfs marched away down the tunnel, singing a happy tune. I tried to get to my feet and follow them, but my legs were too wobbly.

"Wait!" I called. "Come back!"

The only reply was the fading echo of their song. I sank wearily back to the floor.

I slept for a long time. I had no way of marking the passage of time down here in the darkness other than the grumbling of my stomach. I was hungry when I woke up. Unfortunately, there was no food at hand. I was stiff from sleeping on the hard floor, but most of my weariness was gone. I was restored enough to get up and walk.

Groping blindly, I found the passage that Marley and his crew had taken and followed it. I had no idea where it led, but it really didn't matter. One way was as good as another. With a little luck, I would find my way to the surface or back to Castle Bloodthorn.

A little luck soon found me. I rounded a bend and came upon a patch of glow-in-the-dark mushrooms. They gave off a pale, peculiar, purplish phosphorescence, but it was better than nothing. I plucked a few to light my way. They might continue to glow for an hour or so before giving out.

Without the mushroom light, I would have missed the assortment of edible pastel fungi growing on the walls another eighty paces down the tunnel. I was no expert on cave survival, but I recognized these particular plants as identical to those served as a garnish of exotic salads in one of Caratha's finest restaurants. Pastel fungus was a great delicacy in Caratha and quite expensive. I ate several hundred crowns worth for free. The fungus feast didn't fully satisfy my hunger, but it did improve my spirits.

The tunnel roof got lower and lower, until I was forced to bend over double to go on. This continued for quite some distance. Finally, I reached a three-way fork and was able to stand erect. As I did, I noticed some words and arrows carved on the wall at eye level. They indicated that the left tunnel led to Castle Bloodthorn; the right passage to to the Kingdom of the Evil Gnoles; and the middle way to the Vile and Execrable Temple of Hoary Hargel, one of the more mysterious and blood-stained of the Demon Lords. There didn't seem to be many pleasant creatures living underground. Then again, it wasn't a pleasant place.

I didn't care to call upon evil gnoles or benighted disciples of Demon Lords, so I headed back to Bloodthorn. Acheron thought I was dead, which meant he would be very surprised when I returned. I would make it a nasty surprise indeed.

20

A concealed pit filled with iron spikes, an acid-spitting snail, an iron portcullis, and a minor cave-in all failed to stop me from reaching the end of the tunnel, where I found a disappointingly blank wall. By this time my mushroom had fizzled, leaving me once more in the dark.

The wall was obviously man-made. Well, not so obviously man-made, since Bloodthorn was of demonic construction, but it was obviously *made*, as opposed to being there naturally. The almost imperceptible cracks between the large blocks of stone making up the barrier gave it away. That meant I was back beneath the castle, which meant there was some kind of secret catch or lever to open a hidden door here. Unless it was one of those doors that required the saying of a magic word to open. I didn't want to consider that possibility.

It took me fifteen minutes, but I found it. Twisting a projection shaped like a one-winged swan wrestling a diced artichoke caused a section of the wall to swing open with a groan. Armed with a sharp rock, I sprang through the gap, causing an immediate chorus of startled feminine screams.

I was in a cell shared by eight nubile young girls clad in tunics of dirty white linen. The bars that made up three walls of the cell reached to the ceiling. The floor was lined with straw. Frightened by my sudden appearance, or perhaps just my appearance, which was itself frightful, the prisoners cowered against the far side of their cage and wailed.

In the guttering torchlight I saw that this was but one cell of many. The adjacent cells were also packed with young girls, but others held men, women, and children of every age and description. All pressed themselves against the bars of their pens, straining to see what the commotion was.

Other ears took notice as well.

"Pipe down, you wenches, or I'll take my belt to your worthless hides!" bellowed a bulb-nosed, pig-eyed, scruffy-looking jailer as he approached the cell. "Or maybe I'll just gag the lot of you with a greasy—What in the Assorted Hells!"

He started back in surprise at the sight of me, but wasn't quick enough. My arm shot out. I grabbed his throat and pulled him against the bars hard enough to knock him unconscious. He slumped to the floor. Fortunately, the keys were on his belt. I snagged them and set to work finding the one that opened this particular cell.

The prisoners cheered.

"Quiet!" I said. "We'll have more guards upon us!"

"Wh-who are you?" asked one of the girls, a freckle-faced redhead who couldn't have been more than fifteen.

"Jas—" I started, then caught myself. No need to terrify them further by revealing my true name. "Just Jake," I said. "Who are you?"

"Dalainia," she said. "Dal is short. I'm from Goatgloss. That's in Brythalia."

"Mm-hmmh," I said, busy with the keys. All the prisoners watched my progress anxiously.

"The wizard's men sacked the town and brought all the people here. The survivors, I mean."

"Sorry to hear that."

"I'm a virgin," she said. "We all are. In this cell I mean."

"That's nice."

"I think they're saving us for some kind of Dark Magic Society ceremony. Going to sacrifice us to demons or somesuch."

"Some people are rude like that."

"You look awfully familiar, Jake."

"I can't imagine why."

"Here they come!" yelled an excited man down the way. "Two of them!"

"Drat!" I cursed, fumbling for another key. My luck held; this one fit. I swung the door open just as two of

Acheron's mercenaries reached the cell, knocking down the first one and using the distraction to punch out the second. I tossed the keys to Dal and picked up a fallen spear.

"Free the others!"

"Here come two more!" called my eager informant.

"Thanks! I see them!"

I rushed to meet the guards, spear lowered. I windmilled my spear as we met, knocking theirs asunder and tagging the jaw of one man with the spear butt. Before the other guard could recover, I rammed my point through his belly.

I glanced over my shoulder. Dal was more handy with the keys than I was, already having six cells open. Grateful men and women poured out of them.

"Arm yourselves!" I said. "You've got a hard fight ahead of you!"

In the guard room at the end of the cell block were several more spears, a few swords, a couple of whips, and an assortment of knives. The nearby torture chamber, currently not in use, yielded more weapons. The prisoners were villagers, farmers, and travelers captured by Acheron to be tortured, abused, and killed for the amusement of the Society bigwigs he hoped to enlist in his cause. Most were Brythalian or Orphalian, but there were a few other nationalities in the mix. There were about thirty grown men, roughly twice as many women, and twenty or so children.

"Any trained warriors among you?" I asked, as I pulled on a coat of studded leather. Several caravan guards and a couple of Ganthian mercenaries answered my call; but all the men, be they merchant, shepherd, or farmer, were willing to fight. As were the women.

"To the fore then. I don't believe there are many guards, but this is a place of deadly magic and deception, so be wary as you make your escape."

"Aren't you coming with us?" said Dal, who had finished her task of opening cells and wormed her way through the press to stand beside me.

"No, girl. I've got business with the wizard and a

friend to find as well. With luck, I'll keep Acheron busy enough that the rest of you can get away."

"But—" said Dal.

"To the back, lass," said a grizzled, gray-haired veteran fighter who bore the scars of many battles. He gave her a gentle push. "You'll be safer there." He held out his hand. "Cedric O'Suggill," he said. He was at least three times my age, but his grip was strong. "I was a captain with the Haravian Free Companies during the Shadowcrown Wars. I'll get these good folk out if any can. You do what you must."

"Thank you," I said. The Shadowcrown Wars had ended forty years before, but I had no doubt this Cedric O'Suggill was still a doughty fighter. He was the man for the job.

"It's you we should be thanking, lad. You given us a chance at freedom, and that we didn't have 'til now."

"Just doing what seemed right," I said, loud enough for all to hear. "The Gods be with you all."

"And with you," they chorused.

I left the escapees and threaded my way through the dim corridors of Bloodthorn, seeking a way back to Acheron's main hall. I failed to notice a slim girl slipping through the shadows in my wake.

I tried to ignore the disturbing carvings and bas-reliefs on the walls as I crept through the gloomy corridors of Bloodthorn. Most of them depicted horrible beings doing horrible things to innocent human beings. It was raw and unsettling stuff, like the chili dogs sold by Carathan street vendors. Certain antisocial artists who built their careers around insulting and outraging the public with their work would have given much to be able to reproduce the shocking scenes and subjects depicted there.

I didn't encounter any guards or giant spiders or wandering demons, which was a welcome surprise. I worried about stumbling into some fiendish mechanical or magical trap, but didn't come across any.

Without mishap I climbed the central spire and reached a kitchen. I knew it was a kitchen because of the cooking smells, the large boiling pots, the shapeless hunks of meat roasting on spits, and the bevy of surly cooks and scullions bustling hither and thither. I had never thought about evil wizards having kitchens, but I suppose they have to eat like everyone else.

There was a constant flow of serving men and maids in and out of the room, exchanging trays of soiled plates and empty glasses for platters of odd-looking hors d'oeuvres. Their uniforms were somewhat suggestive. The men wore tight black pants, bare chests, and bow ties. The women wore outfits best not described in much detail, but they were also black and included lots of stiff lace. All this told me that the main hall was nearby, perhaps on the level above. I had only to follow the servers straight to Acheron and his guests. But first I had to get through the kitchen.

Peering in the door, I surmised that most of the help wasn't working for wages. The head cook, an ugly, hairy man with a face like a rotted pumpkin, functioned more as a slave driver than a chef. He held a short whip in his grubby right hand, and I knew of no dishes which required a whip for their preparation. Which wasn't to say there weren't such dishes. I just didn't know about them and didn't want to.

The brutish chef was a harsh taskmaster, buffeting his assistants about the head at the slightest provocation, using his lash frequently, and pinching the serving maids' exposed and bruised bottoms whenever they came within his reach. He also spat a lot and wasn't particular about where it landed. I wouldn't want to eat anything that came out of this kitchen.

If I could take out the head man perhaps the others wouldn't give me any trouble. In fact, they might be grateful and as eager to escape this place as the prisoners below. If not, they could quickly alert their master, Rom Acheron, to my presence. Then the fat would be in the fire.

Fat in the fire. The image appealed to me. The ugly chef was leaning over a fire pit to inspect the meat, his broad backside making a tempting target. I resisted the temptation. If I pushed him into the coals, he would scream out. I had to do it another way. I flashed across the room and stuck my spear through his neck. He died with a gurgle, and I eased his blubbery body to the floor. The others stopped what they were doing and gaped at me in amazement.

"Not a sound," I said, lifting the bloody spear. "You're all slaves, aren't you?" A few nodded. The others remained frozen with fear and wonder. "Your freedom may be at hand. Is the wizard through there?" I asked, pointing at the other door.

Three serving girls bobbed their heads up and down.

"You all want to get out of here, don't you?"

Everyone nodded.

"Okay, but I need a little help first. You, bring along one of those flour sacks. One of you women grab a tray and take it in as you normally would. The rest of you can go if you know the way out. If not, wait here and I'll come back for you."

No one moved. I grabbed the nearest serving wench, a sloe-eyed brunette, by the arm. "Pick up a tray and go. You, hurry with that flour."

"What can *I* do?" said an unexpected voice behind me.

I turned. "Dalainia! What are you doing here? Why aren't you with the others?"

"I wanted to come with you," she said eagerly. "To help you."

"Of all the stupid— I'm probably going to die in there!"

"I'll come die with you," she said reasonably. Only now did I notice the smitten look in her eyes. Just what I needed. I was not trained to handle this sort of thing at all. Evil wizards, gastral grabbers, Demon Lords, and deranged terrorists I could deal with. Moonstruck teenage girls, no.

"Look, just stay here where you'll be safe. I'll come back for you." I hoped she didn't read too much into that. You never could tell.

"You just said you probably won't survive."

"If I do, I mean."

"But I can help you. I can carry the flour sack."

"No, you can't," I said.

"Sure, she can," said the husky serving slave to whom I had assigned that task.

"No, she can't," I said. "It's too heavy."

"I'll carry the tray."

"You aren't dressed like her," I said, pointing at the bemused slave girl now holding a dish of jellied trout brains, gecko eyes, and yak cheese on lettuce. "I need her to go in as a distraction."

"I can change clothes with her."

"The girl has good idea, master," said the sloe-eyed slave.

"You aren't built like her," I said to Dal. "Her outfit won't fit you." I turned to the slave girl. "And don't call me 'master.' "

"Okay, master, I won't."

"Just because I'm not busting out all over doesn't mean I can't help," said Dal, her voice getting screechy. "Unless I'm just not good enough for you. Is that it?" She was near tears.

"Don't get sulky. This is dangerous, don't you understand?"

"*I* understand, master," said the slave. "That's why I say let the girl go. She can have my uniform. I don't like it anyhow."

"*You* are going."

"Yeah, why?" said the slave, suddenly hostile. "Why not Talarah?" She pointed an accusing finger at a curvaceous blond. "Or Cherilyne?" Cherilyne was a tall woman with brown eyes and chestnut hair. "Or one of the men? Why does it have to be Ushara? I think if you make me go, I will raise a fuss and the wizard will reward me for turning you over. What about that?"

"He picked you," said Talarah.

"Right," agreed Cherilyne.

"But he's a crazy man, going to fight all those wizards with a spear and a bag of flour. We're better off not to get mixed up with him. Maybe I'll just scream now. How about that?"

"Then I'll have to kill you," I said gravely.

"Oh." Ushara pursed her lips. "Then maybe I won't scream. But I won't go either. There's going to be bad magic for sure, and I don't want to be caught in it."

I threw up my hands. "I give up! I can't make any of you help me if you don't want to. But I've got to act fast, before Acheron starts asking what's going on back here."

At that moment another male server came through the door. "What's going on back here?" he asked. "The boss is wondering where everybody—" He stopped short. I thrust the tray of brains and eyeballs into his hands.

"*You*," I said carefully, "will take this back to the hall and act as if nothing is amiss. You with the flour, come on. The rest of you can do whatever you like. I really don't care at this point."

Rom Acheron and his guests surrounded the Pool of Visions, intent on the scene it displayed. I couldn't see what they saw from my vantage point in the servant's entrance, but I could hear Mercury's amplified screams and the cruel laughter of Halogen and the Society wizards. Acheron himself, his back to me, gleefully made signs and hand passes over the water, shaping and controlling whatever horrible illusions he was inflicting upon my friend. The sight made my blood boil.

"Take the snack tray around," I told the serving slave quietly. "Act casual. Then come back. After that you can go."

He was about as casual as a drunken rhino in a glassblower's shop, bumping into wizards, nearly tripping over his own feet, and shooting a steady stream of nervous glances in my direction. But Acheron and the others didn't notice, being too interested in Mercury's torment. They accepted the slave's presence with the same indifference they showed to the walls and the ceiling. That was good. I wanted them at ease—relaxed and off-guard—not wondering why the slaves hadn't returned with more goodies.

"Good job," I whispered. "Now get out of here. You with the flour too—I'll take the bag now." The slaves quickly vanished.

Dal was still with me. "What are you going to do?" she asked.

"Crash the party."

"All alone?"

"Yes."

"That's very brave of you, Jake."

"Right. Now why don't you run along?"

"No way." She furrowed her brow. "I can't help thinking I know you from somewhere."

"What I know is that you need—*mmrmph*!"

She cut me off with a brief but sincere kiss. "That's for luck," she said, lowering her eyes and blushing.

"Thanks," I said, exasperated. She was going to present real problems if we survived all this. "Now stay put."

I propped my spear by the door and lifted the forty-pound bag of flour by two corners. I stepped into the great hall and spun around like a discus thrower, giving the bag momentum before heaving it into the air. It arced over the heads of the sinister sorcerers and landed in the middle of the Vision Pool with a tremendous splash that sent black waves sloshing over the rim in all directions. The startled wizards jumped back as the water, hot with magic, scalded their hands and arms.

I snatched up my spear.

"Acheron! I'm back!"

He turned. I hurled the weapons with all my might. The sharp blade split his breast bone and sent him toppling back into the Pool of Visions, which boiled and hissed and steamed as it attacked his flesh. The others stared at me in shock for a moment, then broke into laughter.

Rom Acheron laughed too. An invisible veil was lifted from my eyes. Pool and cackling company both dissolved into fading sparkles. The true Pool of Visions and the true assembly, a live Rom Acheron among them, were twenty yards away from where they had seemed to be. That spot was marked by a split sack of flour and a spear.

Acheron ceased his mirthful laughter. "Very good, Cosmo. Very dramatic entrance." He gestured absently at the pool. "Had we not watched your entire progress from the time you entered my dungeon, your desperate plan might have succeeded and I would be dead. You are resourceful, but you will never be a match for Rom Acheron and the Dark Magic Society."

"You're Jason Cosmo!" squealed Dal, stepping through the doorway. "That's where I know you from! I served you at the Dancing Donkey! I spilled wine in your lap! Do you remember?"

"Vaguely," I said, not taking my eyes off Acheron and company. "Now run for it!"

"Don't bother," Acheron said. A pair of huge, furry hands shot up out of the floor to seize us and hold us fast. "You are both in my grasp, as it were, and there will be no running. Now it is time for you to experience the true depths of my evil brilliance."

"I can hardly wait."

21

"You heroes are so arrogant."

Acheron sauntered around the Pool of Visions with his hands loosely clasped before him. "You think yourselves so clever, so keen, so daring, and your enemies such fools. 'That stupid Rom Acheron thinks I'm dead.' You thought it. I know you did. You thought it would be easy to slip through my castle while my attention was elsewhere, catch me by surprise, and make an end to me. Then, of course, you expected to escape in a daring and improbable manner. A classic scenario."

He stopped a few feet away from me. I struggled to escape the grasp of the gargantuan hand, but to no avail. Acheron smiled thinly and strolled over to Dalainia. Her eyes were wet with tears and wide with panic. She whimpered as he took her chin in his gloved hand and tilted her head back. "And while you're at it, why not rescue those poor hapless folk the vile sorcerer has imprisoned in his dungeon? That's the noble, heroic thing to do. Of course, they're all dead now." I saw a brief scene of the animal-demons below feasting on the remains of the escapees. He twisted Dal's head to the left, then to the right, scrutinizing her features.

"Leave her alone!" I said.

Acheron's cronies laughed. The illusionist ignored me.

"We all know that goodness is its own reward, but sometimes there are other compensations. This young girl seems fond of you, and why not? You are her hero, her savior. She owes you her life and will follow you anywhere, do anything you ask. Not that you would ever ask her to do anything interesting." The wizards snickered and jeered. "After all, you are a man of principles, a hero of the first order, a moral exemplar."

"Acheron, I swear I'll—"

The hand clenched and cut me off.

"Tsk, tsk. Always swearing this and promising that. Always puffing up your muscular chest and strutting and posturing and spouting empty threats. I truly wish you heroic types would find something original to say. For centuries the champions of evil have had to endure the same tired litany of clichés. 'I'll get you yet!' 'You'll pay for your crimes!' 'It's just you and me, evil wizard, and now you will die!' How trite. Of course, I admit we villains have an affection for theatrics too. I indulge in them myself, as you will soon see. But with much more flair and style than you could ever hope to achieve." He stroked Dal's pale cheek. "As for this wisp of a girl you feel so protective toward, you don't truly want her. I'll give you a hand in disposing of her."

He snapped his fingers and the hairy hand holding Dal contracted, slowly squeezing the life from her. She tried to scream, but her scream became a wheezing groan as her ribs imploded, her organs were crushed, and her skin burst. Blood and guts and broken bones spurted between the fingers of the murderous hand. Rom's guests watched Dal's death with amused detachment.

"No comment, Cosmo? Have you nothing bombastic to say? Ah, of course."

The hand relaxed enough that I could speak. I glanced at young Dal's crushed and mangled body, then looked to Acheron with white hatred in my eyes. "You sadistic bastard! I'll—"

"More hollow threats?"

"I'll see you in Hell, Acheron."

He shook his head. "Good try, but overused. Perhaps there is nothing fresh and original to be said in a situation like this."

I cut loose with a string of traditional Darnkite oaths and epithets that would make even Vixen Hotfur blush. Acheron paled and unconsciously backed away. Then he smiled.

"*Very* impressive. Unprintable, but certainly original. I wasn't aware heroes knew such words. Frankly, I didn't understand half of what you said, but it was deliciously vile. Don't you agree, my friends?" The others assented. "However, Master Cosmo, I fear you have vented your spleen in vain. This poor, pure, innocent girl whom I just murdered . . . she never existed!" Dal's body and the horrid hand holding it vanished. "Nor, I am sorry to say, did her fellow prisoners. All your noble work was for naught."

"What are you saying? Do you mean—"

"Yes! Exactly! The grok, the gastral grabber, the fish, the dwarves—"

"Dwarfs."

"Whatever. The mushrooms, the pit, the wall, the jail and the jailers, the kitchen staff—all products of my imagination. You never left this room, Cosmo! Your mighty struggles, your supreme effort, your desperate plan—fluff and air! All in your head and put there by me!"

If that was all true, then Acheron *had* been merely toying with us before, when we first entered Bloodthorn. Those illusions had been shadows on the walls compared to what I had just gone through.

"Why?" I asked.

"Why? Why? You ask why? Because you had the temerity to criticize the quality of my illusion magic to my face and in front of my peers! I take great pride in my work, Cosmo. I don't suffer such insults gladly. 'The seams showed' indeed! No seams showed in my last little production, did they? You never doubted its reality for an instant. You never questioned how limestone caves formed in an obsidian mound. You never wondered that you barely managed to escape each danger only to encounter another. You just happened to be rescued by friendly travelers, just happened to find food and light when you needed it, just happened to find the correct path back here. I suppose coincidences like this are so commonplace to you that you accepted them as a natural sequence of events."

"Well . . . Yes."

"Then it was a masterful illusion, don't you agree?"

"Yes, I suppose it was. And what about Mercury?"

"Look around you, Cosmo. Observe the truth. No hairy hand holds you—you are chained to the floor. And there beside you is your companion. Do you see that?"

"No."

"No? What do you see?"

"Purple cows eating blue grass under a green sky."

"No sign of Boltblaster, me, or the great hall?"

"No."

"Must be another illusion! Not bad, eh?"

"Pretty good."

"You will henceforth see whatever I wish you to see, whenever I wish you to see it. You are completely in my power. Don't deceive yourself into believing otherwise."

The polychromatic pastoral setting faded and I was once again in the great hall of Castle Bloodthorn, a few yards from the Pool of Visions. My hands and feet were bound in iron manacles attached to the floor with a heavy chain. To my right, Mercury was similarly bound. He lay on the floor, seemingly unconscious.

"Merc!"

"He is alive," said Acheron, who stood before me. Beside him was a purple cow chewing its cud. "Unconscious, but I will wake him if you wish." He kicked Merc in the ribs. The wizard stirred and opened his eyes.

"Boltblaster. I see that you have learned your place. It is fitting that you kneel before me."

"Having your thugs break both my legs kind of made that choice for me," said Merc. "This is definitely not by choice."

Acheron spared me a knowing and warning glance. Merc was still in the grip of an illusion scenario and I had best not interfere, or else. The purple cow transformed into a purple tiger and growled.

"Nevertheless, the posture becomes you," called Eufrosinia the Cruel. "You were always too proud to suit me."

"I never tried to suit you, Eufy," said Merc.

Irritated that the self-styled Lady of Pain had interrupted his own gloating, Acheron sought to regain the limelight. "When we are done here, Mistress Eufrosinia, you may have him to do with as you will. A little gift from me."

"You are too kind," said Eufrosinia, licking her lips. "We have much to discuss about old times, don't we, Mercury?"

"You promised him to me!" said Halogen petulantly. "You said he would be mine to kill!"

"So I did," said Acheron, waving the deposed king's objection away. "We will have to find some means to fairly divide him." The guests laughed at his joke. I didn't find it amusing at all. Neither did Merc.

Acheron turned his gaze on me. "Then there is Jason Cosmo, our old enemy the Mighty Champion reborn, returned to Arden to once more take up his blade against the evil we represent. Slayer of the Evil Emperor, Banisher of Asmodraxas, Harbinger of the Age of Hope, and key figure in the downfall of our late, lamented Overmaster Erimandras. A durable pest."

More laughter. Evil wizards are easily amused.

Acheron mounted a small podium which appeared from nowhere between Merc and me. The room went dark, except for a spotlight centered on the illusionist. "I promised you a real show, Cosmo. Pay attention." He raised his hands for silence, and his guests stopped all conversation among themselves. "Allies! Fellow Society masters! Honored guests from afar! You are here today at my invitation, here to share my victory, here to learn why Rom Acheron should be the next Overmaster of the Dark Magic Society!"

He gestured grandly at Merc and me, caught now in spotlights of our own. "Behold what I have wrought! The two greatest enemies of the Dark Magic Society lie helpless before you! Revenge for the humiliation at Fortress Marn is ours! You have seen how I toyed with them, manipulated them, stripped them of their greatest possessions, and lured them to their destruction. Sinshaper did not achieve this! Necrophilius did not achieve this! Nor did Vectoroth! Only I, Rom Acheron, had the genius and the daring to make war on our enemies while my opponents make war on each other! The record speaks for itself—Rom Acheron acts while others do nothing! The evidence is plain before you. They practice the policies of division, of factionalism, while Rom Acheron stands for a united Dark Magic Society, ready to face the challenges of the 990's and the dawn of the Next Age."

"This is the worst torture yet," said Merc, who still believed his legs were broken. "A campaign speech."

"Think about it, my comrades," continued Acheron. "It has long been our goal to enslave all the peoples of Arden and restore the Empire of Fear by the dawn of the Next Age. That time is less than a decade away. If we are to achieve our dark dream of domination on schedule we must have a leader who is bold in his thinking and masterly in his capacities. We must have new ideas, we must have competence, we must have proven ability. You dare not pledge allegiance to anyone who will give you less."

"Merc!" I whispered. "Your legs!"

"Yes?"

The purple tiger bared its fangs and crouched to spring. I decided not to take a chance. It just might be real.

"Uh—how do they feel?"

"Broken in six places."

Acheron spoke with increasing volume and tempo. "I promise you today that the defeat of Jason Cosmo and Mercury Boltblaster will only be the beginning! The Rom Acheron regime will be one of unequaled ruthlessness, unrivaled decadence, unparalleled progress toward the complete and eternal triumph of evil! We will utterly break the forces of good, body and soul! We will tear down their citadels, obliterate their armies, devastate their lands! The time for skulking in the shadows has passed! The Dark Magic Society must be ready to assume its rightful place as the supreme power in the world!"

Images of the glories he spoke of flickered in the air above the Pool of Visions. His audience murmured their approval.

"To take us there, we need a man who has fought tirelessly for wickedness and corruption all his life. We need a man who has taken food from the hungry, robbed the weak, deceived the gullible, and treaded upon the downtrodden. We need a man who can command not only respect, but fear. We need a man of dishonor, of low principles and lax morals. We need a man of power, brilliance, and vision. My colleagues, *I am that man*!

"I have proven that I can vanquish our enemies. You have seen my power. Now hear of my vision and my brilliance. For too long the Dark Magic Society has confined itself to the Eleven Kingdoms, ignoring the ancient nations of the southern continent. No more! As your Overmaster, I will reach out to our fellow evil-doers in those distant lands. I will seek to bring them into the Dark Magic Society, swelling our numbers and our resources. I have already begun this process. With us today is Swanballah the Damned, conscienceless court mage of the Majahrajah of Manjiphar."

A spotlight fell upon a swarthy man with a face like a pickled prune. He wore a red turban and loose black garments.

"Also, cruel Tloques, witch-priest and major pharmaceutical exporter from the mountains of Meru." Tloques wore an elaborate headdress of quetzal feathers. Brightly colored feathers and fabrics made up the rest of his outfit as well. He wore a belt made of the skulls of infants.

"From the rocky wastes of Pharistan comes the fierce and fanatic Yatollah Khomanni." The bearded Yatollah wore coarse brown robes and an olive turban. His eyes burned with boundless hatred.

"Finally, there is the sorceress, Nyarla of Thotep, ambassador for the dread arch-mage Tsorthas, who has ruled the island of Sanskaara for over a thousand years and has until now had naught to do with our Society." Nyarla was a tall, thin woman with jet-black hair and wine-purple eyes. Vestigial black horns grew from her brow, and she had fangs like a vampire. Whether she was one, I couldn't tell. I got the sense that if she wasn't, she was something far worse.

"Our cause is one and we should stand together as one until our mutual enemies have been trampled down beneath us. Then we may sort out our own differences at our leisure without interference. That is my vision. Now hear of my brilliance.

"I know how to weave evil plots of great complexity and subtlety in the grand old tradition. I shall now reveal the intricate depths of my cunning. The very scheme which laid low these heroic clods will also place two kingdoms, Orphalia and Raelna, squarely in the hands of the Dark Magic Society. Listen well!

"After surviving the disaster at Marn, I realized the time had come to make a bid for supreme power. Yet I knew what many would say: No member of the Twelve has ascended directly to the Overmaster's throne since the Society's founding. The struggle for supreme power is always between the Three. Isogoras the Xornite is gone, and neither Necrophilius nor Sinshaper has what it takes to do what must be done. But I knew that the constraints of tradition would freeze me out of the race. I might aspire to join the Seven, but no more. Unless I was willing to take a chance and prove that only I was fit to be Overmaster.

"I soon devised a bold and far-reaching plan. I recruited the terrorist Zaran Zimzabar to massacre the leaders of the Eleven Kingdoms gathered for the wedding of Mercury Boltblaster and Raella Shurbenholt. I also schemed with Duke Thule Nethershawn. With promises of magical aid, I persuaded him to stage a coup after the massacre. He believed that I would help him become King of Raelna in return for his cooperation in future Society operations. In truth, I merely used him to plunge that land into chaos, giving him enough help to destroy the existing government, then abandoning him before he could consolidate his power. I will place a more pliant puppet on the Prism Throne."

"Who?" Eufrosinia asked.

"You shall see soon enough. While playing Thule for the fool, I directed Zaran to free Halogen and convey him to Voripol, from whence he was transported here by a hidden teleportal. At the same time, he laid a trail for Cosmo and Boltblaster. It was by my design that they survived the wedding massacre. It was at my command that Zaran delayed them and took their magic treasures. I drew them onward to my lair and to their present humiliation.

"Meanwhile, the great nations of the north fight for possession of Orphalia, as we see." Images of the ongoing combat at Voripol appeared in the pool. "Little do they suspect that mine will be the hand that claims that prize. With the aid of certain potions prepared by my alley, the Apothecarian, it was a simple matter to make the shallow-minded Halogen my willing pawn. My agents have recruited a measureless mob of monsters in the Incredibly Dark Forest—ogres, goblins, bugaboos, trolls, ratlings, wolves, even a dragon." The horde of monsters appeared in the pool. They were ready to march. "Tomorrow I shall join them and we will march on Voripol to crush the combined might of Ganth, Raelna, and Brythalia. By week's end, King Halogen will be restored to the Orphalian throne, to rule that kingdom for the Society. Immediately after his coronation, he will wed the bride I have selected for him, the woman he has always desired—Raella Shurbenholt!"

22

With a dramatic swish, the curtains flew open to reveal a striking woman dressed in evil chic. She wore leg-hugging black boots that rose to her thighs and fingerless gloves that reached her elbows. The rest of her outfit was a black G-string and corset and a cloak of sable tatters that swirled around her like the wings of a bat. Her long red-gold hair hung loose and wild around her shoulders. Her ice-blue eyes glinted with deviltry, and her blood-red lips were set in a cruel sneer. She posed alluringly, slim fists on bare hips, one foot casually propped on a leering human skull.

Shouts of amazement swept through the room. Acheron let his guests babble for a moment, enjoying their stunned reaction to his surprise. He was clearly pleased with himself.

"Raella?" said Merc in disbelief.

The woman didn't answer, didn't deign to look down at Merc lying pitifully on the floor. Halogen crossed the room and slid his arm possessively around her waist.

"Mine at last," said the ex-king with a smirk. She kissed him sensuously and played her long nails across his chest.

"Indeed she is," said Acheron smugly. "Her spectacular death was the most masterful illusion of all. She was actually drugged, bound, and borne here to me by a courier pigeon from Hell. Unlike Halogen, Raella has—had, rather—a strong will and a deep devotion to goodness. But with over a month to work, a combination of the Apothecarian's drugs, Vrilya's enchantments, and my own illusions has corrupted her sickeningly pure heart. Every human has a dark side to his or her soul. Some foolishly suppress their sinful desires, their malevolent urges, but the proper encouragement can bring them to the fore. We have recast Raella Shurbenholt in the Society's image, brought the seething cauldron of her hidden lusts to a satisfying boil, seasoned to taste, and let simmer until she was ready to serve. We have made her our witting and willing tool. She will wed Halogen, joining their realms together in the service of the Dark Magic Society. Is that not so, my darkling?"

"It is not," she said, pushing Halogen away. Caught off guard, the once and would-be king fell heavily to the floor. Raella planted a stiletto heel on his chest, pointed a finger at his face, and drilled a smoking hole through his forehead with a beam of eldritch green fire.

"You aren't supposed to do that!" cried Acheron. "We rehearsed this a dozen times! You say, 'Yes, my lord,' and kiss him again."

"I'm rewriting the script," said Raella, slowly stalking Acheron. She moved with a rolling, liquid, feline grace. Frightened and bewildered, the illusionist gave way.

"You used me, Acheron." Her silvery voice took on a throaty, seductive quality that caressed the ears like the wanton fingers of a courtesan. "You invaded my mind, body, and soul with your drugs and visions and potions. You stripped away what I was, stripped away the thin veneer of virtue and decency that kept the dark parts of my soul in check. Unfortunately for you, you did your work too well."

"What do you mean?"

"You thought you had shaped me into the perfect instrument, eager to serve you, do your will, worship your evil. Fool that you are, you never realized that, once unleashed, my evil might exceed your own. You speak of vision, brilliance, and power. In all of these I am many times your better. I will not serve you, Rom Acheron."

"No?"

"No."

"Well, I'm sure we can reach some other—"

"I will destroy you!" Green lightning exploded from her eyes and enmeshed Acheron. The powerful attack lifted him from his feet and hurled him across the room like a scarecrow in a cyclone. He crumpled into a ball of scorched crimson robes.

Acheron's allies reacted quickly. The Apothecarian hurled a glass vial at the angry Queen. With an outstretched left hand she reversed its flight and sent it to shatter against his own face. The contents melted his features away in a cloud of putrid red vapor. He screamed and dove headfirst into the Pool of Visions. The water boiled around him but did not wash off the horrible chemical that ate through his skull and dissolved his brain. He thrashed wildly for several seconds, twitched, and sank to the bottom of the bubbling basin.

Meanwhile, Vrilya pointed a slim silver wand at Raella and spoke a command. From its opaline tip leapt an intense beam of violet light. Raella caught the beam in her right hand, twisted it like a cord, and yanked the wand from Vrilya's grasp. The witchlight vanished as the wand left her hand. An emerald bolt from Raella's eyes ended the enchantress's brief dismay by removing her pretty head.

Poskav the Slug opened his flabby mouth wide and belched up a tremendous mass of nauseating yellow slime. The loathsome goo oozed across the floor toward Raella, its acidic secretions burning a track into the floor. It slid over Vrilya's body, absorbing and consuming it, and glided on toward the Queen.

Raella vaporized the blob with a wave of her hand. Then she struck whimpering Poskav with another optic green bolt. His grossly fat body exploded in all directions, spraying the chamber with gore. Bits of his body stuck to the walls and dripped from the catwalks above.

"This has got to be the most disgusting scene I've ever been in," I said, wiping a bit of esophagus off my cheek.

"Raella!" said Merc, forgetting that he thought his legs were broken, and leaping to his feet with tears of joy in his eyes. "I thought I had lost you. I thought—"

"Raella," she snorted derisively, turning in place to confront him. Her cape swirled about her revealingly. "You knew me by that name, but now I take another. Now you may call me Morwen Hellshade, Queen of Darkness!"

"Uh-oh," I said. "This is not a good sign."

"Wh-what are you talking about, Raella?" asked Merc, a stricken look on his face.

"Raella is a fine name for a sweet, goody-goody champion of mercy and justice, but I am no longer what I was, my pet. I am evil now, evil to the core, and I have renamed myself to reflect that reality."

"Okay," said Merc. "But do you still love me?"

She considered this for a split second, then spat. "Love! I loved you once, but such petty emotions are far beneath me now! I have no need of love."

"Oh. I see." Merc fell silent.

By now Acheron was back on his feet, albeit unsteadily. He leaned heavily against a ruined tapestry, his hair on end and his breathing ragged.

"At her!" he ordered his remaining guests. "She has gone mad!"

"We are not yours to command, Rom," snapped Eufrosinia, her own voice strained. "She is your creation. If you can't control her, it is fitting that you suffer the consequences of your folly."

"Well-spoken," said a hauntingly familiar voice. One of the bronze doors flew open and a stooped, emaciated man in black entered. He leaned on a sablewood staff topped by a grinning silver skull. He was flanked by two yellow-fleshed ghouls with eyes like burning coals. I had met him before on a Malravian mountainside. He was Necrophilius the Grave, master of death magic and Rom's rival for the Overmaster's throne.

"How did you get in here?" demanded Acheron.

"With my pass key. Just thought I'd drop in and inspect my castle," said Necrophilius.

"What?" said Acheron stridently.

"You leased this stronghold from Darklair Properties, Inc., did you not? I happen to own a controlling interest in Darklair. There is always a good market for prime evil real estate. It also pays off when one of your enemies rents from you." A swarm of prying eyes, the animated flying eyeballs of murderers, flew out from behind the tapestries. Necrophilius had developed the prying eyes as an unobtrusive mode of surveillance. "Makes it easy to keep tabs on him." He nodded to Raella/Morwen. "Do finish him, my dear. He's of no further use to anyone."

"Gladly," she said, raising her hands and pumping so much arcane energy into Rom's cowering form that he glowed, expanded, and burst into a shower of green sparks. We all had to shield our eyes or be struck blind by the glare. When it was over, there was nothing left to mark the passing of the illusionist save the ashes of a tapestry and a warped, flowing, superheated section of the iron wall behind it.

The remaining bronze doors opened, and thick white mists flowed into the chamber, heralding the arrival of more ghouls, as well as animated corpses, shimmering spectres, shadow-fleshed nightgaunts, flickering wraiths, smiling vampires, and other terrors from beyond the grave. A swarm of screeching bats fluttered above the crowd. Over twenty more living human beings—evil mages all—followed Necrophilius into the room. Among them was Vectoroth Plaguecaster.

"This party has definitely died," I observed.

Necrophilius rapped his staff on the floor for attention. "Ladies and gentlemen, I will get right to the point. Rom Acheron is dead, as he deserved. He set his aim too high, seeking to exalt himself above his station. In so doing, he violated the ancient customs of our Society which forbid engaging in outside operations during an internal power struggle. We all know why this is forbidden—the Society is at its most vulnerable when it is in the process of choosing a new Overmaster and reorganizing the Ruling Conclave. This is not the time to undertake risky operations. Acheron made a mistake and he has paid the price, as have those who joined him in his folly."

"Hear, hear," said the surviving magi.

"I confess that I am making a show of strength by bringing my supporters and my minions with me today," the Deathmaster continued. "This is for the benefit of the uncommitted arcane masters who came to hear Acheron state his case. The time for fence-straddling is over. You must choose whether to support me or Sinshaper, and you must do so now. It may interest you that I already have the support of nearly eighty per cent of the remaining arcane masters in our Society. This includes those who previously supported my lieutenant, Vectoroth Plaguecaster. He never truly betrayed me. When I perceived that Archeron was attracting dissidents to his cause, I ordered Vectoroth to make his own bid for Overmaster, giving dissent another outlet and draining potential supporters away from the upstart illusionist. There is no further need for that deception. So I put the choice to you. Declare for me now or die."

Eufrosinia, Chossos, Thecia, Last Gasp, and the Blue Fear immediately pledged their undying support to Necrophilius and assured him they had been for him all along and had only come to Acheron's castle to take advantage of the free cocktails.

"Good," said Necrophilius. "By the way, I have it on good authority that the last of Sinshaper's supporters will desert him one way or another by tomorrow, so we should be able to formalize my ascension to supreme power in the near future."

This announcement produced a general round of applause accompanied by murmured comments that Sinshaper was clearly a loser and unfit to be an apprentice street sweeper, let alone Overmaster.

The Overmaster-to-be held his hands up for silence. "Now I bid greetings to our sister and brethren from the southern continent. Acheron was correct when he spoke of the need for greater intercontinental cooperation, and I will be pleased to treat with you once I am confirmed as Overmaster."

The foreign mages nodded in acknowledgment of his offer. He turned his attention to Raella. "And what of you, dear Morwen? A lovely name, that. Will you now join the Dark Magic Society? With your demonstrated power and ruthlessness you will easily win for yourself a place among the Twelve on our Ruling Conclave. Perhaps even the Seven. Or the Three."

"Morwen Hellshade serves no master," said Raella. "I have no need for your niggling Society."

"If the membership fee is a problem, I'll gladly waive it in your case. We offer tremendous benefits and opportunities for a sorceress of your caliber."

"Did you not hear me? I want no part of your order."

Necrophilius shook his head sadly. "If you will not serve us, then you must be destroyed. We can't allow someone as dangerous as you to act as a free agent." He looked her over and sighed. "A pity." He raised his staff, which glowed with the power of a mighty death spell.

"Foolish old man! You and all your lackeys combined could not slay me! You are nothing! In time you will all kneel before the Queen of Darkness! I will conquer the world!"

"A fine ambition," said Necrophilius. "But I implore you to be reasonable." He gestured to take in the assembled mages and undead terrors in the room. "You are but one. Even your power has—"

He broke off as Raella disintegrated two sorcerers and

a dozen ghouls in her way, blasted a twenty-foot hole through the roof, and flew away into the night, leaving molten iron and dead bats to rain down on the chamber.

"—limits," finished the Deathmaster lamely, lowering his staff. "Well, we shall attend to her later." The other mages breathed a sigh of relief that he hadn't ordered them to pursue her at once. "The last order of business is the disposition of Jason Cosmo and Mercury Boltblaster."

"Merc, I think we're in trouble," I said. Intently staring through the breach Raella had made in the roof, he ignored me. I started calculating the best means of escape.

"Boltblaster is mine," said Eufrosinia.

"Acheron made that promise," said Necrophilius. "It is not longer valid. But my promises are, and I promised these two months ago that they would suffer no more harm or interference from the Dark Magic Society under my leadership. We will therefore set them free."

"What?" cried Eufrosinia and several others, including myself. "What about Marn?" she said. "What about the Superwand?"

"Do you question my will?" said Necrophilius, raising his staff. "I was not at Marn, and the Superwand is no longer of any concern to this Society."

"As you command, Overmaster," said Eufrosinia. She bowed.

"Very good. Cosmo, Boltblaster, you are free to go." Our chains fell away. "Your weapons and other belongings will be returned. My ghouls will escort you to the teleportal chamber and send you back to Voripol. I regret that I can offer you no other choice of destinations, but the Society must keep the location of its teleportals secret. In fact, the one in Voripol will be removed after you make use of it."

"Thank you," I said sincerely, abandoning my silent effort to count the number of potential foes in the room. "You're a great fellow for an evil wizard. Thank you. Come on, Merc." I took my stunned friend by the arm. "Thank you so much. I wish all of you the best of luck. We've got to run and I hope never to see you again, but thank you. Come on now, Merc, let's get out of here while the getting is good."

23

The teleportal was developed by the Empire of Fear as a means of fast, safe transport for the Emperor and his chief servants. An extensive secret network of teleportal booths connected all points of the far-flung empire. Most of these portals were destroyed during the Great Rebellion, and the knowledge of their making was lost. Today most people, even wizards and scholars, considered teleportals to be a myth.

A few of us knew better. The Dark Magic Society still operated some of the surviving portals. Merc and I had used one ourselves to escape the destruction of Fortress Marn in Malravia. Now we traveled by teleportal again, stepping into a glass booth in Castle Bloodthorn and, a pop and a flash later, emerging from an identical booth in a secret cellar of the royal palace at Voripol. A pair of ghouls met us there and directed us to a hidden door that led to the concealed chamber Rif and I had discovered during our search for Halogen. It hadn't occurred to us to seek a second secret room opening off the first. Our mistake.

We mounted the steps to the courtyard. That is, it would have been a courtyard if there had still been a court. Nothing remained of the Orphalian royal castle except shattered and scattered rubble. The same was true of the city as a whole. We saw only ashes, cinders, rocks, and bones all corpsy and pale in the moonlight. Our view was unobstructed by even a hint of a wall. The destruction of the city was complete, its ruin total. In the surrounding hills burned the campfires of the rival armies which had wrought this devastation. Tomorrow they would renew their struggle, continuing the battle for this sad and blood-soaked bit of land.

"Alive," said Merc, gazing off to the north. "Alive."

"Excuse me?" These were the first words he had spoken since I led him from the great hall of Bloodthorn.

"Raella is alive."

"I noticed."

"And she loves me not."

"Well, she obviously wasn't herself, Merc. I don't think she really meant that."

"Of course she meant it!" he exploded. "She meant every word she said! Acheron turned her into an abomination! She's alive, but everything that made her Raella is dead!"

"Surely we can capture her, cure her."

"There is no cure for what they did to her, Jason. Her personality has been eaten through, stripped away. Her humanity is gone. Now she is only power and passion and darkness." He looked me in the eye. "But The Gods help me, Jason, I love her still. Had she asked me, I would have gone with her, joined her in whatever madness she undertakes. If she still loved me." He shook his head. "But they took even that. I mean nothing to her. Less than nothing."

"So what are you going to do about it?"

"I have to stop her." He turned his eyes northwestward, toward the black eaves of the Incredibly Dark Forest. "I owe her that."

"Stop her? Stop her from doing what?" I followed his gaze. "You don't think that she—"

"Acheron had an unholy horde ready to march," said Merc. "She knows it. What else would she do?"

The Battle of Voripol started again just after dawn. Merc and I picked our way through the three-way melee until we reached the Raelnan lines and demanded to see the commanding officer. We expected Cull Crossmaster. We got General Vixen Hotfur.

She was overseeing the action on the Raelnan east flank, holding the line against a determined Brythalian advance. Her hair was coiled under her helmet. Her face was streaked with sweat and grime. Her buckskins were splattered with gore. She was obviously enjoying herself.

"I was wondering what had become of you heroes!"

she said as she dueled a pair of Brythalian thugs. "How has it gone? Did you get Zaran?"

"We did and we didn't," I said.

"So I hear. Feel free."

I drew Overwhelm and fell in beside her. "It's a surprise to see you here, General. The last I heard, you were running amok down south."

"King Rubric's horde of mongrels hightailed it up here to join their master, so I brought Halehart and the Reaver and gave chase. Crossmaster's in the stockade, by the way. Confessed all to me."

"And you didn't have him hung on the spot?"

"Thought we'd give him a fair hearing first."

"Generous of you," I said.

"This is the biggest bloody scrap I've ever been in! A beauty, isn't it? Near as we can figure, there's a hundred thousand boot-kickers slugging it out here!"

"Good," Merc said, slashing and thrusting savagely at the Brythalians with a borrowed saber. "We'll need them all."

"What do you mean?"

"We've got a very big problem," I said, looking around for another foe. After the first ten or so went down before me like so much timber, the Brythalians stayed out of Overwhelm's reach. In fact, their whole advance faltered.

"Is that so?" Hotfur asked.

"It is," said Merc. "Raella is alive."

"What! Where is she?"

"She's . . . on the way," I said, sheathing my sword. "That's the problem."

"Problem? I don't think I take your meaning, lad."

"You will," said Merc. He explained.

"Sheepcurd!" exclaimed Hotfur when he finished.

"My sentiments exactly."

We tried in vain to arrange a temporary truce between the three armies, but Myrm Ironglove refused to parley unless Raelna surrendered Hotfur, Mercury, and myself to his custody, or at least sent him our detached heads as a gesture of good faith. In truth, Hotfur wasn't too keen on treating with Ironglove either. He had, after all, murdered her father. Or had her father murdered, which amounted to the same thing. Her message to Ironglove was more inflammatory than deplomatic. ("To the murderous muck-sucking illegitimate Tyrant of Ganth and Trampler of Her Liberties" was the salutation.)

King Rubric of Brythalia, however, was another matter. Brythalia and Raelna had been rivals since time immemorial, but there was no real hatred or rancor between them, just clean, healthy great power competitiveness. Nor was there any personal animosity at work. Furthermore, Rubric had the largest army on the scene and felt secure enough to call a time-out to hear what we had to say.

We held the parley near what used to be the Voripol city gates. Of course, it took us a while to figure out just where the gates had been. Brythalian and Raelnan troops sealed the area from any Ganthian interference. Merc and I went forward with Hotfur to meet Rubric and two of his generals who took absolutely no part in the proceedings but were only present to make the delegations equal.

"Well, She-Fox, what's this I hear about Raella being alive?" Rubric boomed. Word traveled fast on the battlefield. "Out with it, woman!" Rubric Tallshanks was neither handsome nor intelligent nor diplomatic. He succeeded as King of Brythalia through a combination of toughness, bluster, cunning, and good luck. A battle axe of a man, he had a loud, lusty voice and towered over everyone present except me. Though we had left our weapons behind, he wore his greaves, arm guards, and breast plate. He probably had a prohibited dagger hidden somewhere on his person. We all did.

"I'll let Boltblaster explain," said Hotfur.

"Let's have it then, wizard."

"Boo," said Merc unexpectedly. The big king took a step back, and his escorts reached under their cloaks for the knives which weren't supposed to be there. Like most Brythalians, Rubric had a healthy fear of wizards and wizardry. Merc just wanted to reinforce it. "Raella *is* alive," he said. "Her death was a ruse by the Dark Magic Society."

"The Society?" Rubric and his generals made holy signs and sent quick prayers up to The Gods. "They have turned her to a rose?"

"A *ruse*. They have turned her to evil. She calls herself Morwen Hellshade and is marching here from the Incredibly Dark Forest at the head of the largest army of monsters ever assembled. We must join forces against her or we will all be destroyed."

"Who is this Morwen Hellshade?" asked Rubric.

"She's Raella."

"I though Realla was a rose."

"No, Morwen."

"Morwen is a rose? And she is in league with the Society?"

"Something like that. If she wins here, nothing will prevent her from marching across Orphalia, Raelna, and your own kingdom. The only way to stop her is to work together."

"Stop who?"

"Raella."

"What about this Morwen?"

"She is Raella."

"Morwen is Raella?"

"Yes."

"Raella is Morwen?"

"You're catching on."

"If Raella is alive, she is still Queen of Raelna, even if she is Morwen. Or a rose," said Rubric suspiciously. "How do I know this alliance you propose isn't some kind of trick?"

"We don't rely on tricks, man!" said Hotfur.

"Of course you don't," said Rubric sarcastically. "That's why they call you the She-Fox."

"That's different."

"Raella isn't really Raella," said Merc. "The Raelnan army won't fight for her now."

"How can Raella not be Raella?" said Rubric. "I mean, even if she is Morwen, she's still Raella."

"I told you—the Society brainwashed her and turned her to evil."

"They washed her brain? Those bastards!"

"Not literally, you oaf!" Merc was losing patience fast and he didn't have much to begin with.

"Who are you calling an oaf, little man? I am King of Brythalia!" Six hands darted for concealed weapons.

"And I am a wizard."

"Oh. Right." Three hands withdrew. The other three followed. "As you were saying, they cleansed her mind."

"No, they corrupted it."

"I thought you said they—"

"I did. Forget it. I assure you that the Raelnan army is not going to fight for Raella when she gets here. *I'm* not even going to fight for her, and I love her."

"You will fight against the woman you love?"

"Yes. I'll kill her if necessary. If that's the only way to save her."

"You would save her by killing her?" Rubric's look of perplexity deepened.

"It's a wizard thing," Merc snapped. "You wouldn't understand."

"Wizardry never has made sense to me," Rubric conceded.

"I'm not surprised."

"Can your magic match hers?"

"Usually. But we're sending for the League, just in case."

"More wizards. I don't like all these wizards horning in on the action."

"I'm not fond of the League myself, but you work with what you've got. It's going to take power to stop her."

The Brythalian monarch turned to Hotfur. "Do you believe all this, She-Fox? Are you going to take up arms against your own Queen?"

"In these circumstances, yes."

"Very well. If all is as you say, I am with you. We will stand together against these monsters. But once that is finished, all bets are off."

"So be it."

*   *   *

We spent the next three days preparing to meet the expected onslaught from the Incredibly Dark Forest. Raelnan and Brythalian soldiers worked side-by-side digging trenches, erecting bulwarks, setting artillery in place, devising strategies, and ignoring the Ganthians. They lined up on the battlefield each morning, but no one came to fight them. After a couple of abortive attacks were crushed by Raelnans and Brythalians working in tandem, Ironglove pulled his legions back to their encampment to sulk.

Five hills surrounded the valley containing Voripol. Ercan the Reaver and the Army of the North fortified the heights to the southwest. Hotfur and the Army of the Longwash occupied the south-central hill. The Brythalian position was on the east end of the valley. The Army of the South was in the rear, ready to fill any breaks in the line. The three small hills to the north and northwest were under Ganthian control. Raella's army would most likely come from the northwest, meaning Ironglove and the legionnaires would bear the brunt of the attack. This thought didn't disturb anyone.

Hotfur's signal corps included a junior wizard capable of sending messages back to Rae City. The She-Fox explained the situation to Chancellor Vannevar and the Provisional Council and asked them to send a plea for help to Timeon and the League in Caratha. Merc didn't like the idea, but he had to admit that with his own powers gone, we needed master sorcerers on the scene if we were to have any hope of stopping Raella. Ormazander, Episymachus, and Valence arrived on flying carpets in the afternoon of the third day after our arrival. Half a dozen arcane sub-masters accompanied them. Timeon was in bed with the flu.

"This will not be easy," Ormazander said after Merc and I fully explained the situation. "Because of her divine blood, Raella is potentially one of the most powerful spellcasters in Arden. Her innate capacity for magic far exceeds that of most mortals. She has always specialized in protective and informational magics, but from her studies she is familiar with many powerful destructive spells and will surely use that knowledge against us."

"I know that," said Merc.

"We may not be able to take her alive," said Episymachus.

"I know that too," said Merc. "But if it comes to killing her, no one does it but me."

The Leaguers flew an aerial reconnaissance mission to confirm the position and numbers of Raella's horde. Their report was not encouraging. Hundreds of ogres made up the vanguard, and goblins accounted for most of her force. They weren't much as individual fighters, but there were droves of them. All told, we faced nearly a hundred thousand foes. The monsters were encamped about two leagues northwest of the Ganthian position. The Leaguers caught no glimpse of Raella, but she was there somewhere. Most of her minions were nocturnal creatures. She would wait until nightfall, when her forces were at peak strength and ours at low ebb. Then she would come.

By this time, Myrm Ironglove figured out what was happening and decided he wanted no part of it. The Ganthian legions abandoned their positions and retreated to the southwest. The Imperator clearly intended to let his enemies fight among themselves, then return with reinforcements to pick up the pieces. According to the League scouts, the Seventh and Tenth legions had crossed the Crownbolt onto Orphalian soil. Ironglove could afford to sit out the battle and wait for a chance to prey on the weakened victor. Only Barons Bismuth and Tungsten and their remaining knights crossed over to stand with us against the invaders. They joined the Brythalian contingents.

Ironglove's move gave Raella an unobstructed path to Voripol. We didn't have the time or the warriors to fortify the area the Ganthians had left open. The mood in the Raelnan and Brythalian camps was bleak. The Raelnans were disheartened by the fact that it was their own Queen they faced. The Brythalian army, composed of conscripts and the lowest class of mercenaries, was plagued by mutiny. Fighting the brave and disciplined Ganthians and Raelnans had been bad enough, but asking them to face the nightmare denizens of the Incredibly Dark Forest was too much. Whole companies deserted, hacking their way through any loyal troops who tried to stop them. They headed south, where the foes were less deadly and the plunder was good.

By the time the moon rose and the first hulking line of ogres appeared on the far ridge, the defenders of Orphalia numbered less than fifty thousand. We held the high ground, but that was a scant advantage. On the face of it, the combined Brythalian-Raelnan-Orphalian army was doomed. This battle had "heroic last stand" written all over it.

Our only chance of winning was to take Raella out of the fight. Deprived of their leader, the monsters might lose heart and flee back to their lairs. This unpleasant task, of course, fell to Mercury, the League, and me.

24

The ogres thundered into the valley. Their war cries echoed off the hillsides and made even the most experienced warriors tremble in their boots. Twelve to fifteen feet tall and dressed in skins, they came on at a ground-eating pace. Row after row of ogres charged down the slope. Armed with tree trunks, stone clubs, and giant hammers, they were confident and cocky. No puny little humans could hope to stop their charge. The ogres would feast tonight.

In their wake came goblins by the thousand. Three or four feet tall, with pointy ears and glowing saucer eyes, the goblins chittered and squeaked as they charged. Like ogres, they considered human flesh a great delicacy. Not as good as fried potatoes, but close to it. The goblins bore small bows, short swords, and tiny spears. All their weapons were coated in poison paste made from powdered toadstools and ground gagroot. The chieftains rode on the backs of big slavering wolves or unblinking grok lizards. Mixed among the goblin-folk were squadrons of their larger cousins, the burly bugaboos, The bugaboos were similar to goblins in appearance but reached six feet in height.

The ogres and goblins were the mainstays of Morwen's army, but a variety of other monsters rounded out the horde. A few big, spindly trolls marched with the ogres. Trolls needed moisture to live and most didn't stray far from water, but these looked tough enough to survive in the volcanic Fields of Fire at the uttermost south of the world. Interspersed with the goblins I saw a hairy black spider as big as a rhino, weird red-fleshed norgs, a band of dastardly dregs, and some other horrors I couldn't identify. Eight or nine manticora flapped in the air above the dark host along with the biggest bat I had ever seen.

"Come on, you ugly sons of bricks!" said Hotfur. "Closer, closer—Now!"

At Hotfur's command a catapult crew launched a load of burning pitch. It traced a red arc in the air and splattered over a pair of ogres in the first rank, igniting their greasy fur. The shot was a signal for all the artillerists to open fire with catapult and ack. Pitch, boulders, and steel-tipped arrows as long as spears rained down on the ogres in the valley. Despite their losses, the behemoths did not falter in their advance. If anything, they came on faster, thus reaching the concealed pits all the sooner.

The pits weren't deep enough to trap an ogre, nor would the sharpened stakes at the bottom damage one in most circumstances, but in this mad charge an ogre would fall into a pit only to have the one behind tumble in after. The weight of the second drove the stakes through the first. And when the third ogre fell in, it was nearly impossible for the victims to get disentangled and escape. And still the boulders and arrows fell.

"Ready below!" yelled Hotfur.

The first ogres to get past the pits easily jumped the trenches at the base of the hills and ripped into the bulwarks, shattering timbers with their clubs or ripping them apart with platter-sized hands. But these lower defensive works were unmanned. They were only intended to delay the ogres while the archers and crossbowmen on the higher slopes picked them off. It took a great many arrows and quarrels to bring an ogre down. You could make one look like a porcupine and still not wound it fatally. But it only took one good shot in the eye to drive an ogre mad with pain. In such a state, the monster would go berserk and was as likely to attack his fellows as his foes. More likely, actually, since his foes were out of reach. The archers concentrated on head shots.

The goblins swarmed into the valley. The catapults squashed them by the dozen, but the vicious little humanoids were as heedless of their losses as the ogres. Unable to leap the trenches, they laid down felled trees and rough-hewn poles to serve as bridges. Quick and sure of foot, they streamed across like ants and scurried through the breaks in the barricade to work their way up toward the archers. Small and fast, they made more difficult targets than the lumbering ogres. Many goblins were able to get their own little bows in range and repay our archers in kind. The goblins had the advantage of being able to find cover behind the smaller rocks. They could also see better by moonlight than could humans.

"Wizard, I think it's time," said the She-Fox.

"Aye," said Ormazander. He lifted his staff and the tip glowed like a small star. This was a signal for his fellow wizards on the other hilltops to release their flares. Dozens of tiny white globes of light streaked over the valley like small comets and burst into brilliance. Their combined radiance approximated the light of day which the nocturnal goblins hated and feared. Thousands of screams bounced off the valley walls as the goblins threw down their weapons and shielded their eyes from the painful glare.

"Look there!" said Hotfur, pointing west to Ercan the Reaver's position. The manticora attacked the catapult crews, believing their power of flight would protect them from harm. But even as we watched, archers and ack gunners brought down three of the winged terrors. The rest retreated.

The giant bat whirled and wheeled above the battlefield, then flew away to the north to escape the painful and unfamiliar light of the flares.

"Where is she?" Merc asked, scanning the valley for a sign of Raella. "She has to be directing this mob from somewhere."

A bolt of fire fell from the sky and blasted the Brythalian position, scouring the hilltop clean and killing all upon it, including two Leaguers. A second tongue of fire licked the middle slopes. The third column of flame fell on our central hill, destroying an ack and its crew. It was as though the night itself had joined the war against us.

"By the Nine Noses of Nalor!" exclaimed Hotfur. "What was that?"

We heard the beating of huge, impossibly powerful wings. A shadow passed across the moon, and waves of fear swept through our ranks. The soldiers muttered and prayed and looked anxiously upward, not knowing when the fire would fall again.

"Did you see that silhouette?" asked Merc.

"A dragon," I said. "And on its back . . ."

"Raella."

The dragon made another pass over the Brythalian hill, scorching it twice more with blasts of primal fire. This was more than Rubric's conscripts could bear. They abandoned their positions, threw down their weapons, and fled screaming down the far slope into the night. This left Rubric with only his personal guards to defend him. Accepting the inevitable, the Brythalian monarch fled too. Only the hardy knights of Orphalia remained steadfast, gathering on a prominence to fend off the ogres, who now climbed the hill unimpeded. Feri Halehart and the Army of the South hurried to their rescue.

"She knows what she's doing," I said. "She went for our weakest link first."

"I suggest we get out of the open," said Ormazander. Hotfur was already giving the necessary orders.

"Take me up," said Merc, grabbing the Cyrillan wizard's arm.

"Are you mad?" said Ormazander. "You want to challenge a dragon in the air?"

"We're got to capture her. The plan, remember?"

"Snatch her from the dragon's back? Impossible!"

"Take me up or I'll kill you," said Merc. He meant it.

"Hop aboard," said Ormazander. They mounted one of the flying carpets and took to the air as the dragon wheeled around and dove toward General Ercan's position. The Reaver had already cleared his hilltop, and his ack crews bravely trained their weapons on the swooping dragon. Most of their quarrels missed or bounced off its scaly hide, but one passed through its leathery left wing. Enraged, the monster wheeled about again and blasted the offending ack crew to cinders. This time it came low enough into the light that we could see it clearly. It was a big one, larger than any two ships of war and blacker than black except for its luminous green eyes. Perched on its back, where the neck met the shoulders, Raella rode in a kind of modified howdah. Her cape flapped behind her in the wind and she laughed as the dragon brought death upon her own subjects.

Her laughter had always been pleasant, ringing with cheer and light. Now it was chilling, hideous sound. The dragon banked back up into the darkness above the light. Merc and Ormazander streaked after it.

"That was Nightfire," said Valence as we scrambled for cover. "It had to be. That dragon is over fifteen hundred years old. He's the same one that laid waste to the Kingdom of Terrengia at the behest of Uliziah the Unkind."

"I've never heard of Terrengia."

"When Nightfire lays waste to a place, he lays waste to it."

"You've got to take me up," I said suddenly.

"What?"

"They can't handle that thing alone. Take me up."

"You hate flying!"

"I know. Take me up. Now."

The flares dwindled and the goblins renewed their attack. Above, looming shadows and jets of flame marked the dragon's position. I joined Valence on his flying carpet and we look off, climbing steeply. Too steeply. I already regretted my decision. Part of the enchantment of a flying carpet is that passengers will not fall off, even if it flies upside down. A kind of holding spell keeps them in place. Of course, one can always jump or be pushed, but that is another matter. I really hated flying.

We soared up behind Nightfire and narrowly escaped being swept from the sky by his thrashing tail. Valence was a skilled pilot and eluded the attack with an inverted barrel roll that made me toss my cookies.

"Okay?"

"Fine. Fine. Where's Merc?"

"There." He pointed.

Ormazander approached Nightfire from above and behind, swooping down between the dragon's beating wings. As they skimmed over Raella's head, Merc jumped down to join her in the howdah. His weight knocked it askew and pitched him out. He clung to the harness that held the seat in place. Raella, securely strapped, laughed and struck him in the face with the back of her hand. Meanwhile, Nightfire singed the rear of Ormazander's carpet with his breath. The League wizard lost control and went down on the east side of the valley.

"Thoughtful of you to drop in, lover," said Raella. "More thoughtful for you to drop back out."

"Raella, you must end this madness!" cried Merc.

"What madness? Yours? Gladly!" She struck at him again, but this time he released his hold on the harness and grabbed her wrist, pulling her half out of her perch.

"Can you take me in closer?" I asked.

"No," said Valence. "He's diving."

Nightfire, ignoring the wrestling match on his back, swooped down for another run at the Reaver's emplacement, this time staying well out of ack range.

"What is Merc trying to do?" I asked as we climbed. "First he tells me there's no cure for what happened to Raella. Now he's hanging onto the side of a dragon trying to reason with her!"

"I think it's an elaborate form of suicide," said Valence. "Ever read any tragic plays? Full of this kind of stuff. By the way, did you figure out how to operate the Ring of Raxx's power to communicate with squirrels?"

"Yes."

"And?"

"I'd rather not talk about it just now."

We made another pass over Nightfire. Green light flashed as Raella fired her emerald eyebolts pointblank at Merc. He escaped an energetic decapitation only by releasing his hold and plunging into the milling horde below. He was only two hundred feet from the ground when he fell. He might have survived, but it was doubtful. In the darkness I couldn't tell.

"Merrrrrrrrc!"

Raella turned at the sound of my scream and laughed. She had just sent the love of her life to his death and she laughed about it. Merc had been right. All that had been Raella was gone. She was Morwen Hellshade now.

Nightfire attacked the central hill again, giving Morwen's minions the cover fire they needed to get past the archers and reach the acks and catapults. Ogres ripped the war engines apart and tossed the pieces down the slope. Brave Raelnan troopers closed in for hopeless hand-to-hand combat and fell in droves. Twenty men died for every ogre they brought down.

The pair of League sub-masters still on the central slope helped fight the monsters with spells of wind and ice and fire, but they ventured too far forward and got riddled with poisoned goblin arrows. The monsters gained the peak which Hotfur had abandoned for fear of dragon fire.

"We have to slay that dragon!" I said.

"Easier said than done," replied Valence. "Many champions have faced Nightfire in the past. Great warriors, arcane masters, entire armies—he defeated them all. Even the Mighty Champion of old failed to kill this wyrm."

"Well, the Mighty Champion of new is going to try! When he comes up again, zoom in head on."

"Did you say head on?"

"That's right." I drew Overwhelm from its scabbard.

Nightfire swung around for another run at Hotfur's hill, but before the dragon could dive, Valence flew past his muzzle, wheeled around, and came right at him as I had ordered.

"I hope you know what you're doing," said the wizard.

"So do I."

Nightfire opened his gaping jaws wide to sear us with a gust of heat.

"Go under him!" I cried. "Close in and full speed!"

A billowing column of flame rolled out of the dragon's mouth and blossomed toward us. At the last possible instant Valence took the carpet down so that the fire passed overhead. It was close enough that I could feel the heat through my helmet, as if I had stuck my head in an oven.

Nightfire snapped at us as we dipped past his neck to skim along below him at incredible speed. Placing more trust than I wanted to in the enchantment of the rug, I stood and held Overwhelm aloft with both hands, tensing my body. The jolt when the blade pierced Nightfire's breastbone nearly yanked me from the carpet, but the holding spell didn't fail. Valence kept the rug on course as I split the dragon open from throat to loin. We banked and dove under his twisting tail and skimmed across the hilltops before rolling into a steep climb.

Meanwhile, Nightfire's unhinged ribs gave way, dumping his innards on the creatures below. The disemboweled dragon's carcass followed. His wings crumpled and he fell like a mountain, crushing hundreds of goblins as he landed where the royal palace had been. Morwen went down with him.

"Amazing!" said Valence.

"Take us in low. I want to see if Raella—Morwen—survived the crash!"

We hovered above the ancient dragon's broken body. All the monsters were still running in the other direction. I willed Overwhelm to cast its light and scanned the area for Morwen, dead or alive.

An emerald bolt of power ripped through the center of the flying carpet, ruining the enchantment. Valence and I fell. The wizard hit the rocky ground, breaking a leg. I struck Nightfire's body and slid across his warm scales,

landing on my feet face to face with Morwen Hellshade.
I held Overwhelm at the ready.

"You!" she spat. "You meddling moron! How dare
you attack me!"

"How dare you betray everything that you were!"

"How dare you kill my dragon!"

"How dare you kill Mercury!"

"How dare you—" She faltered.

"Yes?"

"Never mind. Die, peasant dog!" Green lightning flared
from her eyes, but rather than strike me, it all flew to
Overwhelm and was absorbed.

"You missed me!" I exclaimed. "Ha!"

"Die!" she repeated, firing emerald bolts from her
hands. I deflected them both with my sword and strongly
wished my shield wasn't still strapped across my back.

"You die!" I made a great leap forward, intending to
strike Morwen's evil head from her body. She made a
greater leap, rising twenty feet into the air and hanging
there. My sword cut empty air.

"You pathetic worm! This time I will obliterate you!"

"No!" I said. "I won't let you win! I won't let you
desecrate what you stood for anymore!" I cocked my
arm to hurl Overwhelm like a spear. I knew the magic
sword would fly true to the mark and pierce Morwen's
empty heart. "Forgive me, but by Holy Rae, this ends
now!"

"WELL, IT'S ABOUT TIME!"

25

Dawn exploded across the sky, rudely shoving
the bewildered night aside about six hours too soon. The
confused moon scampered over the western horizon like
a whipped dog, utterly unable to compete with the glory
of the sun. The early light that shone down on Arden
was no product of pale flares. It was the genuine article,

the real stuff. I felt the solar warmth flooding my body with strength and renewed vitality. The goblins and other monsters threw up their hands in despair (those that had hands) and howled and fled the way they had come, routed by the hateful light and the presence of the Light Bringer—the one and only Goddess Rae.

One hundred feet tall for this appearance, she wore a gown of radiant sunbeams and a tiara of small stars. Her red-blond hair, clenched into tight curls by some unknown process, bounced around her shoulders. She hovered above the battlefield, careful not to let her feet touch the ground in violation of the Holy/Unholy Non-Intervention Pact.

"It's about time, I say!" repeated the Goddess.

"About time for what?" I asked, lowering my sword and craning my neck to peer up at her. Morwen cowered before the shining Goddess, shielding her eyes and shrieking profanities. A flick of Rae's hand froze the fallen Queen in place and ended her outburst.

"About time you asked me for help, of course," said Rae. "You know I can't help you unless you ask me to."

"Did I just ask you for help?"

"You said 'By Holy Rae, this ends now!' which is close enough. You should be ashamed, Jason Cosmo! You are my Champion and here you are trying to kill my Chief Priestess."

"But I . . . but she. . . ."

"Well?"

"I don't know what to say. Forgive me."

"Hmph!"

"Please?"

"Really, Jason." She crossed her arms and stuck her nose up. "It's inexcusable."

"Pretty please?"

"Double hmph!"

I sighed. "Pretty please with sunbeams on top?"

She smiled. "Well, okay. You're forgiven. I suppose it isn't your fault anyway. I saw what really happened at the wedding in Rae City—Isn't that a charming name?— but I couldn't just tell you without breaking the rules against interfering in mortal affairs, although I think there ought to be an exception when my own High Priestess is involved, but the Executive Council said even that would violate the Non-Intervention Pact so I just had to watch when that nasty wizard took poor Raella to his castle and did whatever to her, though I don't see why we have to follow that silly old treaty anyway because the Demon Lords sure don't. Still, I would have given you a little hint, but I had to wait until you called on me for aid; so of course when you did I was at the hairdresser. Do you like my new perm?" She shook her head and made her curls bounce and throw off bright sparks like solar flares.

"Smashing."

"Thanks, you're sweet. So I missed my chance to come rescue you, because by the time Gloama got to me it was too late. But now you finally called on me again and here I am."

"Can you cure Raella of . . . whatever they did to her?"

"Of course, silly. I'm a Goddess."

She scooped Raella up in her giant hands and breathed pure light over the afflicted Queen. Morwen Hellshade's garments vanished. A perfect replica of Raella's golden wedding gown replaced them. The Queen blinked as if recovering from a trance.

"O my sweet Goddess!" she exclaimed, dropping to her knees in Rae's hands. "I have betrayed you, dishonored you—"

"Oh, hush!" said Rae. "It was beyond your control."

"Mercury!" cried Raella in anguish. "Goddess, what have I done? I killed him!"

"Or at least you give it your best shot," said Merc, skimming into view aboard a flying carpet piloted by Episymachus. "As I plunged to my doom, your fellow Leaguer here witnessed my descent and caught me in mid-air just in the nick of time."

"I should have known," I said.

The carpet sailed up to the hands of the Goddess, and Merc leaped to Raella's side. They embraced and kissed.

"Oh, Mercury, I'm so sorry!" said Raella.

"Enough," said Merc. "If anyone is to blame it's me

for accepting Rom Acheron's vile deception too readily. It's over now. We're together at last."

"And so you shall remain," said the Goddess Rae. "I hereby complete the ceremony that was interrupted and proclaim you husband and wife. Kiss the bride, wizard."

The royal couple needed no encouragement.

"Excellent!" I said. "Who could ask for a happier ending?"

Of course, it wasn't over yet. Morwen Hellshade's fleeing army of horrors ran straight into the pikes of the Ganthian legions. Ironglove had brought his forces back into the hills he had earlier abandoned, trapping the monsters in the Voripol valley. He later claimed this had been his intent all along, that his apparent flight had been a ruse, another example of Ganthian military genius. This was certainly possible. It was also possible that the Imperator had seen which way the wind was now blowing and didn't want to miss a share in the spoils of victory.

Whatever his reasons, the frightful fiends were now surrounded. Raelnan troopers, Ganthian legionnaires, and Orphalian knights took heart at the sight of the hovering Goddess and the unexpected arrival of day and poured down the slopes to massacre the leaderless monsters. Halfway through the slaughter, even Rubric returned with what remnants of his army he had been able to round up.

Raella and Merc watched the one-sided battle from their safe vantage point, but Rae insisted that I take part in the fray so she could brag to Lucinda Everfair and the other goddesses about what a fierce and heroic Champion she had. I did my best to oblige, seeking out and destroying the most dangerous of the monsters.

Once the day had been won, Raella called for a parley to decide the fate of Orphalia. Mindful of the Goddess Rae's presence, the other leaders quickly agreed to the terms Raella proposed. The Kingdom of Orphalia ceased to exist. Its former territory was divided into three roughly equal sections and assigned to the control of Ganth,

Raelna, and Brythalia. Voripol would be rebuilt and granted independent status as a free city. This arrangement displeased Barons Bismuth, Tungsten, and von Zinc, but they were in no position to complain.

Personally, I thought it would have been wiser to guarantee Orphalia's neutrality and independence so that it could continue to serve as a buffer between the three superpowers. Raella's plan seemed a bit ruthless and opportunistic. It had something for everyone except the Orphalians themselves. I wondered if there wasn't still a bit of Morwen Hellshade left in her, but I kept these thoughts to myself.

A few days later, back in Rae City, Raella held court in the Grand Plaza before the Solar Palace, in part because the throne room was still wrecked and in part to show her jubilant subjects that she was indeed alive. Mercury, as Prince Consort of the Realm, was enthroned beside her.

Raella was at once stern and magnanimous in victory. She confiscated the lands of Thule Nethershawn and his allies, doubling the Royal Demesne at a stroke. She praised the members of the Provisional Council for their efforts to secure the realm in her absence. She had special medals struck to honor the warriors who had driven the Maceketeers from the city, and conferred knighthood upon Devra Highrider, Colonel Gerron, and Captain Taurus. For the She-Fox she had a special reward and mission.

"General Hotfur, it is Our wish to reward you for your valiant efforts on Our behalf. By your courage, devotion, and leadership, you did as much as any to make this day of victory possible. It is Our decree that Our new Orphalian holdings be called Vixeny in your honor. We do furthermore now create and confirm you Princess of Vixeny and command you to order and secure that portion of Our realm, that it may become the birthright of Our firstborn. You will relinquish this holding to him or her on the day of his or her majority, but the title, precedence, and honors We bestow today shall be yours henceforth."

Hotfur, clothed again in the full-dress uniform she despised, knelt before the Queen for the ceremonial laying on of hands which confirmed her new title.

I was next.

"Jason Cosmo, Champion of Blessed Rae and dearest of friends, you have made it clear that you will accept neither gold, nor land, nor title in reward for your noble and heroic actions. Nevertheless, it is Our wish that you accept a small token of Our affection, gratitude, and regard." An attendant handed her a slim jewel case of polished mahogany. She opened it and lifted from its velvet resting place a golden medallion with a brilliant sun jewel in its center. "This amulet, blessed by Rae Herself, bestows divers beneficent powers and useful protections upon its owner, which We shall explain to thee in private." She slipped the chain over my neck and kissed my cheek.

"Thank you, Your Majesty."

"No," whispered Raella. "Thank *you*."

The time came for me to return to Caratha. By now Sapphrina and Rubis should have returned from Zastria, and they would be worried about me. Raella loaned me a horse from the royal stables, and I was ready to go. But I wanted one last word with Mercury. He met me by the stable gate.

"It all turned out for the best," I said.

"Yes it did," Merc agreed. "For once." He smiled.

"You're smiling much more than I've ever seen."

"I've got a lot more to smile about."

"I hope you two will be happy."

"We'd better be," said Merc. "We've earned it."

"I still don't see why the Goddess Rae couldn't restore your magic abilities."

"She could have, I suppose," said Merc, "but I didn't ask. I mean, would you want to take a chance on letting *her* fix anything?"

"Utter blasphemy—but point well-taken. So what will you do?"

"I'm not worrying about it for now." He turned thoughtful. "Jason, I want to thank you again for all you did, for making my fight your own."

"Merc, it *was* my fight."

"You're a true hero, Jason. And a truer friend."

"That's what it's all about," I said, swinging into the saddle.

About the Author

Dan McGirt was born in Sylvester, Georgia, in 1967. He received a B.A. from the University of Georgia in 1989 and is now studying law, which involves learning obscure Latin phrases such as *res ipsa loquitur*. In his spare time he likes to brush up on quantum physics, read comic books, and avoid stepping into the paths of large, fast-moving vehicles. *Royal Chaos* is his second book.